BACK ON TRACK?

BACK ON TRACK?

A Murder Mystery By

Lawrence Gordon

Order this book online at www.trafford.com
or email orders@trafford.com

Most Trafford titles are also available at major online book retailers.

Printed in the United States of America.

ISBN: 978-1-4269-5715-4 (sc)
ISBN: 978-1-4269-5714-7 (hc)
ISBN: 978-1-4269-5716-1 (e)

Library of Congress Control Number: 2011901657

Trafford rev. 04/27/2011

 www.trafford.com

North America & international
toll-free: 1 888 232 4444 (USA & Canada)
phone: 250 383 6864 ♦ fax: 812 355 4082

BACK ON TRACK?

Preface.

The idea for the book came from a city break I took to the Christmas markets of Cologne and Aachen well into the Twenty First century. I enjoyed it so much I decided I'd write a novel based upon some of my experiences, but giving the novel several nasty twists.

Travelling before Christmas, celebrating a major wedding anniversary the main subjects, a retired couple, visit Cologne as part of an organised rail trip. Progress in the book is quite leisurely to begin with as only the occasional encounter proves challenging or sinister. The peaceful atmosphere is shattered when one of the main characters disappears. What happens next could be a nightmare for anyone travelling abroad.

In writing the book I owe thanks to many people, too many to record here. But my special thanks must go to the following people who have supported me throughout my writing endeavours.

Firstly, to my wife Avril, the most patient and tolerant person I know allowing me the time in which to write despite our many problems at home.

Secondly thanks must also go to Anita Betts, Helen Mitchell and Jill Hilditch for acting as my extra pairs of eyes in writing this book.

Thirdly thanks also to Rebecca Smith and Laurence Daren King for their skill and expertise guiding me when I needed their help.

Any similarity in this book to anyone living or dead is purely coincidental.

Chapter One.

After nearly forty years of marriage to my good lady wife, Libby, our Ruby Wedding Anniversary was fast approaching and was going to be some celebration. How we were to celebrate was the problem. Should we celebrate with family, family and friends, or just by ourselves? After much soul-searching and then having made our choice what was to transpire when we did celebrate exceeded our wildest dreams. Perhaps that should read nightmares because we were utterly unprepared for what was to follow. The fact that I am writing this by myself may give some indication as to what may have occurred that December.

Always one to celebrate an anniversary of almost any type if it involved family, particularly if it was our children or our grandchildren, my wife was absolutely desperate to celebrate the occasion of our Ruby Wedding Anniversary big time. That we chose to hold this momentous event out of the country, for us was novel. We began organising it in the autumn before the due date in December. We wanted it to be not only the anniversary of our lifetime together but we hoped it would be a magical and really special celebration. Little did we know or appreciate that autumnal day what would be in store for us as we set in motion a series of occurrences that would change our lives forever and I do mean forever.

'Are we doing anything special for our Ruby Wedding Anniversary?' my wife asked me one Saturday morning at the end of summer, 'because if we are not then I'd like to arrange a party for the family and some friends. What do you think Tony?'

'You know I'm not keen on parties Libby' I replied, 'particularly if there is there an alternative?'

'Well what about a city-break somewhere now we have the time and are retired and perhaps just prior to Christmas too on or around the actual date we married? That would be a change and all we would do is pack our bags and go, not mess around with food and all those party things. We could maybe have a party when we get back. Does that seem OK to you Tony?' Libby asked as she continued preparing our lunch that Saturday afternoon.

Me, I've never been able to tolerate parties, all that false chit-chat, the ogling of the opposite sex as people get more and more tipsy and the noise of the music. Not my style. An old Dodo I know I'm told often enough. So not being a party animal I agreed with my lovely wife that any celebrations would be private between the two of us or with close family. You know the type of thing I mean. Hence the reason why that autumn travel outlets were to become a second home as I collected many different types of city-break brochures from the holiday firms in and around the small town we lived in near Birmingham. Selecting the right trip became more interesting surfing the web on my new PC meaning I could practise my pretty basic, and they were basic, computer skills searching for the best deals. We decided it would be in our best interests if we were away for a short time just before Christmas, and if it were all possible, on or around the date of our Anniversary which would be Sunday December 14th. Anywhere in the world would do, hot or cold, so long as we could be away together.

Me, I am Tony Russell an ex-PE teacher now retired after thirty odd years in teaching having towards the end of my career risen up the educational ladder in secondary schools to become a senior teacher in several schools close to where we lived. In college I used to stand six feet four inches tall and weigh about fourteen stones: now it's over sixteen stones and still counting if the scales are to be believed, which of course they never are. Many years ago I used to have jet-black hair too but that turned prematurely grey long before I went to PE College. Since then most of my hair has disappeared on top which leaves me looking well-bronzed in summer above what is left of my hairline, and so to compensate for the lack of hair above I have a Zapata moustache. I love watching all ball sports and was lucky to have played football and cricket for far too long as my aching bones can testify.

My wife of almost forty years at the time I refer to was Libby Russell also a former PE teacher. Libby taught firstly in the London Borough of Islington and later, after transferring to be nearer me, also taught in Birmingham where we married. Libby, five feet six with beautiful blue eyes, looking as gorgeous as the day we met in December 1965 was the only woman I really loved. She used to have mousey hair but since the first grey hair became visible had several new shades since. But for me to suggest her weight you must be joking: that would have been more than my life was worth and though not an issue with her she kept the details close to her chest. Libby played county netball for Warwickshire before she had our two children Miles, now thirty seven, and Caroline now thirty four. Caroline is married and has two lovely girls Ruby and Catherine and lives happily with her husband William. Miles also a teacher is no longer married to Susan his former wife and has no children we are aware of. I say that because he was never without female company whilst he was growing up the lucky blighter. How times have changed. Our family holidays often took us, if not to the seaside in Britain then to France where we stayed either in tents close to some of their amazing beaches or later in gites.

However, going on holiday at the beginning of December had never entered our heads before as we were always involved in the frenetic build up to Christmas with our family. A break just before Christmas, and one of such personal importance to us, would be a new experience. Having looked at the mega-amount of options available for a break at home in the UK, or close-by in Europe, we eventually came to a decision and stuck to it. That year, for our big wedding anniversary, we would visit Germany during Advent when the Christmas markets and fairs were taking place. They would, we hoped, bring that extra touch of magic to our lives for not only were they supposedly unique but might also bring back to us the childhood magic of Christmas we so missed. You see, like many in Britain, we had become fed up with the non-stop razzmatazz and the over the top commercialisation that had taken over our high streets for the holiday period. So we longed to find and experience a more traditional Christmas, one without the mass-produced goods we see in our shops. And with no television wall to wall with their incessant and begging adverts would, for a short while, enable us to bury ourselves in what we hoped would be the true spirit of Christmas. Not only that but we looked forward to the occasional glass of mulled wine or two, or three, toffee apples to test our teeth and the aroma of hot chestnuts baking on an open fire, grilled sausages, pancakes and chips permeating the atmosphere of frosty and snowy days. At least that's how it was portrayed in all the brochures we collected from the High Street. We decided that type of break could only be experienced first hand not on some television screen. Our problem was deciding which markets and which fairs to visit.

Cologne, Dresden and Nuremberg were top of our cities to visit list as we sorted through mountains of brochures all proclaiming the merits of their markets. In the end it became a question of distance and the time we would spend travelling to get wherever we were headed for. After much discussion over some nice German wine, Cologne won by a mile, several actually, and was our preferred destination. At least that was what we hoped for when we chose that venue from the tour brochures. Going to Cologne meant we could also visit Aachen on the Belgian border and so the choice became easier and very straightforward. Cologne it would be then so booking our break after checking out a myriad of tour companies and speaking to friends, we eventually chose a company with the quaint sounding name of Pineapple Rail Tours, a travel firm based in London. The tour we chose meant we were scheduled to spend three days and nights in Cologne with the final day Sunday, the actual date of our Anniversary. After a last check on price and hotel it turned out I could not have picked a better time or place to take my lovely wife to: her comments not mine. For the next few weeks before we travelled Libby regaled me so often as to how she was so looking forward to visiting Germany, she would have burst if it fell through in the end. The thought that it was to be only the two of us, and no-one else in the whole world that we knew of, would not I hope disappoint her.

I'd always enjoyed travelling by train or 'going on holiday' as the kids put it later when they could talk, ever since we married. What I didn't like was the lead up to it: the preparation, getting the clothes ready, the toiletries, checking the passports were in date, checking the insurance and so on. Those chores were the adopted domain of my wife Libby who just loved the excitement of the planning and preparation. That was so long as I kept out of the way you must appreciate. Meanwhile I tried to tie up any jobs and loose ends around the house prior to our departure or, wickedly, read the daily newspaper in the mornings and avoid working. Like for example on that late, cold, damp and wet November in Birmingham whilst Libby was out shopping for the 'things we needed for our holiday.'

We were a good team together and yes we had had arguments down the years, mainly about the children, or my drinking, but by and large we were very happy together. It was too late if we weren't at our age. That had not always the case when Libby lived in London I might add, what with the distance between our respective homes being well over a hundred miles. With new careers unfolding in teaching and our own personal sports' teams to participate in at the weekends, the relationship became tenuous and cooled off for a time to say the least. That was never more clearly illustrated than when we were back together and I would venture occasionally to London to visit her flat. Arriving unannounced to find some 'bumptious cockney thoroughbred' flirting with her over a cup of coffee in her kitchenette got me all hot under the collar. Strange thing that jealousy of mine, so I had to find a way round it. I did it by asking her to marry me and was grateful and lucky she said yes.

Those days of self-imposed doubt have long since gone and on the particular morning in question, a Thursday in early December, a week before we were to leave for our break, Libby decided to go shopping for a few last minute items and call in at a chemist's in our local shopping centre to pick up some travel sickness pills for my regular condition. Travel sickness had blighted my holidays since I was a child and whether the pills ever had a placebo effect on me or not to be honest I didn't care. Without them I became ill on any type of journey on the ground or in the air and would need a day to recover. If I forgot to take them I would always lose at least one day of the holiday. Looking back I wished I had gone with her that morning, but regretfully I chose not to go with her as there 'were things to do' around the house.

On her very, very late return from the shops Libby looked dishevelled, shocked and ill when she came in through the front door. I was busy in the kitchen and was not prepared for the way she looked or what she was about to tell me.

'I'm so sorry' she cried 'I've been in an accident, crashed the car and been assaulted by some nasty bastard who was also involved in a hit and run.'

'You've what?' I screamed at her.

She ran towards me, I placed my arms around her hugging her close. Only then did she tell me in between sniffles how on her way home she had been deliberately cut up by some bloke in a sports car. She said she gave him a one-fingered salute for his efforts and he tried to force her off the road which he had succeeded in doing, and whilst skidding to a full-stop himself hit a pedestrian. Libby said she having come to a stop when she collided with a lamp-post managed to eventually get out of her car to check for any damage to her beloved VW Golf. Only then did she notice a limp body in the road. It was when walking towards the body, that for a second she thought she had hit, when she was confronted again by the thug in the sports car who had stopped a few yards ahead of her to check on the condition of his prey, both Libby and the pedestrian now bleeding profusely and motionless in the middle of the road. Libby recalled how the thug grabbed hold of her shouting threats that he would kill her and placed his hands round her neck and was just about to throttle her when some chap in the gathering crowd of people across the road shouted at him to stop what he was doing. Releasing his grip on her neck the thug ran back towards his car, took one look back at the body in the road, quickly got in his car and sped off injuring a stray dog in the process. In complete shock at what had happened Libby failed, for obvious reasons, to collect his car number as she sobbed her heart out on the side of the road. Then, having been comforted by a complete stranger at the roadside, the kindly Samaritan asked if she was OK to continue her journey home when a police car and an ambulance arrived.

Libby was checked over by a paramedic for any injuries, all the time Libby asking how the pedestrian was who was by then being carried towards the ambulance on a stretcher. A police-lady took Libby's address and a brief statement, before asking her if she needed treatment at the local Infirmary before going to ask for any witnesses on the pavement nearby from the small crowd that had gathered to oversee the proceedings just as the ambulance drove off with siren blaring. Libby said that after first reversing away from the lamp-post, made a cursory check that the car was safe to drive and, still in shock after what had happened drove home.

I sat her down with a cup of strong coffee as she was still shaking and it took some time for her to recover before she was able to recall her eventful and a somewhat puzzling trip to the chemist and shops.

'I cannot believe he drove off. Who would do such a thing?' she asked speaking about the thug involved in the accident.

I told her that he could have only been someone without a conscience when, bursting into tears she said

'The police said they will be back to check my statement later because when they finished briefly with me they followed the ambulance to the hospital with the hit and run victim in. Will we have to forego our trip to Germany?'

I had just managed to get the words out of my mouth when the door bell rang. The police had arrived. After explaining to Libby what they wanted her to do on that occasion they took a full statement from her of what she had experienced. When the police had left Libby said she'd asked if it was ok for us to travel. The police said that she would be needed, perhaps in court in future if they had made an arrest, but so long as they knew where we were travelling to it would be alright to go ahead.

By the time she had begun to recover a little it was well after two o'clock. She sidled up to me, put an arm round my shoulders and said that the lady assistant who served her had looked uncannily familiar. From somewhere in the dim and distant past, she said, something rang a bell in her head about the woman but she was unable to recollect immediately what it was. A place or face from where or how far back in time she did not know, only that she thought she recognised her because of the scar below her left eye.

'Do I know you?' she had asked the lady who had her back to Libby as she searched for my tablets on a shelf. The woman replied that probably not as she wasn't from the Midlands originally but 'from down south.' Still Libby was convinced she knew her from somewhere previously but could not remember from where.

'I then went to the supermarket to get a few things for lunch and was quite taken back by Anne Thompson on the till who was very chatty asking when we were off on holiday.' Libby recalled.

Libby was quite surprised by the reaction of the shop assistant who, as she packaged up rolls and cold meat, showed an enthusiasm beyond the call of duty asking Libby a load of questions about our forthcoming holiday.

'I suppose it was at the point in the conversation when I said I'd been next door for your travel-sickness pills that was the catalyst for her questioning' she said 'after all it wasn't rocket science to assume we were going on holiday sometime soon was it? I mean you don't seem to want them if we go shopping on the bus, do you?'

Where were we going, with which tour firm? What hotels were we staying in? How we were getting there? How long were we staying and why were we going in the first place? As Libby was remarking on the list of questions asked of her I began to wonder if she had invited the assistant to come with us. Surprisingly to Libby the woman seemed really interested in the markets we were visiting in Germany. Libby quite happily told her everything about our intended trip, and much to my consternation, even the dates we were to travel. The assistant said she hoped we would have a safe and pleasant journey and told Libby to be aware of pick pockets and thieves around the markets that had doubled in numbers over the last few years. Libby was bemused that someone who was not a close friend could be so interested in some-else's choice of holiday.

However, Libby was more concerned about the woman in the chemists than she was about the supermarket assistant. She was absolutely adamant she had seen her before somewhere, if not in Birmingham, then somewhere. Then again Libby could see someone and imagine them being, or looking like, some film star or other, or even a colleague or acquaintance she had worked with previously at her various schools. What she could never do, however, was remember their names. Just another of life's complications that we seniors acquire as we reach the autumn of our lives, so I'm told.

It seemed to be a long afternoon as Libby became a little less fraught thinking about the scrape she had had with that idiot in the sports car. She kept returning to the topic of the injured person who had been knocked over and every now and again burst into tears at what had happened.

'I was still dazed when I got out of my car after hitting the lamp-post and didn't see the person who was hit and lying in the road be they man or woman,' she said 'do you think you could phone the hospital or police station to see how they are?'

'I suspect it will be on the local news sometime later if the police still want more witnesses' I replied.

Throughout the rest of that day I could see her turning things over in her mind and half hoped she would relent and lie down for an hour or two and get some rest but could see it was a non-starter. Apart from the fate of the pedestrian, what seriously troubled Libby about that morning, was who the shop assistant was and how was it that she knew her? That woman, who just happened to serve Libby that morning, gave my wife such a headache trying as she did to remember her. There then occurred one of those moments in life, a Eureka moment, giving Libby the answer to her puzzle. She startled me saying she knew the lady came from London, or at least someone similar to her did. I stared at her blankly waiting for her to carry on her explanation. She claimed that years before, a person looking like the woman she met in the chemists but younger, used to visit her boyfriend who just coincidentally lived in the same block that Libby lived in at the beginning of her teaching career. And yes, the woman also had a scar above her eye, but for life of her could Libby remember which eye, or the woman's name and that of her boyfriend from all those years ago? Not then anyway because it certainly wasn't the name on her lapel that morning, a one Ms Allsebruckovski, or something. It all became too much for me to take in so I nodded politely in what I thought were all the right places when Libby looked over in my direction. It was to take some time before we were able to change the subject for obvious reasons.

The morning's main topic and incident were never far away as we talked them over between us for remainder of the day. I even began to rake up that on several of my visits to Libby's flat there had been some very peculiar people living there in the same high-rise block. And as for some of the visitors or interlopers who hung about those high-rise flats, well we have other names for them now. Druggies, alcoholics and just general thugs who you hoped would pass you by on the street without accosting you, making a person very wary not to promote conversation with them. I seemed to remember that all types of human life being evident in that tower block in one form or another. And it came as no surprise to read that people living in those conditions held grievances against their neighbours for the most trivial of reasons. That was the real problem with the area Libby had lived in as a newly qualified teacher and with little money to buy a flat elsewhere it was some problem. But that was London. So, at the chemists that morning, there had been no instant connection made by Libby as to who the lady assistant was. Nor in fact was Libby overly concerned as to why the lady in the supermarket had been so inquisitive or enthusiastic asking all the questions about our forthcoming break. Libby just accepted that some folks were plain nosey.

The TV news that evening was awful: the elderly lady who had been hit by the driver after he swerved away from Libby had died in hospital. The effect on Libby was dreadful and crying she went upstairs where she sobbed her heart out uncontrollably.

Later that evening we checked our passports were still in date for the umpteenth time. I had placed our return rail tickets to London in one envelope unsealed and the main rail tickets for Europe in another envelope, again unsealed. We even checked the first aid package together that we always carry with us when we leave the house to go on holiday. You know the type: plasters, Immodium, Germaloid spray, aspirins; tablets for blood pressure this that and the other and of course Libby's make-up bag. It always makes me think that what we take orally at our age to keep us alive has a price to pay at the other end of our bodies later. Hence the 'mixed' first aid package. But the make-up preparations, applied so methodically each morning before Libby set foot outside of the house and went anywhere, served only to make her look her best. That is to all who saw her, except when she looked in the mirror herself of course. "Is that a spot I see before me?" "Oh no, not another line on my face" were comments that were often heard coming from the direction of her make-up mirror. That was if anyone was prepared to listen as she applied her make-up.

Ah well, more preparation ahead I thought as we packed our wheelie cases that last evening at home taking care to check that all buttons were on shirts, trousers ironed, zips working perfectly, socks clean and without holes and of course a couple of jumpers, not cardigans just yet, for the German Winter. I insisted we went out that night rather than cook at home but I'm not sure that going out for a hot chicken curry was a good idea as we were to travel by train to London the following day. But then we had always visited the Mother India restaurant every Wednesday since the kids had left home. It had become an enjoyable habit as the boss 'Mo', created new challenges for us with his different curries and spices each time we visited. Creatures of habit that's what we were, but why worry, and who cared anyway? After all we were retired.

That last evening Libby was very subdued for obvious reasons. I'd only insisted we go because it might take her mind off the accident that morning.

It was late when we arrived back home and locked up one last time before we left for Germany. Once in bed I had difficulty getting off to sleep and lay awake for most of the night. I couldn't help but think if anyone had ever slept the night before they went away on holiday such was the anticipation and excitement? One other thing that did keep running over and over in my mind was Libby's trip to the chemist and why the shop assistant was so damned nosey. I said nothing to Libby at the time but couldn't help chewing over in my own mind at how brazenly inquisitive the woman had been. And as for the prang in the car, well that just made me wish she had gone elsewhere to do the last minute shopping, because we left the food in the fridge anyway.

'I'll never forget that bastard's face' she said as she climbed into bed that last evening before we holidayed. It was an ominous statement and though we did not know it at the time, one that would come back to haunt us later.

Next day was Thursday and Libby had not had a good night, queried whether we should be going away, and after hearing my reply got on getting ready as we would be leaving for an overnight stay in London. Panic set in as soon as we as we got out of bed. I mean it was manic as we went from bed to toilet, toilet to shower, shower back to bedroom simply to get dressed. I was just glad we got the order and function of the rooms in the right order, or we could have been changing clothes at our age had we had an accident of memory. Then it was time for Libby's make-up to be applied. Breakfast was express fast: decaf coffee and cereals for 'madam'; caffeinated coffee and a boiled egg for me. Still there were little niggles as we tripped round each other sorting ourselves out and trying to make ourselves 'look' and 'smell' nice. Surprising how everything seems to take so long to get ready despite every last detail being planned ahead for weeks. We never seem to leave the house in a relaxed disposition. There was always at least one member of the family in a sweat as we bumped into each other, tripped over luggage, had one last look at passports and then dashed back upstairs to clean our teeth. "Brush, do not rush" I can hear my late mother telling me as the electric toothbrush went to work.

Critically, just when you didn't need it, the waft of new perfume hits the nostrils to send the old hormone racing round the aging body. The dream over, reality returns when you hear

'The door bell's ringing love can you see who it is? Have you checked the central heating clocks and boiler?" It was Libby barking at me as she added the last touches of eye shadow and applied her lippy for the millionth time in her life. I usually muttered something under my breath asking her which she wanted me to check first. It wouldn't have mattered one iota for there, outside our front door, was the taxi ready to take us to the railway station and our train to London. It was still only half past eight and Libby was beginning to fret. The local rush hour had already begun round our neighbourhood as schoolchildren were either being ferried in parents' cars or walking to their school. The roads were usually blocked at that time as the traffic crawled along slowly whilst being overtaken by school kids still making their way on foot. Making matters much worse that particular morning was the fact that the queues of traffic were longer and slower than usual because the weather had decided to turn wintry overnight.

'Come on babe it's the taxi what's keeping you?' I asked knowing that the make-up re-construction job of that morning was still not finished at that precise moment. The taxi driver gave us a reminder on his car horn that he was still waiting and time was money, our money. Curtains were gingerly drawn back as inquisitive neighbours wondered whose car horn it was that was tooting loudly not once but twice that cold morning. Soon afterwards, and with the taxi loaded up, we were travelling to the station. I said travelling but flitting in and out of the traffic like skaters on ice more like, whilst we hung on to the taxi's straps, not each other, to prevent us colliding and rolling around on the rear seat or even the floor. Lord knows why the driver took the route he did because it would have been smoother over fields. What was it the shop assistant said? 'Have a safe and pleasant journey.' If only, and we hadn't gone five miles. Only the cases at our feet were static but not Libby's brain. Oh no. As usual I knew it was ticking over and over checking and double checking if we had included and were carrying everything we needed for the holiday. I knew this was true because it was the only time she counted on her fingers which she was doing rapidly at that moment when not hanging on for dear life. I of course, old clever-clogs, had checked over and over again in my mind what was needed and was satisfied all was well but then I had little to concern myself with as Libby had made her list!

After darting in and out of first this lane and then that lane, the traffic queues being much longer after the few snowflakes that fell, we eventually arrived intact at Birmingham International rail station. Seeing off the taxi driver, though what for I could not imagine after such a journey as we had almost become a feature of his cab, we jumped onto the escalator with our cases and bags and arrived in the main upstairs concourse of the station each of us miraculously in one piece.

That's when the fun started, or to be more accurate, when we panicked. You see I had ordered the train tickets over the internet and in so doing had missed a vital cog in their purchase. I had not clicked on the box that indicated we wanted the tickets by post, but had left it blank. That is how we came to be using an automatic ticket machine for the first time. Libby was apoplectic with worry at the thought of me and all that new technology colliding. All I had to do was retrieve our tickets from the machine: that is what I set about trying to achieve. Yes we had ordered them from the Mr Branson I told the silent screen, and I had inserted my debit card as requested, and it was recognised. So what was I to do next? Where was our code on the paper ticket? What code? Lights were flashing on the screen. Libby's face was utter terror. I needed my glasses. With them on maybe I could see the code on the paper ticket. It was tucked away in a corner of the ticket and so small I should have used a magnifying glass to find it. I entered into the machine the letters and numbers tapping the screen gently and waited, staring back threateningly at the screen in front of me and daring it to fail. Then, as if I'd played and won money on a one-armed bandit at the local pub, the train tickets fell out of that machine and into their slot. I cheered and attracted unwanted attention from passers-by. Libby gave me one of her looks that would have melted the Antarctic so I hurriedly picked the tickets up out of the ticket tray where they lay. I still had that silly smile on my face that to all intents and purposes indicated I had 'won' a prize on a one armed bandit and placed the tickets safely in my wallet. I followed Libby, she who had flounced off in disgust in front of me, glad the technological ordeal was over for both of us.

We decided that a coffee was necessary to calm the nerves after all that nervous activity we had undertaken, that youngsters take easily in their stride. I could see Libby was dying for a cigarette but smoking was definitely out of the question once and for all since we had 'grown' a grand-daughter. How about a white wine I thought as I caught sight of Libby clocking the aperitifs et al behind the coffee machines? But in my continued imaginary response I told myself she would have to wait till we got to London. Coffee it was to be. Bloody mind games.

'I know it's difficult after all that happened the other day, and I don't want to appear cruel but try and relax love, you are after all an innocent party' I said trying to help her situation. The look she gave was not promising but she held my hand as we entered the café and sat on stools.

The coffee warmed us both up and with only five minutes left before the train was due to arrive, and it was on time according to the information boards, we descended by escalator to platform four. Libby was none too pleased as we waddled down to the freezing platform traipsing our cases behind us and returning to a different set of weather conditions from those of the day before. Preparation for the German markets I thought as we moved along the platform to the Gold Section. God it was cold outside on that platform the easterly wind cutting through us like a sharp knife. We soon lost any warmth the coffee had given us when, approaching our platform with its wheels squeaking in the platform's sleepy atmosphere was our express. Oh that wonderful warm air-conditioned Virgin Train was early, just what Libby wanted to get out of the icy cold temperatures on the platform. I'm sure I could hear her quietly thanking Richard Branson as she sank into her seat. We sat in coach F, First Class seats 29A and 30A having accepted the offer from the tour company for

London bound travellers. And then that heavenly aroma of freshly cooked bacon rolls met the nostrils, one of which I would soon eat, the fragrant smells passing through the carriage like a magic carpet wafting past the nostrils. Standing to take my overcoat off I couldn't help but notice out of the carriage window as the train pulled away slowly a red and damaged Toyota sports car at the very end of the car park with two people sat in it. It was the equal of one Libby had described to me the day that she had been forced off the road. Were we being stalked and followed I asked myself? Such silly thoughts are reserved for silly people I said loudly in my mind and put such thoughts out of my head.

I sat down, ate my bacon roll, winked at Libby and no sooner had I appeared to close my eyes than I was being hissed at and kicked under the table. Libby's attempt to wake me up as we passed through Camden a mile outside of Euston station was a lot more enthusiastic and devious than some footballers I'd played against. Outside the carriage and alongside the railway track, as if it had been specifically placed there for Libby, someone had kindly left a sign which had written on it 'Euston Station one mile' and that is what precipitated her attack on my shins. It began to strike me as strange at that bruising moment, before the train came to a halt, how people were already standing up or walking to the exit doors ready to disembark the train. It was after all a terminus so why the rush?

What was apparent when the train did get to the platform and stop, and we too had got off the train, was the speed of the passengers who seemed to be in some sort of race to get off the platform and up the ramp near the buffers where the train had stopped. The race even continued as the majority headed pell-mell and disappeared lemming-like into the cold and anonymous abyss that London was that day. At the time of year and especially in such a cold winter spell that blanketed the countryside as we travelled down from Birmingham – Libby told me as we walked along the platform because of course I had slept most of the journey - there must have been lots lonely people out there in the City of London. Libby and I just tootled happily along the platform aiming for the dimly-lit underground taxi rank beneath the bowels of the station. All the time it took from train to taxi, and despite lugging along her own case, Libby clung to me leech-like in case we were separated such was the effect that the thug of a driver had had on her confidence the day of her accident, and particularly since it had involved a fatality.

'What's the rush?' she kept asking as we dodged in and out of the human traffic that was Euston Station. 'The hotel won't go away!'

"Holiday Inn, Regent's Park please" I said to the cab driver trying to ignore Libby's breathlessness which I was accused of causing as we walked with a bit of a run to the taxi rank. Midday in London is crazy at the best of times, and a permanent rush hour unlike anywhere else in the UK. But we experienced a safe and comfortable journey to our hotel for a change. No sliding about on the back seat that time and I paid the cab driver, walked into the hotel lobby and checked in. Once in the room I was not really surprised to see my wife check all the cupboards and drawers prior to her allocating me my 'pants and socks drawer' after commandeering the rest of the drawers for her 'smalls', jumpers and anything else that was not stopping in her case overnight. In particular the three, yes three, make-up bags.

'Oh and that part of the wardrobe is for you to hang your jacket up' she just happened to tell me as I was hanging said item over a rather nice chair back.

'Put the kettle on for a cuppa Love please' she asked politely now, 'I am so thirsty and my throat so parched after that train journey.'

What is it about women that they always have to drink tea at those moments? Why can they not have a half glass of beer like we parched men?

'I'm not a bloody valet or butler your ladyship' I muttered under my breath for fear of being given a rollicking if heard. I opened the room fridge so quietly, and it squeaked. I was found out.

'Don't start drinking yet Tony it's only just after three o'clock. If you start drinking now you know what you'll be like come seven o'clock when we go for a Chinese meal after the show' Libby said like only she could! That was it. We were only staying for one night and it was as if she had said 'no drink yet little boy, we are off to a show and then a Chinese meal if you are really well-behaved then you can have a drink.'

I could see she was still thinking of her nasty experiences her eyes still bloodshot from her crying. I went along the peaceful and less bumpy route for once and made us both a cuppa. Having drunk my tea I then laid down on the huge super king-size bed, kicked off my shoes and promptly fell asleep in that gloriously warm room. No kicks from the other side of the bed after my forty winks just a nudge in the back as she was adjusting her make-up once again and making sure I had time to look my best to go out with her.

Not long after we'd left the hotel we found ourselves on Tottenham Court Road heading for theatre ticket outlets around the Shaftesbury Avenue area.

'We Will Rock You' was the show we fancied, mainly I think because I started to sing the songs from Queen's Greatest Hits as soon as I saw the advertising boards for the show. Libby said I was singing like a little boy out to impress his mum, totally out of tune of course. To try and shut me up she produced and gave me some exceptionally sticky toffees to chew. Her plan worked because I couldn't sing another note as my jaws wrestled with the sticky toffee. She told me later she had bought them at home the day before for just such an occasion knowing I would participate with the cast whatever the musical. I was more concerned about my fillings from then on as we spent the next two hours clapping, dancing and singing along with a very young and lively audience, to say nothing of the rendition on the stage. At least all the activity had taken her mind off the trauma of the day before.

Exhausted after the musical and our physical workout we set off back out into Shaftesbury Avenue looking for any available cab. Being London we soon found one within minutes and we were whisked away at snail's pace through the interminable traffic to the Phoenix Palace in Marylebone a place we had visited previously and so having had a good meal in very pleasant surroundings wanted to return. On arrival we noticed there were just two other people eating in a restaurant that easily catered for two hundred. Picking a table with so many spare ones to choose from reminded me of being in a supermarket car park when you arrive early before anyone else and cannot make your mind up where best to park. However, there we were at the start of a holiday whose main aim was to celebrate our big wedding anniversary, and we were both starving hungry.

'I could eat a horse' said Libby as she looked around the surroundings.

'This is a Chinese not a French or Belgian restaurant' I replied with a grin on my face. She ignored me and began taking her coat off.

Being inside and warm again, away from the deteriorating weather conditions outside that had turned very wintry and much colder with the heavy December frost, made us feel safe.

Having been guided to our table by a charming hostess a waitress approached and asked if we wanted drinks and starters. Did we want a drink? I ordered the drinks while Libby pored over the menu looking for some tasty starters and ordered food for both of us: pancake rolls, spare ribs, prawn dumplings and crispy seaweed that soon arrived at our table as did our drinks. The first I had I don't think touched the sides of my throat as it disappeared. Before leaving our table the waitress smiled knowingly though I'd like to think she was impressed by my bad habit, and asked if I'd like another drink. I nodded politely. What we both liked about Chinese food was the fact that nearly every mouthful had a different combination of taste. The meal that night was no different the range of tastes being excellent. Another drink arrived before I had placed the second glass back on the table. The looks I was getting from Libby because of my enlarged thirst I continued to ignore. We both commented on how much we admired the variety of Xmas decorations in the restaurant which were a combination of both Eastern and Western cultures kept separate and without any overlap. Filling two sides of the restaurant our Western trimmings were of Santa Claus and fir trees whilst the Chinese trimmings were all dragons and pagodas blending in enchantingly. It promised to be a magical holiday and a theatre trip and meal in London seemed like a good way to begin celebrating. Libby sipping her favourite Chablis looked entirely at home in that restaurant: seemingly chilled out at long last and though she had not mentioned the previous day's problems for several hours, I knew they were still at the forefront of her mind. But for that moment at least she appeared comfortable in her surroundings and ready to indulge herself with her chosen meal. After munching through our starters the mains of chicken, prawn and beef dishes with rice arrived and went down a treat helped notably with the accompanying beers and wine. Contented, or rather bloated food-wise, we settled the bill and made ready to face the elements outside again. Our sheepskin coats, that had been Libby's idea, were most welcome as we got ready to walk back to the hotel and take an early night back in the warmth of the hotel bar where a night cap or two would be most appreciated.

We walked briskly back to our hotel and on arrival went directly up in the lift to the bar and following a couple of smooth nightcaps retired to our room. I switched on the TV for any late news and crept into bed promptly falling asleep. It was then still only ten o'clock when Libby quietly, rubbing her eyes asked

'I wonder if the old lady who died had any family?'

I told her that it was possible but from where we were we could only hope they were being comforted.

I left the TV on still talking to us both so it was no wonder I awoke after a short nap and wondered where I was. Peering sleepily around the room I decided the time had come to turn off the TV with the remote control thinking Libby was fast asleep. What happened next was bound to happen. I woke Libby in the process of leaning over to find the remote control to switch off the TV. With the sound and vision off Libby woke up, not quite as bright as the button that she was normally, and with her eyes almost entirely closed. She then proceeded to berate me because she had been watching some film or other on the TV at that moment. I passed her the controls, grunted and rolled over and went back to sleep vaguely noticing Libby return to the dressing-table mirror to remove her make-up. I don't remember much at all after that.

Chapter Two.

Next morning was Friday and we were both up with the lark ready to face the elements and ready to travel to Germany. Libby had had a better night's sleep and was more like her old self so whilst she was in the shower I made the customary pot of hotel tea. My wife would not, I mean could not, function if she did not partake of that first cuppa. When applying her make-up later she had to have a cup of decaf coffee close by. Having showered and dressed I went downstairs to purchase any of the day's newspapers since there were not any left on the hotel corridors it was so early. It was after all only five forty five for Heaven's sakes. I was no good without a newspaper first thing in the morning and usually began reading it in the 'library' of the house or hotel we were staying in. The winter weather according to the newspaper was to deteriorate rapidly in the UK with heavy snow having been forecast for the rest of the week. The forecast for weather on the Continent, and Germany in particular, looked as though it would be Christmassy since there was already several feet of snow in the Alps. Although we would not be so far south visiting Cologne the winds were blowing from the south so it was possible that the weather would be what we hoped for when we were away.

At half past six we left our hotel room for a breakfast of cereals, fruit and yogurt. Not I might add the lovely sausage, bacon and eggs that were sizzling on adjacent hot plates! That was because after the previous night's sumptuous Chinese banquet a fry up the next morning was definitely out of the question for both of us for health and weight reasons.

Later in our room I watched some news programme showing highlights of the snow in Northern Britain and ice and frost elsewhere. We seem to take great delight that other areas have the heavy snow at that time of the year whilst hankering after it ourselves, until it arrives. A knock on the room door soon aroused us from our semi-comatose news and weather watching state.

"Time to go," I said still thinking of the breakfast fry up I had declined a couple of hours earlier, "It's the guy for the cases to take down stairs," I added.

"Just adjusting my make-up," was Libby's reply as if I wasn't expecting such a comment.

In the lift with the hotel porter and our cases with their silly Pineapple Rail Tour labels I wondered why, if there were three people in the lift as we descended to the ground floor with our cases, how on earth was the lift meant to accommodate ten people when the three of us were pushed for room inside the lift at that precise moment. It could have been worse. We had after all eaten the healthy breakfast and not the fatty and tasty alternative unhealthy breakfast we could have had. Oh no! But what did I care now.

Just as the lift slowed down approaching the ground floor of the hotel Libby made what I thought was a stupid comment at that moment because it failed to make sense to me.

'Walking back to the hotel last night I thought I saw a person I recognised. I know you won't believe me Tony but she looked incredibly like the woman in the chemist's back home where I bought your tablets. I know it was dark and the mind plays tricks in the dark but she and her companion I couldn't place at the time, strange as it seemed. And I forgot to mention to you till now. Ah well they did seem familiar somehow. You know you glimpse a face but cannot put a name to it. Or think you recognise someone, and in a place as big as London I bet many people have doubles or doppelgangers don't they?'

I raised my left eyebrow thinking 'Here we go again, leave it off Libby' when we arrived at the ground floor the lift doors opened and we made our way to the check-out desk, settled our bill and asked a porter to call us a taxi. When the taxi arrived we were whisked the short journey to the station through the bustling throng that is London's morning 'rush hours', not 'hour', and into St. Pancras International Rail Station.

It had been many years since I had last been at St Pancras station. I used to come down from the Midlands or the North on a junior school day out or with family. And yet there we were on that early December morning standing in brilliant sunshine with clear blue skies all around, the glass windows in the station roof glistening like sparkling diamonds. As we stood outside that magnificent building it was difficult not to smile for a second in admiration of what the architect achieved. Only a slight pause as it was time to move on having experienced the coldest and frostiest night of the winter thus far. I remembered the cabbie before he could remind me on his horn and so paid and thanked him for his services. We walked slowly with our luggage into the station's concourse and shops whilst still over awed by the beauty of glass and brick.

Our lazy walk was made worse not only by the incredible cold outside but the cold inside near the entrance too. Unfortunately the sun, though low in the winter sky, had little effect on the warmth in the place. The light was refracted so that rainbows of light cascaded down onto expectant and excited passengers chatting away whilst waiting to board their trains. Libby and I just stood back admiring the whole scene: red-brick walls cleaned of all smoke and grime from the old steam engines long gone; lamp-posts from the Edwardian era. Other passengers too having once entered the immaculately clean but busy station prior to boarding their train, were to be seen surveying their surroundings. Many stopping to gaze at the magnificent station clock for example, others mesmerised by the range of shops particularly the confectionary shops with windows full of chocolate.

'Why don't we come here more often?' Libby lamented ruefully 'with all these sweet shops I could have a ball.'

I ignored her as she paused opposite a window displaying a Christmas tree. No ordinary one either, just pure chocolate, the type someone like my Libby would have liked to have delivered to our address at home. Every week!

Moving ever closer to what I hoped was our planned rendezvous point, and increasingly excited at going away from the UK for a while I couldn't help but think again of the previous occasions I'd been on the station. As a young lad I had maybe stood on the same spot I was then stood on, only forty or fifty years before.

Our trip that December was to include three nights in Cologne in a good and comfortable hotel one of our aims being to visit some of the Christmas markets the Germans accomplish and celebrate so much better than we British. And of course our prime aim was to celebrate our anniversary. If I didn't remember the latter, and the present I had taken along for my beloved, I would be placed well and truly in the doghouse for years.

Having experienced the mythical Advent festival of 'Winterval' in Birmingham, and having heard constantly that Christmas lights and decorations were being banned in some British towns and city centres, we hoped for a different experience in Germany. It wasn't that any other religions ever objected in the UK but just that some jobs-worth justified and earned their salary for being so bloody politically correct. I could not help but wonder what and why we had altered and mutated our Christmas. How on earth would our grand-children ever experience the magic of Christmas we had as kids, albeit in the past? That was not so in Germany thank goodness which was another reason for our holiday.

Back inside the station noises varied: trains hooted as they left for Brussels, Paris, or further afield: announcers spoke in English and French one after the other describing platform alterations, destinations and the weather en route to those destinations. Standing underneath the international platforms we were somewhat shielded from the hustle and bustle going on above us. On those platforms we were aware of the scraping and clunking of cases, trolleys and pushchairs all making the station vibrate with holiday noises. Foreign languages abounded everywhere: French, German, Dutch and Slavic languages from further east in Europe, Japanese, Cantonese and Mandarin such was the pull of London on tourists. Yet even amongst all that the smell of fresh coffee wafted through the air from out of the station bistros and cafes as waiting passengers took one last drink before the platform barriers opened and they passed through to the HM Customs to board their trains. The smell of fresh bread too filled the spaces left by the coffee smells, be it of toast in the toasty sandwich makers or croissants in continental cafes as travellers 'got in the mood' for their holiday, or grabbed a late bite before they mixed with the coffee smells again. The M and S shop was packed – always is; perfume shops were busy; newsagents had enough papers to go round and off-sales had customers perusing their goods. The pre-travel atmosphere became intoxicating.

Exhilarated as we were to be going away just before Christmas, though it was not something we had experienced before, it was certainly something we could have got used to given the chance.

'Look, those people over by that pillar have all had orange stickers slapped on their cases,' Libby pointed out, 'do you think they are they on our trip too?'

'I can't see any Tour manager hovering by,' I replied, 'they usually have to at the departure times,' I said sarcastically. 'I know the company we are travelling with said the rep' would have a large pineapple on his jacket lapel. So perhaps that's not our group.'

'See, over there by the entrance to the platforms, I can see a pineapple on the lapel of a tall bloke who is holding court with some passengers.' Libby had him spotted I-Spy style from yards away and she continued 'and the passengers have all got pineapple stickers on their cases. That's them for sure. That's the group we are travelling with, it's got to be. But they are mostly old folks and I can't see many as young as we are.'

It turned out to be the wrong group when we got near them and enquired of their destination. They were off to Switzerland as it turned out: not our trip. Hovering close by and behind another column we found our fellow travellers who were off to Germany.

Libby had alluded to the ages of the folk in the previous group as being old: as young as we are she had distinctly said which was unbelievable because we too were both retired. To even consider the words 'As young as we are' in such circumstances was exceedingly rude, and utterly false.

The 'big station clock' upstairs showed it was after ten o'clock and there we were hanging around waiting to check in eventually, and with our train due to leave at midday there was still plenty of time to mingle. Several people, seemingly without partners as they call them nowadays, had by that time already appeared to have formed friendship groups both male and female. All were well-wrapped up against the cold weather which could still be felt inside the building and probably why the cafes were full of trippers drinking warm drinks.

'British Café Society even if it is under a roof is keeping the wrinklies warm' Libby thought she had whispered quietly in my ear.

'Good Lord woman watch what you're saying,' I said whispering loudly in response to her comment re' the wrinklies, 'if they hear you we'll be outcasts on the holiday. Anyway we're in our early sixties and you have only just retired from teaching so we can't talk.'

My comments went down like a lead balloon as Libby wheeled her case over more closely to the group with me trailing in her wake knowing she had not heard a word of what I'd said after all. Approaching the group with both a weak and nervous smile we introduced ourselves to the person who we assumed was the group leader when he'd finished talking to the people in front of him. Well it had to be him with his pineapple sticker on his left lapel and his name sticker on the other: Dennis Johnson. A yellow pineapple sticker on a blue jacket standing out like a belisha beacon: sartorial elegance I thought not and him with a goatee beard stuck on his chin too. What did he look like standing legs astride a black briefcase with a small rucksack slung over his right shoulder as he talked, probably one or both containing our rail tickets and labels. I watched Libby's face the moment she encountered our tour guide from the front and saw her trying to control her astonishment at what I knew she would think was his lack of dress sense. Either that or she knew him.

That was when and where we each received our own Pineapple labels for our cases and our hand luggage, each with the address of our hotel of course. It was also our first and most revealing meeting with the tour rep at the quaint Pineapple Rail Tours Desk adjacent to the ticket barrier. I assessed the numbers of the group to be about twenty to twenty five persons strong from what I could make out and we had become one of them. At last we were in possession of that valuable 'pineapple identity'. We were members of the party! Checking the identities of our fellow travellers appeared to be a regular formality carried out several times before we each received our Eurostar tickets. Then, and only then were we allowed to proceed forward and stand in one of the lengthy ticket queues to the trains. All that time Libby and I spent familiarising ourselves with the tour rep's face in case we became separated. At least that is what I thought at the time. How anyone could forget his sparse and meagre goatee beard was a thought that I knew had Libby transfixed for a moment? I looked over towards where she was stood staring at the bloke like somehow she knew him. I disturbed those thoughts when I said to her drily

'Smiling at people who have pineapple stickers on their luggage could be come a sport don't you think?' She just ignored me as usual because she immediately began talking to a lady and her man friend who had her back to the tour rep. The lady was explaining some of the procedures involved in moving from our current position to the ticket barrier when the 'Pineapple' rep turned and beckoned us all to go towards him for more information. His arms were flailing about for a minute that reminded me of when our daughter Caroline was a cheerleader at her dancing school.

'I just wanted to tell you that we shall be moving into another waiting area the other side of the barriers in a minute. We shall then pass on through security and passport control which is on the other side of the ticket barriers.' Johnson's broadcast was meant for our group in particular but it was hard for the passing crowds to ignore it and they stared at him in disbelief. His arms began whirring again once more rather like an epicyclic gear system as he pointed and 'conducted' us towards and beyond the barriers.

There was further information to come as he blurted out

'For those of you who have not travelled with us before you need to know the following information: take your outward rail ticket and place it in the barrier like you have to for the Underground and pull it out of the machine from the other slot when it pops up. When do we proceed from here?' he said responding to a little lady under his nose, his face reddening not expecting a question at that moment. 'Good question. When our train time and destination appears on the indicator board above us is the answer to that. Normally half an hour before the train is due to depart.'

There was a slight pause in his answer, his mouth open without any words coming out, but it was only a temporary lull as he continued

'Ah but we can go through now I think. I have checked, seen and spoken to each person I think, and recorded the attendance of everybody in our group.' With a final flourish of his arms on the station concourse he bade us follow him deeper into the bowels of the station and nearer to our departure platform.

'Is it going to be like this all holiday with us treated like imbeciles? And what slot did he mean?' asked Libby fiddling with her rail tickets.

'I don't know what you're going on about, now keep listening because it's my first time here too' I grizzled back in reply as I looked in my holdall that had every known device that man or woman would need on a holiday. Except for a penknife of course, because now we were grown up we are not allowed even to carry one. I thought that was a stupid rule as when we were kids in school we used to sharpen our pencils with them and nearly every child had their little penknife, and no-one ever got hurt, I think.

'This is my fourth trip with this company' said someone close 'and we have always had great holidays with them. The reps have been superbly helpful but this guy sure is different to say the least.' They continued looking at and talking to Libby 'It's only getting here from across the other side of London that is murder with all the traffic and crowds so early in the morning.'

Only days later would I realise the importance of what those words would come to mean to both Libby and me at the end of our break. At that moment though, being new to rail travel on the continent of Europe, we were about to be surprised by the recollections of some people as we listened to the non-stop conversations around us. It seemed rude to listen in as members of the group jousted verbally endeavouring to score points off each other as they reminisced about rail trips of old. But that is what people do when they go on holiday isn't it? One couple had incredibly been on seven rail trips all with Pineapple Tours. Were they mad or just sad I asked myself? I pointed this couple out to Libby but she had already spoken to them she said, and had begun classifying the group into their perceived careers she thought they were currently in, or used to be in. In fairness I said there were several people who were younger than we were in the party but as yet Libby had not had any contact with them. I say yet, but it didn't take much for her to start a conversation with anyone. I had always told her she could start a conversation with herself in an empty house and be quite content to discuss the merits, for or against, any situation she cared to. That really pleased her: which way I'm not sure. Was it to be on her own in the house or simply happy that I had acknowledged her need to be alone? I shall never know.

Two rough looking but well dressed chaps stood next to the tour rep chatting away animatedly, in particular one with a flattened nose. At least he spoke 'awfully' well despite the nose looking as though it had met a bus at sometime in his life it was so mashed up. I imagined he was definitely one to avoid at all costs. Perhaps he was an ex-boxer or security guy judging by the size of his frame. With my fertile imagination beginning to run amok I was brought back down to earth just as a Scottish accent pierced the air. Nothing unusual in that you may think but over and above everyone else's voice? Give me strength. It didn't matter that the voice was informing all who were prepared to listen, and many who had little choice, that our train's Eurostar number, and the places en route it was to stop at, were now listed on the information board. The voice was so loud and just coincidentally happened to be one of the persons who had been on seven previous rail trips. I saw Libby look disgustedly in the direction from where the noise came from, and then back to me, with a pained look on her face that indicated she was not happy. Perhaps, we were to discuss later on the train, the lady had been co-opted as a deputy rep or tour organiser after all her trips with the company. I sincerely hoped not because that would have been an even worse scenario than the one we were faced with then.

'Come people' I heard the tour rep state firmly taking back the organisational reins once more, 'let's get on our way, but please let's keep together till we are the other side of the barriers and into Customs.'

Just like all those bloody school parties I went on as a kid or as a member of staff, and I'd been on plenty of those I recalled. My reminiscing was brought to a halt as Libby abruptly stopped dead in her tracks in front of me and nearly had me, my case and hand luggage all over her.

'And the problem is?' I asked sarcastically noting she still had both her rail tickets in her hand. 'Use the ticket that says London to Brussels, the Eurostar ticket, and place that in the slot next to your right hand like Sir said.'

Technophobe or not that's my lady Libby! She was not amused but with a little help from Johnson, who was loitering at the barrier for just such a hold up, she was on her way blaspheming at me for showing her up she said. Me? I'd run through the information about our tickets not thirty seconds earlier, but was she listening? I know damn well she was not! But that was all part of the excitement of going on holiday, wasn't it? We cleared the checks on our hand luggage, my jacket, coat and pocket scans made by a plastic-looking table-tennis bat waved all over me as an alarm went off. To cap it all there were more checks to our clothing for some perverted reason that I never found out why at the time when another security officer said gruffly 'Remove your belt and shoes sir and place them in the tray.'

That's when I started to smile to myself as I began to see the comedy of it all unfolding as people began to put shoes back on, re-fit belts into trouser loops and get dressed again. Thank the Lord that was all we removed I thought as I looked around and saw people trying to balance or wobble on one leg as they replaced their shoes or leant on friends and family to complete getting dressed. It was a pantomime that had been decreed necessary by whom I knew not, but it had a funny side to it. When we had all performed those regulatory tasks it was full steam ahead to another queue where we would proceed through passport control. I say proceed but it was more of a cursory glance at our passports by the British Officers, followed by the 'real check and stare at your face' by the French Customs Officers. The strained look I got from the French Officer appeared, to me, to question the validity of my photograph in the passport as he stood glaring at me while I stood in front of him. I imagined his thoughts being 'Can this really be a picture of that rostbif opposite me?' I trundled past him thinking I knew at last why Anglo-Gallic relations had always been difficult in the past. Necessary checks in 'unsafe' days I suppose even if 'Thierry' did come over all super efficient.

And then, as if by magic, it happened and we were free again. In front of us was a myriad of shops, cafes and bars allowing us time to re-mingle with our fellow travellers, or simply sit and chill out before we boarded our train to Germany.

Chapter *Three*.

Our train was scheduled to leave at midday and there we were
waiting almost an hour early at 11.00am, not the anticipated half
an hour before departure. We were only on the trip because we
were celebrating forty years married to each other and although the
years had passed it still brought a tingle to my spine when I thought
about it. It didn't stop the need for a drink, the compulsory visit
to the toilet and the chance to stretch our legs. All much needed
before we left London at our age and this extra time gave us
the opportunity. Only one problem: which order to do them in,
because to have got it wrong would be plumbing the depths so to
speak? Only the brave would have taken a drink first! So one at
a time, first Libby and then me, would leave our comfy seat and
head off to the loo to satisfy our immediate toiletry needs. On the
occasion I am referring to I remained sitting tightly cross-legged
flicking through the day's newspapers hoping I too wouldn't have
a plumbing accident when I suddenly felt a shadow hanging over
me darkening the area I rested in. It was his nibs the tour guide
just checking we were OK and had our tickets to hand ready to
board the train when called, by which time Libby had returned
looking refreshed.

'Don't I know you?' he asked ignoring me and looking straight
at Libby. 'Haven't you been on rail tours with us before?'

'I don't think so as this is our first time travelling by rail to the continent,' Libby replied, 'if we've been away on holiday it's normally been with our children or grand-children.'

'Sorry, I just thought your face was …… familiar. Well you know how it is one sees so many people in this job. So where are you from then?' Johnson asked.

'Birmingham for the last forty odd years or so. We are both retired now so can holiday when the schools are not out as they say. How about you Dennis? Where do you hail from?' Libby asked ever the inquisitive and mischievous minx.

'I'm from London. I used to work on the Underground before I retired. That's how this job came along and as I can speak German fluently because my dad was German they were only too pleased to employ me' Johnson continued. Much more forthcoming he carried on 'Of course it is much easier when you are single.'

'How do you mean? Surely a knowledgeable man like you hasn't been single all his life.' Libby was showing her nosey side but she would say she was only making polite conversation.

'No of course not I was married to my wife for four years, well nearly. Big mistake living with such a jealous woman I can tell you. Thank God there were no kids to suffer her too like I did. Since me there have been several other blokes in her life so I hear. I used to feel sorry for her because she couldn't settle down again but who cares she is history to me now? Heard she was living with some Russian or other last I heard of her. Anyway, where was I? Ah yes if you two know what to do next here, when they notify us of our impending departure, I'll see you in our carriage later when I have more information OK? Byeeeee.' And with that he was off to engage another unsuspecting couple on our tour and perhaps impart his personal history to them.

'You didn't have to go so far with the Third Degree' I said to Libby, 'Himmler would have had you in his team, no bother, questioning Johnson like that.'

'I just wanted to be sociable that's all' was the riposte I received from my good lady. 'There wasn't anything contentious. He seems like a nice chap but terribly hurt. Needs ironing around the edges and should shave his silly beard off, dress himself properly and he could be quite presentable. I did it for you and you're presentable despite it taking me forty years!' Ouch!

I turned to reply and caught sight of the smirk on her face and knew she was winding me up so I went to the much-needed loo instead - at long last. When I returned Libby decided she should 'go for a wander' to see if anything was worth buying, as if she had room in her case for anything else. I could see she was beginning to relax more and I really hoped the rest of the journey would take her mind off the last forty eight hours and by meeting new people it would perhaps act as some sort of healing therapy. Minutes after she returned and sat down again next to me I caught her staring at someone. They walked past us with their face covered by a large scarf type thing, a pashmina I think they call it. Anyway she stopped reading her book abruptly and really stared after the lady.

'OK?' I asked her.

'Just for a moment … it's nothing' she said and carried on reading her book.

'What's nothing?' I half enquired as she pretended to carry on reading.

'Like I said it was something and nothing. I saw that lady in the toilet area looking at me rather strangely so I thought. And there she was again walking past staring at me. Now she's gone again. I thought she looked familiar that's all. Something weird struck me about her. Just beneath her left eye seemed ……. It was nothing' she again replied and buried her face deeper in her book. I knew when to lay off her in circumstances like that after years of experience and practice. To carry on would mean I was only wasting my time.

Not long afterwards the announcement we had been waiting to hear was read out over the Tannoy.

'Would passengers for Lille and Brussels please make their way to Gate 9 and have their tickets available to be checked.'

That was the call we had been expecting and so we both stood and lemming-like prepared to add to the already formed queue by the ticket barrier.

Unbeknown to us at the time as our tour group made its way towards the ramp, the lady with the scarf over her head whom Libby had thought she recognised, was likewise moving towards the ticket barrier to board the same train with a tall swarthy companion.

Having had our tickets checked a last and final time by the ever-efficient Eurostar personnel we followed the stream of fellow passengers and their luggage up the ramp to the waiting carriages. Our 'Outward' tickets' numbers showed we were in coach 8, seats 27 and 28, non-smoking. St Pancras to Brussels Midi, arrival 15.03 hrs: very impressive giving the arrival time too I thought! Of course I went the wrong way at the top of the walk-way looking for our coach having lost sight of our Tour Guide who, by the time I realised he was missing, could have been on another train. My immediate about turn unfortunately meant I bumped into other passengers who had clearly done likewise but who were by then also travelling in the opposite direction from me and an increasingly pissed off Libby. Collisions were inevitable in the frenetic chase for seats despite the fact that all seats were allocated beforehand. That included Libby too who, as I pivoted turning sharply, and without prior warning having realised the error I had made on my radar, bumped into me with such force she almost disappeared up my nostrils she was that close behind me. I was so happy that I had been brought up to believe looks could not kill. The look on Libby's face when we collided could have altered that theory had there been witness to our collision!

Moving on as you do in that predicament we pretended to be happily looking for our coach number as we smiled cheerfully dodging the moving throng. Upon finding it, because I recognised several of our party clambering aboard, I managed to drag our cases onto the train hauling Libby behind me as I did. Once aboard we set about looking for our seats in a queue that was progressing at a snail's pace along the carriage. There followed the inevitable delay as someone tried to lift their case onto a luggage rack and that's when I took hold of the situation. It was easier, and subsequently quicker, for me to 'assist' them with their luggage. Crawling slowly through the coach still searching for our seats we found we were amongst 'friends'. Friends Libby had spoken to both on the station concourse and in the waiting area prior to boarding the train.

Perspiring profusely after running round first trying to locate our carriage, and then lobbing cases onto luggage racks, and despite having taken my coat off, it became even more noticeable how very warm it was aboard the train. Not warm, hot. I had lost more weight perspiring from the carriage heating than from that other more noble exercise of lifting several cases onto the luggage racks. I would have much rather preferred to ride my bike than be in such a frantic atmosphere. However, sorting the hand luggage and where to place it was my next chore when we had at last located our seats. I thought I was being polite in helping three ladies from our group lift their cases onto the racks close by but they would have none of it and told me in no uncertain terms 'It's OK we can manage ducky'. Three to avoid I thought at the time but I was to be proved completely wrong as the tour developed.

For a train Leisure Select was extremely comfortable and made even more so by the young stewardesses who attracted the attention not only of the 'bruiser' with the flat nose during the journey south, but also more mature gentlemen who were having problems with their partners because of it. One of those young ladies appeared just before departure with a menu card that quickly became the centre of attention on our table at least, and with the other travellers too after the lady had left our carriage. Checking out the lunch-time offerings we noticed the usual introductory and preliminary conversations had started up amongst members of our group who had found themselves opposite other fellow members at the tables of four. Libby and I were, however, at a table for two and were quickly both of us stretching out in our comfy seats playing footsie under our table. But not the type we played nearly forty years ago when we courting. Even England footballers would have been impressed as we 'kicked for space' under that table whilst Libby selected her Belgian cheese quiche, and I chose my chicken fillet from the menu, not a football programme.

A gentle pull on the seat told me that the train was on its way at last to our destination for the weekend, Cologne. Well Brussels and a change of train to be precise. Our first stop would be Ebbsfleet in Kent a new station on the new section of track. Leaving St Pancras we managed a short glimpse of the East End of London as we travelled above ground before entering a long and winding tunnel as the train picked up speed on our journey. Back above ground after several minutes beneath London in the tunnel I asked Libby to guess how many coaches she thought there were being pulled by our engine.

'You're being a little boy again' she laughed, 'a railway anorak just as if you were aged fifteen again and train-spotting. I bet you are going to hang your head out of the window and collect passing train numbers getting smoke all over your face you little rascal aren't you?'

I pretended to ignore her but it was true I'd enjoyed steam trains as a kid, not diesels, but this was different. The whole train must have had twenty coaches as it quickly threaded its way through the outskirts of East London. By then Libby was in serious conversation with one of the Scottish ladies who seemed to have been every where in the world with her husband by train. She expressed a view that they were confident of being more experienced that any other couple in the group at any rate. Her husband, for his part though, smiled occasionally giving me one of those 'I am sorry she is going on so much but I cannot stop her' looks poor man. He looked so uncomfortable sitting in the window seat. I began to wonder if he'd ever heard of selective hearing. Maybe I could teach him a thing or two about it when Libby was out of ear shot of course!

'Monsieur and madam would you like a drink before your meal?' sang this delightful African-French stewardess as she flitted from table to table.

Champagne was what Libby enjoyed most especially when it was 'inclusive' and it's what she had that cold day on the first leg of our journey. I chose to partake of one of Belgium's finest lagers. As we waited for the drinks to arrive it was very evident from the view outside the window somewhere south of London that it really was becoming a bleak midwinter. We passengers safe in the warmth of our carriage, sat back and relaxed as the train whizzed by buildings and trees leaving them a blur; we overtook speeding cars that could only look on enviously as we sped across the lightly snow-dusted countryside as we continued to enjoy our drinks. Much jollity prevailed amongst the passengers as the alcohol took effect upon our group. The laughter increased in volume and the talking too became louder a sure sign that meant people were beginning to relax if they weren't before. Looking round and studying the faces that were to become a fixture in our social calendar for a few days it was obvious that age was no barrier to travel, particularly rail travel.

'Where are you from?' someone asked Libby in a very posh accent. Hearing those dulcet tones was all Libby needed to 'switch on' her conversational iPod. The charming elderly man who spoke introduced himself as Sid who came from Essex.

'Call me Sid' he told Libby 'and what pray, is your name young lady?'

Being referred to as young lady was the type of flattery that got you everywhere with Libby. And Libby loved it as she introduced herself, and me, to our fellow traveller who having introduced himself to us could not imagine the conversation that was about to be unleashed from my wife's mouth. Lighting touch paper was known to produce a similar effect in setting off the combustibles, only these were questions fired machine-gun like from Libby. It transpired Sid had worked in London most of his life although he never said where, though Libby and I both imagined it was in some important capacity. Maybe he worked in the City as a financier or even a top Civil Servant for HMG. We would discuss this together later at length as our forever fertile minds went into overdrive. It was purely guesswork of course at first but we were to find out what Sid had done job-wise during our journey from Cologne to Aachen's Christmas Market the following day Saturday. The conversation faltered momentarily as the train began to slow down quite suddenly the driver applying the brakes bringing to bear people's ability to juggle and prevent drinks from spilling.

'Ashford I bet' said someone obviously used to the journey.

'Can't be they don't stop there on this run it will be Ebbsfleet' another 'anorak' ventured.

And Ebbsfleet it was: we had barely noticed any train movement at the beginning of the journey or even given so much as a cursory look out of the window because the train had been so smooth not only in its acceleration but it appeared to glide over the rails.

'Not long to the Tunnel' continued the second 'anorak'.

Conversation amongst the group only reduced a little in content or volume as the meals arrived at our tables. More champagne, more lager, more wine arrived making that first meal, the first of several together as a party, that much more pleasurable.

Eating hungrily we hardly noticed the slight dip in the track as we headed towards the entrance to the Channel Tunnel the frosted Kent countryside being replaced by a darkened abyss outside our windows. Twenty minutes or so later coinciding with us finishing our meals we returned to daylight, the French countryside and light drizzle. The chatter amongst us surprisingly changed during those few metres into France and turned to the prospect of what type of weather we might expect in Germany. Memories flooded back to bygone romantic times long ago of white Christmases, not the Christmases we'd experienced for many years without snow or even frost. Sid for his part remained the most optimistic of the lot of us convinced that in Germany the weather would be colder and snow far more likely. A grand old fellow of 81 years living alone Libby 'found out' and travelling by himself on the trip having only just returned from a cruise round the Mediterranean to 'keep the bones warm' he had said.

Travelling at speed across Northern France it was noticeable through the 'blur' that the drizzle had given way to frosted fields and frost-sparkled trees in the countryside. All that was needed were some fairy lights and the scene would have been magical. So far and fast had the train travelled that the luncheon plates and glasses had been cleared away and the train, once again, began to slow down again on that occasion for Lille the only scheduled stop in northern France. Whilst Brussels approached ever closer time-wise, the need to test Eurostar plumbing following our liquid intake at lunch was nigh. It was noticeable to the connoisseur of such things that the carriage door leading to the toilet was being opened and closed more frequently than at any time since we had left London. The increasing need for this bodily function, a sort of liquid gravity failure, is connected to the liquid intake consumed, however little, and gathers momentum with advancing age in the human frame. Hence the increased activity as more people visited the loo particularly from the old stagers in our group.

Whilst we were all enjoying ourselves Dennis Johnson was busying himself visiting each member's table relaying some very important information about Brussels' Midi Station. In doing so his arms again rotated violently appearing to conduct some imaginary orchestra as he spoke. The first point he made, when he arrived at our table, was that if we needed the WC in Brussels it would have to be paid for in EU coinage. Secondly, and equally important, the train to Cologne would leave platform four or five at 15.55 hours and we were to all rendezvous at the designated position close by which he would point out to us when our train had 'arrived' and we had cleared the platform.

'Don't forget your cases and make sure the labels are correctly addressed with the correct name of the hotel on them.'

As those words were given to the last table Johnson visited cue a frenzy of activity as coats, scarves, gloves and hand luggage were placed onto tables as Senior British Citizens made themselves ready for their entry into Brussels.

'Have you any euro coins?' Libby asked making me once more fiddle my way through my trouser pockets.

'But we've both just been' I replied, 'surely you don't want to go again so soon?' I continued all to no avail as it was to turn out later. The entrance fee to the station toilets was fifty cents but a whole euro if you felt generous or had no change. What a pity the English coins weren't the same size as these European coins. I was lucky I found the fifty cents needed which I handed to Libby who almost snatched it out of my hand. Not long to go I consoled myself.

The train had slowed as we passed through the Brussels' suburbs. Staring out of the window it was satisfying to see where many of our taxes had gone on the newly built and paid for EU offices and buildings that stood out against the dimming skyline. The train's wheels creaked and squeaked loudly as it slowed down to a walking pace on entering Midi Station. No sooner had the train pulled alongside the platform and with the train still moving and long before it came to a halt, people had begun leaping off the train with an athleticism to be admired as much as it was foolish, before they disappeared into the station's labyrinthine pit.

'Bang on time at 14.03 hrs' someone commented as we walked towards our leader at the side of the platform.

'Yo' ain't changed your watch mate check again. You mean 15.03 hrs' one of the Knuckle Brothers shouted informatively and as usual was spot on.

Like all stations in capital cities this one functioned as a small town on its own: so numerous were the people working in bistros, flower shops, cafes, toilets and bars that it was easy to think we were anywhere but in a mainline railway station. It was nearly ten past three when our group assembled underneath the platform as requested. We found ourselves coincidentally opposite the Eurostar left luggage department as directed by Johnson so his instructions were good. 'Easy to locate later' someone had whispered to her husband. We shall see I thought.

Libby had struggled along the platform and down the slope with her case refusing any offer of assistance from me. The only problem being the wheels and handle on her case would not do or go where she wanted. Tripping first one way and then another she was glad of the rest when we arrived at what would be our meeting point later. Breathless conversations broke out amongst the more elderly group members until, with his arms flapping about once more, we were brought to order by Mr Dennis Johnson.

'Gather round and I'll tell you at what time we travel on the next train. I have your tickets for the next leg of the journey in my briefcase.'

'Just as well' said Libby in an aside to me, 'we don't have any more tickets do we?'

I told her all would be well and to listen as Johnson continued 'Our next train a Belgian Thalys leaves from platform five according to the information board, which is over there' he said both of his arms pointing precisely to where we had to assemble later. 'In twenty minutes time because the train leaves at fifteen fifty, continental time, please. If you want the toilet, and I know some of you do, it's over there on the right. You will have to pay to go in through a turnstile.'

People were instantly confused as to whether to alter their watches if they hadn't already done so, or test the Belgian plumbing and with only twenty minutes freedom in Brussels in which to 'pee or flee' a race was about to commence. How he knew some folks needed the toilet again having left them minutes before on the train was a mystery to me. Was he psychic?

Cases were left with friends or family as the rush to the toilets commenced. In the lead from the start was one of the brothers from what I could see. He was followed by one of the Scottish men as both seemed to know where they were headed for making haste whilst a slower trickle, pardon the pun, of folks followed. I looked out for Libby who had taken the small change from me and had reminded me again that she 'desperately needed the loo'. I couldn't see her near the front of the race and as I looked around and began thinking I'd lost sight of her I caught a glimpse of her moving quickly through the 'field' and towards the leaders of the toilet pack. I should have known better because she was a regular jogger and there she was in the distance closing in on second place in the rush to the loos.

Fifteen minutes later most folks had returned from the toilets but there was still no sign of Libby. I walked slowly over to the toilets and whilst loitering outside them waiting for my wife it was evident listening to some of our party as the passed me that they were beginning to become even more talkative amongst themselves. It was as if there had been some form of bonding procedure down amongst the plumbing. But there was still no sign of my Libby when all but one or two had left the toilet area and returned to our designated rendezvous point. Minutes went by each one seeming like ten minutes as I waited and then, like a rabbit out of its burrow, out popped Libby.

'Feeling better?' I chanced asking rather cheekily.

'Absolutely fine' Libby replied, 'such clean toilets, so clean that you could eat your meal off the floor in there.'

'Why would I do that?' I countered, 'there are better places to eat and what took you longer than everyone else? The others will be at our meeting place by platform five by now. Look at the time, we'll be late.'

'Tosh,' she said, 'we'll have no problem. Look over there one of the Scottish ladies is eating a roll of some kind. Anyway I had a wash and brush up and put some make-up on. Can't you tell?'

It's at moments like that when your reply can determine the quality of a holiday and your being together comfortably for a few days, or not. I took the diplomatic and easy way out replying 'Yes darling you look beautiful as always.'

We crossed the vast station concourse and arrived breathless below platform five as a couple of fellow stragglers returned behind us.

'See I told you' Libby hissed quietly to me as we rested by our cases that were in front of us, 'you should not be so negative!'

What more could I say? Johnson did, and he went on to hand out our tickets for the journey to Cologne asking us to keep close together pointing out where would be moving towards once all were accounted for. Having proceeded altogether up the escalator and onto platform five we all stood close to the point at which our carriage was allegedly to arrive as the train pulled into the station. It was absolutely freezing standing there. A winter gale blew along the platform acting like some kind of vortex making the air seem even colder in the wind chill. The station announcer poured more 'cold water' on the situation notifying the waiting passengers that the train would arrive eight minutes later than scheduled. It would too.

Chapter Four.

It was seriously cold on platform five particularly for the more elderly among us as we waited for our delayed train. Waiting in the cold it was impossible not to be distracted by the smell of smoke: and it was not from a steam train. It was cigarette smoke and some of us were taken aback to see that smokers were allowed to smoke on a railway station after all the furore about smoking at home.

'Bet those cigarettes are keeping their hands warm in this Godforsaken freezing place' Libby chipped in just as the train with our carriage number arrived at the exact spot that had been designated for Pineapple Rail Tours. The smile on Dennis Johnson's face was an absolute picture because after all he had predicted our carriage would arrive at the point where we stood. However, that smile soon disappeared as he and we fellow travellers watched the doors of the carriage slide back pouring forth its human content that took an age to disembark. That microcosm of panic seemed so unreal: one minute we were stood patiently but cold, relaxed and organised and then we too all joined the melee to get on the train. Observing the tension on passenger's faces for a few seconds as they witnessed that brief lack of etiquette reminded me of cattle being herded out of railway trucks back home on their way to market. It was that bad but without the stench. But we all survived and boarded the train lifting our heavy cases first onto the carriage step and then into the corridor of the main carriage. Once again we began the onerous task of locating our seats trailing our cases behind us. We were still standing in what passed for the corridor when the train pulled out of the station. Suddenly the carriage resembled a geriatric rugby scrum as bodies lurched in all directions throughout our carriage. Cases when they are let go of by people seem to have a mind of their own. That corridor on the train was no different. Those bloody cases responded to every movement of the train, particularly the sideways movement. They seemed to move away from their owners and crash and bump people who were still seeking their seats. Owners of the runaway cases could then be heard apologising to the battered and soon to be bruised folk as they tried desperately to catch their case. Meanwhile those who had successfully placed cases onto overhead racks were bumping into unknown fellow travellers before steadying themselves and falling into their seats. It was from that moment that our group of happy travellers began to gel together as a party. It was also the time when the journey descended into farce and resembled a barn dance as Libby and me became entwined and generally barged around the coach our cases trailing behind us again as we continued looking for the seats that matched our ticket numbers. Adding to that railway circus was the train, having pulled out of the station was accelerating and beginning to lurch from side to side as it passed over the railway points beneath us. And still we struggled with our cases. By the time we had placed our cases aloft on racks, and we had sat down, we were ready for a cooling drink or two. Inside the carriage a new seating plan, craftily engineered by Johnson, had all the group members sitting opposite different faces within our group. We sat opposite the two people Libby had tried all day to avoid, going by their looks that was. Johnson had placed a nervous Libby opposite the only people she had wanted to avoid: they were of course the brothers John and Kevin whom we came to nickname the Knuckle Brothers on account of their faces that seemed to have been fashioned in a boxing ring. Well John's appeared to have been whereas Kevin seemed quite handsome beside his brother.

Then the shock hit us. They were really nicely spoken chaps and came across at that table as nothing like our preconception of their supposed upbringing. Well Libby's if I'm honest. Surprisingly for her

Libby broke the ice first by enquiring of the two if it was their first trip with Pineapple Tours.

'No, this is our ... ' slight pause as John with the broken nose and replete with re-arranged face counted on his fingers and continued 'will be our ninth to date.'

You would have seen Libby's face nearly fall off her head if you'd had taken a photograph at that moment. Her eyes popped out as if on stalks and her bottom jaw almost hit her chest. Further, with mouth wide open and her eyebrows lifted nearly to the roof of the carriage, such was her reaction to the answer I thought she was going to poop!

'Yes nine,' said John as if it was an every day happening, 'and yourselves?' he asked.

'Our first' Libby said, at first defensively, as both of us just sat there amazed at John's reply 'where else have you been with them?' she asked.

'Well last summer we went to Sweden, Norway and the Arctic Circle' Kevin said jumping into the conversation for the first time, 'and although the cost was high and the scenery spectacular the rest of the trip was somewhat puritanical.'

'In what way?' both Libby and I asked immediately in unison.

'For a start' said John, 'the guide and the folks on the trip were not our sort. No comedians or even drinkers. Not like the year before in Japan. Now that was a trip worth going on.'

'Japan?' gasped Libby.

'Maybe it was the pace of the holiday that made a difference because the people all enjoyed a drink and a laugh which of course we do and the whole trip was superbly organised' butted in Kevin.

'That must have been an expensive trip' Libby reckoned prying, 'because none of these trips are cheap so to speak. You must have good jobs and save up throughout the year for your holiday.'

Just like my inquisitive wife to ask the obvious but I too did wonder how two fairly young, possibly mid-forties seemingly unattached gentlemen could afford such regular holidays without a decent career and salary. The answer never came because just at that very moment a waiter arrived with some drinks and a hostess followed on swiftly with some nibbles stifling the answer that Libby so wanted to hear. The conversation with the Knuckle Brothers was placed further on hold as Johnson stood perfectly bolt upright and in a loud voice announced to us all

'That is a freebie so you don't have to pay for either drink or food, but you may have a long wait for another drink.'

How he managed to keep his drink in his can and prevent spillage as his arms waved about as he spoke I will never know because the train picked up speed just as he stood up. We had left the outskirts of Brussels and travelled rapidly across the frosty and lightly snow-covered ever darkening Belgian countryside. Our conversation with the brothers would continue for a while longer until the warmth of the carriage eventually took its toll on our old and tired bones. With our eyes closed after the drinks were finished, we dozed off, me anticipating and thinking of the treats and surprises to be thrust upon us during the next few days.

We were awakened as the train slowed and stopped for a few minutes in Liege after about forty-five minutes during which time both Libby and me had caught up on some much needed sleep. I excused myself and stood up to stretch my legs by walking to the end of the corridor and looking out of the open door. I caught a glimpse of other passengers doing exactly the same and my eyes opened wide when I thought I saw a face I imagined I recognised. I was beginning to think I had become very much like Libby who seemed to recognise everyone, or thought she did, when the doors bleeped and closed. I returned to my seat thoroughly confused and sat down wondering if I had seen somebody I knew.

Before the train departed Libby had woken up from her slumber and asked where we were, closed her eyes again when told and drifted off back into her slumber, by which time my previous thoughts had gone out of my head.

'Next stop Aachen' said John 'should be there before six o'clock I reckon'

'We'll be back there again tomorrow if the itinerary is spot on' I said knowing full well that it was the case but at least the chap was still talking to me. 'They tell me that the Xmas market in Aachen is really beautiful set as it is below and around the cathedral. With all your rail trips have you been there before, you and your brother?'

'Not Aachen but we went a couple of years ago to Nuremberg which was spectacular and possibly one of the nicest Xmas trips we've done' John said. 'The reason we went there was because it is the oldest of the German Christmas markets and so is not only wrapped up with history but also in much sentimentality too. And of course it laid down the marker for the rest to follow.'

Outside the window it was totally dark with only the light of the train illuminating the snow-covered fields. In due course we travelled through the Ardennes in eastern Belgium where the Battle of the Bulge had taken place as the Americans called it, John reminded us. I remember it being so comfortable in that train: the seat was comfortable, the air was warm and the lager had gone down too easily. Dozing off to sleep I became startled by someone who passed through our carriage rather clumsily knocking my shoulder in hurry to get to the toilet I presumed. I was about to apologise to him when I thought hang on a minute, don't I know you? He looked familiar for a fleeting second, but then I thought it too much of a coincidence. Dreaming again Russell I thought, and before I could think anything more of it I felt myself beginning to drift off to sleep. I forgot the incident as I caught out of the corner of fast closing eyes yet another waiter approaching our table.

'May I have two more Stella Artois please?' Kevin asked and looking at me, 'how about you and Libby Tony, would you like a beer too?'

'Yes ' I replied sitting bolt upright in my seat and struggling to open my eyes, 'one like yours and despite the fact that she is still asleep a dry white wine for Libby please.'

'Merci messieurs' spoke the steward and in a jiffy was gone to his drinks store returning within seconds. He neatly placed our order on the table with some nuts and chocolate and proceeded to open and pour the drinks. Then with a polite 'D'accord?' and smile he was on his way to another table and another request.

Before we could even take sip of our drinks the train braked heavily and slowed almost to a stop as we passed the first houses of what was clearly Aachen. It was perhaps testament to our drinking skills down the years that none of us at the table, at that dodgy instant, spilt any liquor despite me holding onto Libby's drink as well as my own.

'What was that jolt? And where are we now?' the sleepy request alongside me came squeaking out of the side of Libby's mouth.

'Aachen', I replied, 'and we will be in Cologne in approximately forty minutes so don't waste that drink John ordered for you my sweet.'

'Aachen? Larkin'? Barkin'? Harkin'?' Libby pondered rapidly machine gun fashion 'how did it get a name like that?' she continued.

'German language of course but it used to be called Aix-la-Chapelle when it was French' John said and continued 'it has passed back and forwards several times throughout history in wars between the French and Germans. They crowned German Kings and Holy Roman Emperors there or something and Charlemagne was a big wig there too. It all went wrong when Napoleon made it French again but again the Germans retrieved it after his fall.'

'What have you eaten today?' Libby asked John I thought quite rudely, 'the Encyclopaedia Britannica?'

'Nah he just likes to keep abreast of places we visit and read up on the history an' all that' Kevin said, 'proper mastermind he is, I tell him he should enter the competition: Specialist subject, places I have visited with Pineapple Rail Tours. He'd be good too, probably knows more than most of the operatives and guides.'

John blushed and appeared to ignore his younger brother, but secretly I thought he enjoyed listening to his family sycophant.

I then watched as some people stood up in our carriage and did stretching exercises as if in a gym for the elderly, whilst others were fiddling with cases or zipping up small bags that had contained rolls or sandwiches brought for snacking. A few folks in our group returned from the buffet car and in essence the whole carriage was a thoroughfare from A to B for people who were, or were not, part of our group. There always seemed to be someone going past: some ignored you even when they bumped into you accidentally as

I found out earlier. Yet some gave you a strange type of look like those in the black and white films either side of the War, the ones containing foreign spies you know the ones, as they tried to move past. Others just smiled as if they knew you or wanted to know you better. Certainly some of either sex, after quaffing lots of alcohol, left little to the imagination. I have to say that on one of these trips to buffet or toilet and passing our table another one of the passengers gave me a particularly funny and peculiar look as he went past as if I'd stepped on his toes not the other way round. I wondered what it was about my feet that caused such looks. Then again I wondered if he'd been the chap earlier who had bumped my shoulder, or the one I saw back in Liege when I was looking outside the door in the station. I felt sure there was something about him …. But I couldn't recall what. Ah well it takes allsorts I thought and put the thought to the back of my mind.

With only minutes to go before we entered the Cologne Bahnhof, Johnson was tearing round the carriage talking to members of our group telling them to collect their luggage together and, when able to get off the train, to wait together as a group on the platform where the cases would be collected and taken directly to our hotel by station porters.

Hardly had the train slowed down on the outskirts of Cologne when I began watching in fascination as locals got up out of their seats and headed for the exit doors when we still had several miles to travel before we arrived in Cologne. Cases and bags were even being taken off our overhead luggage racks and placed inconveniently in the aisles by Pineapple Tour travellers. So inconvenient was it for people to get past I soon realised that was why the locals were getting off first!

'Help Iris with her case' Libby barked at me so rudely I nearly swore at her.

'Who' I asked loudly 'was Iris when she's on holiday?'

'That very elderly lady behind, you sat next to her husband Richard, remember?' she replied. 'They have the same type of cases we have only a different colour. Go on please help them my darling.'

What a change of attitude. How could I have resisted? After all, flattery gets you most things in life. And that is how their cases, along with everyone-else's cases, were placed obstructively in the aisle. Not deliberately obstructive mind you but just enough to cause pandemonium with the elderly members in our group.

'Thank you my dear' said a rather posh voice that was directed at me as I straightened up the two cases alongside their seats. 'What a gentleman he is Richard' she continued turning to speak to her still seated and grinning like a Cheshire cat, husband.

'See I told you' whispered Libby 'that's all it takes to be civil.' At that instant I caught out of the corner of one eye the faces of the Knuckle Brothers who were smirking uncontrollably. His reaction indicated to me that he was better off staying single and not married having heard Libby's comments. At least Iris was happy and it would not be the last time not with all that gin and tonic in Cologne.

Chapter Five.

Like little lost souls we were nearly thirty of us waiting patiently on the platform for the station porters to arrive like Johnson said they would. With arms flapping Johnson announced in a screechy little voice that we should place our luggage next to the trolley cages that porters would then load and deliver to our hotel.

Trying to make conversation in such a busy and noisy railway station like Cologne's was nigh impossible. However, even through that cacophony of sound it was just possible to hear the German announcer on the Tannoy calling out the names of German and International Cities that trains were either travelling to, or from. Names like Hamburg, Berlin, Vienna, Budapest and Amsterdam that conjured up thoughts in me of long overnight journeys where the trains stopped at towns and cities that I'd heard of in my youth. We were summoned by Johnson to follow him along the platform and down some steep steps into the milling throng that Friday night at almost 19.00 hours. It was a different type of experience even if it was only an exercise in crowd dodging as that Advent weekend drew closer. There was an enthusiastic buzz about the place as if something was about to happen. Maybe that something was called Christmas I thought to myself as it just happened to be round the corner!

Out in the cold Cologne air we snaked across newly laid out but uneven paths weaving in and out amongst the road-works as we circuitously made our way to the Four Corners Hotel about 150 yards from the Banhof. Through the automatic doors of the hotel we frozen ones piled into the foyer where the warmth greeted us like a long lost friend. The faces of party members visibly changed colour as rosy cheeks and red noses, at the extremities of those faces absorbed the warmth of the room. A human form of Christmas decoration I stood thinking to myself in the warmth when the air was rent asunder by a commanding figure issuing our room keys. Johnson, having communicated in perfect German with the lady clerk on the adjacent reception desk, was in his element. Give him his due he was perfect for the role he had acquired from the tour company.

'Before I hand you your plastic keys' he began, his arms laden down by the weight of all the plastic in the envelopes containing the keys. I was just imagining all those keys flying out of his hands and across the foyer when he continued saying 'Dinner is at eight o'clock. I know that is soon and you do not have your luggage as yet,' he paused looking past us towards the automatic sliding doors and continued 'Ah, here it comes now.'

As if perfectly arranged by him at that instant the luggage arrived on the trolleys and was being pushed into the hotel lobby by two, despite the cold outside, hot and sweaty railway porters.

'It has arrived as if by Christmas magic' I heard one old wag croak through his or her sore throat, I wasn't quite sure who.

The porters quickly unloaded the cases leaving them in precise lines in the foyer as Johnson carried on talking to us.

'Take your luggage to your room when you have it by one of two lifts over there, unless of course you are young and fit enough and you want to walk up the stairs. Our dining room is round this corner' he walked across to the entrance pointing to it 'and you can sit anywhere like so long as there is a table naturally.' He again paused as if waiting for laughter but we were all looking at our watches, assessing how much time we had before dinner. He persevered 'There is a bar just here too for your pleasure and any notices I have for you will be pinned on this board here. Don't be late for dinner now please' he said pointing at the board one more time and then at last proceeded to hand out the envelopes with our room keys in.

'Blimey it's past half seven already' we overheard from one excitable or plain hungry person obviously not used to rushing. I knew exactly what Libby was thinking at the very same moment and I was not disappointed as she blurted out 'I shan't have time to wash, put on my make-up and visit the loo in such a short time never mind have an aperitif.'

'Then you are not the woman I married' I said with tongue in cheek.

First off their blocks were the Knuckle Brothers who raced up the stairs with their cases like the really fit blokes they were as did some of the other under fifties. However, for the other less fit one couldn't help notice the queues for the lifts were lengthy. With the lifts moving upwards at a speed slower than walking pace and with hardly enough room inside them to swing a cat, the time was quickly ebbing away with dinner-time getting ever closer. Observing the lack of movement Libby asked me for our envelope containing the room key and left the lobby with me there stranded with both the cases. She then proceeded to walk up the back stairs alone. I knew her intention was to find the floor our room was on and locate and enter our room so she could begin preening herself before dinner. That was her intention when she set off without a route map or sat-nav. When the time eventually arrived so that I could at last gain entry to one of the lifts with the cases I was of a mind to beat her to our room and wait outside before she arrived. As the lift slowly ascended to the floor that had our room on it, passing and not stopping at other floors, I couldn't help but notice through the lift's window a squidgy nose peering into the lift shaft as the lift sped past slowly. One guess! Yep, that's right it was her, lost again. Vacating the lift on our floor and leaving the cases outside our room, because I hadn't a key, I walked back down the stairs to the floor below to look for Libby. No sign of her. Of course she was by then, unknown to me, vacating the lift on the floor where our room really was located? I retraced my steps back upstairs and found her stuck outside the room frantically trying to open the door with a plastic key in one hand and beating the unopened door with the other. I moved quickly to relieve the situation. I found it hard not to laugh at her plight as did others in our group who were watching and either in the same situation or, having just given up, just dumped their cases and headed off to the bar. We both briefly tested the plumbing in our room and we too headed for the bar with seconds to go before we had to report to the dining room when

'Hello', someone said 'My name is John, can I interest you and yours in a drink? I saw and heard you on the train and noticed the label on your cases that you are also from Birmingham.'

'Yes pleeeeeease' jumped in Libby 'dry white wine and a beer. Large one I think. Is that right love?' she said looking at me 'Large beer I mean of course.'

'So where are you from precisely? I have a brother-in-law who worked in Solihull near Birmingham' said John, 'and here's your glass of wine er er...... Libby, isn't it? Cheers everyone.'

That conversation continued until we all were summoned by our leader to go through to the dining room and told we were free to sit where we liked and could help ourselves to the food. The eventual charge towards the food, by nearly thirty starving tourists, could have been catastrophic such was our hunger. That it wasn't a catastrophe was down to the Knuckle Brothers forming a safety barrier in front of some hot plates and steel containers to prevent any accident. Of course I exaggerate the situation purely to emphasise our hunger. Interestingly one of two of the older ladies, impressed by the sight of the instant security, commented on the muscular structure she thought John of the Knuckle Brothers must have to have performed that role. Meanwhile

'Over there in the large steel containers there is pork, fish and a selection of vegetables for the main course and a variety of starters to choose from over the other side of the display. Oh and the sweets or puddings are over to the left on separate tables. So folks,' and with his arms again moving like rotor blades yet one more time he continued saying 'as the Germans say *geneissen sie ihre mahlzeit*. Or as we British say bon appetite.'

Some of us chose to sit down at that moment and continue waiting rather than be in the rush for food before plating up ourselves.

'He's got that wrong, hasn't he? He meant enjoy your meal,' Libby said contorting her face as she always did at such a malapropism. 'Isn't that French?'

'Precisely' said one of the ladies we'd seen on the train earlier in the day and who kindly invited us to sit with her and two other friends for dinner. It appeared we'd lost John and his partner somewhere along the way from the bar to the dining hall such was people's eagerness to get stuck into some food and eat.

'Definitely' she continued in her West of Scotland brogue, 'He can be so frustrating. How do you think he cleans his teeth with those arm movements?' she asked before talking to her younger friends, one who was drinking a glass of red wine and the other drinking orange juice. The fizzy wine, or champagne, had been a 'welcome to Cologne' courtesy donated by the tour company. During the rest of the trip many were the times these ladies were to be seen quaffing beer in or around the bars and restaurants adjacent to the markets.

Following our introductions we found we were sitting with Elspeth a Scottish lady and Mary, at that moment without her reading glasses, and Jenny who was a very softly spoken lady. All three ladies seemed good close friends, polite, intelligent and very affable. All of us were just beginning to relax when I spoilt the conversation by mentioning the need for food because the queue for the food had tailed off.

'Would you excuse me please I am absolutely starving?' I asked politely before standing up and sauntering towards the soup pot and past the meat and fish which was now being examined by one or two senior ladies in our group. Libby and the others followed me and by the time we had all selected our first course and returned to the table a range of different starters had been assembled by all five of us: soups, salad with cold meat, salad with cheese and the usual rolls all were in evidence of that on that table.

Conversation continued across the table though greatly reduced as we tucked into our starters such was our hunger. We seemed only to briefly exchange any further pleasantries until the starters had all been eaten. They did though include talk of the coming activities and the Christmas Markets that two of them had already been to several years before.

'Why come back?' Libby enquired, 'Is there much more to see or do that you had not seen or done first time around?'

'That's not why we have returned at all' claimed Mary whom we would later find to be a musical genius capable of playing a wide range of instruments. 'No that was not an issue it was that as friends we decided we needed a break and we were all able to travel at this time. So having enjoyed Cologne so much before it was an easy choice to make to come back here.'

The Knuckle Brothers had finished their first course quickly already had re-fills of drinks from the waitress and were starting on their main course. Having winked at us on the way back to their table with their dinner plates fully laden to the brim they could be heard laughing and joking again as they returned for second helpings only minutes later.

Having collected our plates together Libby and me excused ourselves and left our table and claimed a place opposite the pork and beef. This was when the debating began between ourselves as we quietly discussed the merits of what was in front of us.

'Now what shall I have fish, beef or pork, pork, beef or fish? What looks best?' Libby questioned herself loud enough for me to hear. 'I think .... I think ...... the fish' she said enthusiastically, 'just look at that sauce it looks so appetising. Mmmmm having now tested it with my finger it is .... oh wow, you must have some Tony.'

'No chance,' I said 'just get a load of that pork Libby even the stuffing looks perfect and there are those soft noodles you go on about too which with some of the vegetables will make a real Teutonic meal. But I don't want the potato gratin no thanks not with the noodles as well.'

'Hi Elspeth what are you having?' Libby asked the Scottish lady from our table who appeared alongside her.

'Eh, the fish, some vegetables and the potato too looks really nice but I don't really care for the pork. If I'm honest I'm not really hungry just thirsty,' claimed Elspeth. 'But that's not to say I might not try some later.'

Libby's eyebrows were raised a little as she listened attentively to her associate who, though petit, didn't look as if she could polish off two meals there and then. Back at the table Jenny had the fish and Mary the pork. From my point of view I must say that 'of all the pork in all the world' I had never tasted such a tender and succulent portion like that one I had in front of me for a few minutes, until I ate it. Mary obviously felt the same as me too and was influential enough so much so that Elspeth decided to have second helpings, only this time she too chose the pork.

The main topic of conversation for the rest of the meal focussed on the following day's visit to Aachen's Christmas Market. Had the two ladies who had previously travelled to the Cologne at this time of year been to Aachen's Christmas Market? They had and they said that the market was indeed close by the cathedral and though it was not anywhere near as large as anyone of Cologne's six separate markets, it was still worth visiting for its ambience and the medieval architecture in the town.

'Though the market the tomorrow is not so large the town offers ample diversity of shops many very different from those in Cologne. I found that they were particularly quaint and spent hours looking round them, without spending any money' Mary said.

Throughout our conversation other group members were passing back and forth regularly to collect seconds from the hotplates. As they did there was much nodding and acknowledging the more familiar some faces had become and a smile here and a smile there sealed the recognition. The chatter in the room was quite animated and loud confirming the growing confidence within the group as people became more acquainted. That had to be a good sign for Johnson who must worry about such things in his role. One particular articulate and cheerful chap was a little Irish gent called

Dermot who seemed to be keeping all and sundry entertained on his table with his conversation that never seemed to stop or falter. Also on his table was a tiny lady who reminded me so much of an actress from ITV's Rag Trade called Esme Cannon. Well she did to me and had, along with the others on her table, to listen politely and attentively to Dermot. Even taking a cursory look around the dining area as people were eating it was possible to identify the very polite and reserved people, and what one would call 'first timers' on the trip, because they had remained sitting at tables for two. Perhaps as Libby said they were just 'eyeing up the opposition or competition first.' Either way what had been a group of complete strangers only hours before progressed along in a very positive vein when

'Going for a beer?' the younger Knuckle Brother Kevin asked as he made his way to the sweet and pudding area, then the cheese and biscuit area, then the area containing the yogurts and other milky desserts. What it was to be young and thin? I could just about remember............

'No I think I shall go to our room and have a swill around in the shower and only then have a beer I think. Might even pop over for a look at the floodlit cathedral too' I replied knowing full well my itinerary could change at the closing of an eyelid or two: Libby's of course. I called a waitress over to our table, ordered some more drinks for the ladies and then ventured slowly across to the cheese board. Libby and two of the other ladies had chosen some of the fruit salad to eat and had just sat down when another waitress approached us and asked if we wanted some coffee. She then disappeared into the kitchen to return moments later with a pot of lukewarm coffee.

'I hope that the coffee was from a kettle and not a hot, should I say warm water tap.' No guesses as to who made that comment and so at about eight thirty German time, Libby and I stood and excused ourselves for leaving our newly acquired friends at the table and passed through the hotel reception area, waited for the lift and on its arrival trooped up to our room.

I couldn't help thinking to myself in the lift that it was just typical of the kind of situation where you find yourself on holiday with people you had never met until then and before you know it you cannot not stop talking and smiling along with them. That is how it was that first night with members of our tour group. We seldom spoke or acknowledged strangers at home but there we were, on holiday, having conversations with complete strangers: weird. The lift arrived at the sixth floor after Libby had pushed the correct button for a change. Hey presto within seconds we were playing with the plastic key-card outside our room waiting for the green light on the door to shine before we could enter. On entry both of us flopped onto our beds and as my eyes began to close in the warmth of that room after having eaten far too much at dinner, I was brought out of my slumber when Libby said out very loudly

'What's happened to our luggage labels? They're not on our cases!'

'No worries. Perhaps they are on the floor or under the beds, or more likely they were ripped off or they just fell off when the luggage was transported in those cages from the railway station. I'll get some more off Johnson later tonight or in the morning. It's nothing to worry about.' It was a reply of sorts but even I was none the wiser as to what happened to them but at least it soothed Libby's curiosity for that moment.

When both of us had showered and were ready to go downstairs again for yet another holiday drink Libby said she'd like to go for a walk if it was not too cold outside. So that's what we did only we were not alone because as we were about to go into the cold night a lady in our group was waiting for just such an opportunity and asked us if she accompany us. Even with our first steps outside it was impossible not to be impressed by the floodlit cathedral up on its hill. But blimey O'Reilly was it cold outside? Walking through the railway station was like visiting another world with so much hustle and bustle going on in and around the shops. Out the other side and into the area below the floodlit cathedral cameras were flashing everywhere around us as visitors captured the quite amazing and beautiful silhouette of the cathedral. It was in all probability the most famous and easily recognisable building in Germany but despite that it was too cold to remain still for long and so I cajoled both Libby and Margaret, our new friend, to continue walking across the cathedral's square and around several offices and shopping blocks returning back to the hotel again via the railway station. Fascinating as it was what was equally interesting were the vast number of food stalls that always had endless queues for the really fresh produce at all hours of the day or night: various rolls and salads were stacked up really high in pyramid shapes on their counters. They would become a necessity during our stay in Cologne when supplementing our lunches in particular. More to the point, there was no way I could walk past without stopping to buy something that looked so temptingly inviting and ultimately delicious.

Back inside the Four Corners Hotel the warmth standing in the foyer was a Godsend and much-needed treat for our old bones after a forty-five minute walk in the cold Cologne winter air. Our friend disappeared after bidding us goodnight and so once again the bar and its treasure beckoned. A large pinot grigio for Libby and a beer and whisky chaser for me was a welcome night-cap at the end of the first day of what we hoped would be a memorable anniversary expedition together. Unsurprisingly several of our group were still in the bar at that ungodly hour approaching ten o'clock. Linking up with and buying John a drink and one for the lady who was with him, though not his wife, I turned the conversation round to his relative in the Midlands as he too had been a schoolmaster. The next half an hour of convivial conversation passed very quickly as we swopped information on many subjects whilst standing at that bar. But half an hour was all we would muster after a long day and with all that travelling. So, feeling knackered and after apologising to our fellow drinkers we said goodnight and once more headed for the lifts for what we hoped would be the last time that day.

'Wonder what happened to little old Sid tonight? I didn't see him after dinner did you?' I asked walking into the lift. Inside the lift and with a straight ride to our floor Libby said she thought he would have been too tired after the long journey at his age and was probably tucked up in bed and sound asleep.

Clearly Sid wasn't the only one feeling tired which was why we returned to our room. We made the room a little more hospitable than the war-zone it had looked like before we had left hurriedly for dinner. I placed the chargers on our mobile phones as Libby requested and put our personal radios on the beds. I know what you are thinking: why radios? Well, rather than lay awake at night counting sheep or whatever you do when you get older, we had decided that personal radios were better than a clock radio because that would have woken the whole household. So it was that we came to listen each night to our personal radios: BBC Long Wave 198m for Libby and in my case I had become an avid fan of Radio Five's Rhod Sharp and Dotun Adebayo at weekends.

It had been our intention to carry on that 'hobby' in Cologne that was until

'Can you get anything on your radio? My radio is all funny noises and crackling' Libby asked.

I told her I couldn't get either of our regular stations after fiddling with the small dial and could only get English records on a German radio station with German DJ's which was not exactly what my wife wanted to hear from me, or the radio.

'Good night love' I murmured, 'have fun listening' and with that turned my bedside light off leaving Libby fiddling to find some music or other programme on her radio. She had appeared to relax and had not mentioned her accident for well over twelve hours at that point which was good.

I dropped off to sleep quickly dreaming of Aachen and its Christmas Market. What fun holidays can be as you grow older.

Chapter Six.

It was still dark the following morning when I was rudely awakened by a news broadcast being read out close by. Checking that my personal radio was switched off I sat bolt upright in bed and put my bedside light on. Rubbing my eyes so they almost hit the back of my head I peered round the compact hotel room. Libby was missing from her bed but on the floor, trailing round her bed and snaking into the shower were her night clothes. Quietly crawling sleepy-eyed out of my bed and slipping into the bathrobe I had left on the chair at the side of my bed, I sneaked a look into the shower room through the small crack between the door and the wall. There she was towelling herself down at five past six German time. There was my Libby. Pushing the door open James Bond style I looked at her and grinned when she abruptly let out an almighty scream so loud they probably heard her over at the station.

'You bloody Tom what are you playing at creeping around like MI6? You silly sod you could have made me have an accident.'

'Well you didn't but what are you doing up at this ungodly hour? Do you know what the time is?' I whispered back loudly so the people in the rooms by the side of us hopefully had mistaken what they heard. That is if they heard Libby's piercing scream.

'You plonker course I do. And do you know why I am here, because of your bloody snoring. I am surprised the management haven't been to move us to a shed outside you were so loud. We are supposed to be celebrating forty years together not playing silly buggers!'

With that endearing compliment she squeezed past me, told me not be idle and by implication suggested I should put the kettle on for a cup of tea. Second day of the holiday, ten past six in the morning, the lights from the Railway Station across the road shining brightly and there we were half naked giving it the verbal. Some celebration I didn't think.

Peering through the window as I slurped my tea it looked very cold outside. It was Saturday morning in Cologne and cars and their passengers had already begun making their way to work and there I was in the doghouse. I made another pot of tea took the long way round Libby avoiding eye contact and any further international crisis and went into the bathroom. Taking a shower and getting dressed meant I didn't have to watch Libby applying her pre-breakfast make-up. What tickled me then, and still does to this day, was how she could ever apply the make-up to her face looking into a mirror, listening to the TV and trying to solve a crossword all at the same time. She used to say it was because women could multi-task and did enjoy telling me that, especially in the company of some of her women friends.

Any further thoughts on that subject were ended by a clout to my head with a magazine kind permission of Libby as she moved around the room having finished dressing who then announced

'I'm starving. I really am. What time is breakfast please Tony?'

'Seven o'clock Hun but surely you don't want to be seen queuing for breakfast. This is not Spain' I replied.

'No but there are Germans here and it would be nice to be first in the queue even though we're not in a Spanish hotel' she insisted.

'Five past seven I'll do but anything-else and you are on your own. Knowing your sense of direction you're better off with me particularly as you were on the wrong floor last night after we had arrived. Remember dear heart?' My comment was not appreciated and to prove it a waste paper bin hurtled in my direction with several expletives 'behind' it, and enough detritus from the pot of tea to make her point.

We eventually left the room making our way along the corridor and across the landing towards the lift where we were joined on the journey downstairs by little old Sid, Iris and her husband and another couple we had not been introduced to at that time. Elspeth came out of her room just as the lift doors were closing and uttered something horrible that could well have been choice Gaelic swearwords. We all met again at the entrance to the dining area and who should be there to greet us but Mr Pineapple Head himself. Johnson our energetic and eccentric tour guide was once more holding forth.

'Greetings' he said with a fixed rictus smile on his face, 'I hope we all slept well?'

Quick as a flash and with no gap in the conversation little old Sid responded

'We probably did but not all in the same room thank you kindly.' That not only brought a chuckle from a couple of folks but I caught sight of Libby as she turned to take Sid by the arm, patted him on the back and praised him for his acidic comment.

'I hope you are suitably refreshed and looking forward to the Aachen trip the details for which are on the board in the reception area. Don't forget to take a look.' And with that Johnson swept past us to talk to the next set of folks that came from out of the lift.

Back in the dining area the wide choice of breakfast food was already being sampled by some German guests and of course our Group's early risers were already testing the day's breakfast. Sitting down at the same table we had sat at the night before a couple who introduced themselves as Dave and Margie asked if they could join us.

'No problem' Libby said, 'take a seat' she said as she set off to explore what was on offer for breakfast. The choice was wide and before long Libby had arrived back at the table with a bowl of cereals and fruit and the customary plain yoghurt.

'Aren't you going to get some breakfast too?' she asked as I stood to go and have a reconnoitre myself.

'Of course but I ordered the coffee from the waiter, had a sip when it arrived and asked them to pour some hot water in with the coffee if they wanted us to drink it' I replied full of myself.

'You'll have to excuse him Margie he will insist that it is perfect if he pays for it' Libby explained to Margie as our two new friends returned to the table and sat next to each other. Dave and I exchanged knowing glances understanding that if the ladies had discovered the coffee to be lukewarm they would have asked one of us to change it anyway. An example of the Law of Unintended Consequences I think they called it at college. Of course I cannot win with Libby I thought to myself as I wandered over to the cold meats and cheeses none of which would be as tough as my Libby. Picking up my knife and fork and taking a look at the choice of cereals I met Dermot who was casting an eye over the various types of tea on offer. He had already made me aware of his preference for a cuppa. It had to be a pot of tea that had 'normal tea' in it not one of the 'perfumed teas' that seemed to be everywhere. His words not mine.

Within minutes of our arrival the dining room was busy with most, if not all, of our party. They peered into large containers of bacon, sausage, tomatoes, boiled eggs, fried eggs, scrambled eggs and commented to their partner or friend beside them how 'that confounded food' always got in the way of their dieting. Well it was Christmas after all and a blow-out, food-wise, was an integral part of the festive season. Back on our table the conversation varied widely from the approaching visit to Aachen, or as to whether the ladies would have second portions of breakfast. This was followed by what they thought the trip and dinner on the Rhine would be like later that evening. Libby also managed to squeeze into the conversation the reason why we were there in the first place and why we were not celebrating the anniversary at home. Incredibly, even by her standards, Libby even managed to work into the conversation and mention to Margie how interested the assistant was in the supermarket before we left.

After we had all finished breakfast and a good chinwag about the journey from London to Cologne, and I should add a comment or two about our tour guide, Libby and I said a 'Cheerio' to Dave and Margie and disappeared upstairs to collect our scarves and coats. Another brisk walk around Cathedral Square beckoned and was needed to blow away any lingering cobwebs and wake us up from any lasting slumber after all the food at breakfast. The group had been asked to assemble in the hotel lobby for nine forty-five sharp when we were all to march together as a group - sorry walk - to platform 9 to catch our train to Aachen at ten seventeen precisely! At a quarter past eight there was plenty of time for a stroll so we left the hotel for another winter's stroll in Cologne that Saturday morning.

'Oooooh myyyyyyyy God!' Libby pronounced cringingly as she walked out of the hotel's front door 'it is bloody freezing. Look over there I can see monkeys with welding equipment Tony just you be careful now.'

'Never mind' I replied, 'but don't open your mouth out here it could freeze open' I chortled not being able to see Libby's face but having a good idea of what it looked like and what she was thinking.

Negotiating the road-works and the pedestrian crossing outside the hotel we headed once again towards the station. The station that was a town within a city appeared to function as such for most of the day and night. Inside there we were out of the cold wind but it was still bitterly cold. It was even colder when we entered the square below the cathedral which was already busy with people scurrying into and out of the station. With her eyes watering because of the freezing cold wind it wasn't long before Libby wanted to head back to the hotel and the warmth of our room despite us not having walked even as much as a mile. Apart from a supposed accidental collision with some ignorant bloke who gave my wife such a bizarre look it startled her she would recall to me in our room later, we strolled very quickly to maintain what warmth we had. That Saturday morning walk didn't allow for the exercise we had hoped for because we cut it short it was so cold. Returning to the hotel and after taking the lift to our floor, it was a real pleasure to open the door to our warm and cosy room. I collapsed straight on my bed without removing my overcoat and dived under the duvet with my shoes. Whilst I was hiding under the duvet being even more of a juvenile Libby recalled that the bloke who had banged into her in the station had left a nasty bruise on her left shoulder that had become quite painful. She said she thought he could have easily avoided her even in that crowded station passageway but he seemed to target her. Yet again she insisted his face was familiar in a sort of strange way. Whilst she was rambling I removed my duvet and told her his face probably was familiar along with at least another eighty million Germans. She was not impressed and swore at me very naughtily. The matter was then dropped and forgotten for the rest of the day. We completed our ablutions and with still half an hour before we had to meet with the group downstairs at nine forty-five we chilled out for the remaining time.

'I'm going to read yesterday's papers Libby would you like one too or would you prefer a magazine?' I asked. She didn't answer as she was looking through the Hotel Information book so I didn't disturb her. Putting the papers to one side and with only minutes to go before we had to meet downstairs we tidied the room up and made our beds. It would leave a good impression Libby said, for the maid.

Leaving our room and checking that the door was firmly closed we ventured towards the larger of the two hotel lifts along our corridor. Realising that several other group members waited for the lift Libby and I walked down the back stairs to the hotel's lobby. We arrived in time to hear Johnson giving out last minute instructions, with maps, of Aachen and Cologne's Christmas markets before we marched - sorry walked - to the station and platform 9. He did so resemble a croupier as he waved his arms about distributing his literature. Rather like Jack Douglas the comedian in Tourette's syndrome mould Libby would later recall.

We heard several comments about the coldness of the weather as we snaked in twos and threes across to the railway station altogether, as requested by the management, in one group. For example, some folks said they should have brought their scarves and gloves they didn't think it would be as cold like it was. Libby knew exactly what I was thinking at that moment which was not surprising after our thirty-nine years and three hundred and sixty-four days together.

'Shall we hold hands or do you think the teacher will tell us off?' she twittered like some fifteen year-old school girl and continued

'Go on I dare you, we have been married for forty years tomorrow after all!'

I knew Dave and Margie had heard her ramblings as they were walking right behind us. They just grinned at what they knew was a dare. I meekly complied with her wishes and daft as a brush began skipping along like the adolescent I was. Libby instantaneously released my hand from hers out of disgust at my puerile actions so I stopped skipping and a smidgen of sanity prevailed again as we entered the lower reaches of Cologne railway station.

Platform nine, from where our train to Aachen was due to leave after we had negotiated the steep and numerous steps to the platform, must have been as cold and windy as the Steppes of Russia. The Pineapple Rail Tours' party to Aachen that Saturday morning huddled really close together to reduce the effect of the biting wind. Taking out one of Mr Johnson's photo-copied maps of either of the cities we were to visit proved impossible on that windy platform. However Johnson had yet to dish out our latest train tickets but we weren't disappointed or kept waiting much longer as he unfurled a huge wedge of tickets just before the train arrived. The German penchant for immaculate and precise organisation had penetrated their National Railways, and as if to prove the fact, our train was no exception arriving exactly on time. And yes, left precisely on time at ten seventeen. A double-decker train was a new and different type of experience for most in our group and whilst several dashed upstairs to gain a better view of the frosty German countryside Libby and I, with a few others who were the more elderly and sedate members of our group, stayed downstairs and mingled with the German passengers. The train was packed to the gunnels with hardly a spare seat anywhere. Not surprisingly the German Government heavily subsidised the railways making rail travel popular and essential for members of the public.

The whole of the journey took place in brilliant sunshine with wall to wall blue sky. Though there were several stops at minor stations on the way to Aachen it was obviously noticeable that the people getting on or off the train were well wrapped up and fully acquainted with their winter weather requirements, clothes-wise.

Paradoxically we were used to the opposite in the UK. The elderly appear to wrap up well though the youngsters just seem to ignore the cold wearing their trendy t-shirts and jeans. The latter paying the price for their bravado as they aged.

Our group were in good spirits as the train progressed towards Aachen. Libby and I could hear laughter coming from the upper reaches of the carriage where most of the group were. We thought we were able to identify some of the laughter-makers and their voices as the noise got ever louder. Perhaps they were being entertained by Johnson, God forbid. He eventually appeared downstairs in our part of the carriage and began identifying important landmarks in and around Aachen on the map he had given us to our other colleagues in the carriage. That was other than the Christmas market area because that was clearly marked all round the cathedral, on the map. When he finally sat opposite Libby and me he used his own map and a felt-tip marker pen which he produced from his dainty rucksack. He fastidiously marked the points of interest on our map as if he were a real cartographer. I was impressed.

'This is the bit I enjoy most' he said, 'being involved in this side of things. I have travelled so many times to Germany, obviously, since my late father was German and still has relatives here.'

'How did he come to be in England then Dennis was it love or the war?' I asked.

'Dad was originally from Cologne and was politically active against the Nazis a matter that nearly cost him his life' he said.

'Blimey' said Libby, 'so how did he manage to survive the war over here?'

'He didn't, that's the point. He escaped before war broke out and before wholesale arrests were made of dissidents in Germany. He cunningly avoided those arrests often living rough under the stars. He managed to travel to Poland on a false passport but found to his dismay that Poland had been invaded just after he arrived in Warsaw, so he continued travelling eastwards and into Russia at first. A big mistake as they were then allies of Germany.'

'Bloody hell did they capture him then?' Libby persevered.

'Not the Germans at that moment, but weeks later on the Russian-Polish border, he said the Ruskies picked him up thinking he was a spy for the Nazis.' Johnson was really re-living his dad's life at that moment and his speech became quite emotional. 'After some nasty interrogations, he never told me what they did to him, the Russians released him having relieved him of the money he was carrying, which was counterfeit anyway he said. Then he tramped through to Latvia and Riga the capital, managed to find and stow away on a freighter bound for London and hey presto he made it. He met my mum, a Cockney girl, and married her and I'm testament to that liaison.'

'My God there's a film in all that surely?' Libby asked.

'Not now he's gone and so has my mum too and they wouldn't believe me if I tried to write it all down on paper. Dad changed his name too on arrival in England, but I guessed you realised that. It must have saved him being locked up as an alien like many Germans and Italians who lived in England at that time. His name was originally Lantag.'

'I can't believe what I've just heard' said Libby taking another look at our map of Aachen. When Johnson finished his story he just stood up and thanked us for politely listening and again commented that he was sure he knew us from some other rail trip. Then he was gone popping back upstairs to the revel-rousers.

The train continued to rattle along at a fair lick while Libby and I discussed a possible plan of action to see Aachen now that Johnson had been more than helpful to incorporate not only the market there, but its cathedral and of course the shops. We paused from talking only to take in the names of the stations we stopped at before numbering on our map a few items and places we wanted to visit. We then discussed the trip on the Rhine arranged for later that night and what we might expect for dinner. It would be a long day with lots of action but it would also be an exciting and most revealing day.

The outskirts of Aachen came into view and at twelve minutes past eleven we pulled into and stopped at the main Aachen station. Off the train and having left the platform by lift we walked across

73

the station concourse and into the small square in front of the main building. The party had split up quickly into groups of two or three friends or newly made acquaintances many having begun making their way downhill and into the city towards the Christmas market. We teamed up with Dermot, the genial Irishman, who had asked us as we left the platform if he could join with us for the morning.

'No problem Dermot you be our guest' Libby said and the three of us set off for the market and the cathedral not forgetting to walk in the slightly warmer sunshine that shone on one side of the road.

It was at the first set of traffic lights we came across in the city that Libby suddenly remarked casually

'That's the bloke who bumped into me on the station last night and bruised me, I'm sure it is. You know the one I said gave me a funny look as if he knew me, but didn't appear surprised to bump into me. At least that's what I thought at the time it happened. Proper frightened me at the time. I bet he's here in Aachen visiting the sights like our mob.'

'We're a mob now are we?' Dermot asked 'and what made you come to that conclusion Libby if you don't mind me asking?'

'Just the way we all poured off the train a few minutes ago like the natives. Or maybe it's the Christmas spirit' Libby replied.

We crossed the road when the traffic stopped at the red light and walked towards the cathedral. Libby began walking normally again from then onwards: by that I mean she was looking in all the women's fashion shops, lingering long enough as she did at home not just to have a better look at some of the goods in the windows, but in her mind compare prices. I knew she had hit the jackpot when I received the usual good tug on my arm, so strong it almost levered it out of joint as she stopped and stared straight ahead into one shop. I hoped that there would be little chance of that in such cold weather but I was wrong, so wrong. I rescued myself from financial oblivion by saying

'Let's look for a bar or coffee shop, have a cup of coffee or maybe something stronger. Maybe even a cake or sandwich' I suggested 'just so we can warm up a little.'

'What a good idea that is.' Dermot agreed 'Give us chance to reflect and think of the morning's expectations, look at the maps too and I could sure use a coffee.'

Libby wasn't so convinced as she walked away slowly from the shop front, looking longingly over her shoulder at the expensive clothes on view. However, she went along with the idea as long as she could have a cold dry wine, preferably Pinot Grigio. She and Dermot began looking for a good coffee house as we sauntered through the town centre. It was important not only to get out of the cold but it transpired that Dermot, who, having said he was a connoisseur of good coffee, said he had not had a good cup of coffee since leaving London. It didn't take them long to find what they were looking for. Having walked through the main shopping area of the city we came upon a small market in a large busy square, although we were to find the market was not the one that contained the cathedral. Surrounded by lots of quaint Christmassy stalls that filled the square to bursting one could not avoid the heavenly smells of gluhwein and cooked meats that teased our nostrils and reminded us that it really was Christmas.

The square was crowded and it was a pleasure to see faces of both adults and children in that magical world albeit a temporary one. I say temporarily because Dermot our little caring friend had spotted his proper coffee shop on one side of the square: Konig City, selling Plum's Kaffee or something. Entering we found a truly fabulous bar and coffee house that was packed to the rafters, throbbing with the life of both customers and staff and the most amazing smell of coffee.

Once the drinks had been ordered I was glad that Libby again began to relax her recent nightmare crash three days ago. Certainly she had every chance whilst Dermot took centre stage and regaled us both about the life and times of one Dermot O'Leahy. His varied and troubled life had undoubtedly kept him on his toes and his incredibly diversified career interested both Libby and me so much Libby appeared transfixed at his eloquence. He only stood five foot six in bare feet, weighed less than Libby and the beggar had most of his hair. But I tell you what, with the Irish brogue he had, I could have listened all day to him it was so gentle and relaxing. I very nearly had to as well he talked energetically for so long. He claimed he had worked in the desert heat of Australia as a young man and returned, married, to the heat of Luton back in the UK. He'd had such an adventurous life with so many jobs you wondered how he had had time to cram them all in. Listening to our new friend talk Libby and me were surprised how much of our lives and travelling abroad had coincided very closely with that of Dermot's. Incredibly he knew of Libby's friend's parents in Luton. He had worked for the same car manufacturer as her friend's dad before being made redundant himself. We'd also visited places he'd visited in Australia, in the West Indies and in Canada. There were though so many places in the world that he had visited, listening to him was like listening to a geographical compendium or world gazetteer Libby would recall later in the hotel.

'How have you found time for all these trips if you have been working too?' my lovely wife asked.

'Ah well you see Libby' he began, 'I have run my own window-cleaning firm for years and it has allowed me plenty of flexibility during the year if I wanted to travel, on my own of course, since my divorce came through.'

I shot Libby a glance that I hope meant 'no more questions on that subject' knowing what was about to come from her mouth as it began to open. True trooper that she was she completely threw me when she asked him what his favourite place on the planet was.

'That would be South America' Dermot gleefully answered like a young schoolboy who had just gained ten out of ten for an English test. He said that Paraguay, for him, was such an amazing collection of contrasts, in essence he would like to have lived there not only holidayed there.

'What about the heat?' Libby asked, 'were you never in trouble with the humidity and isn't it always very high there?'

'With low blood pressure I don't perspire as much as many people though the West Indies was really clammy, sticky and sultry when I was there with a partner,' Dermot continued.

'You have a partner, you married again?' Libby asked him.

'Sort of but not married just a close friend,' he said with a huge smile on his face as if he'd anticipated that Libby question.

'What of your children you said they had been in Oz with you and your wife early in your marriage? Do they live in England?' Libby demanded to know which although entertaining between the two of them began to irritate me as an outsider and onlooker, drinks organiser and chocolate biscuit locater.

'Yes my daughter lives in London, and my son, well ...... you know how it is.' he said with lots of thoughtful reflection. 'What about another drink? Tony another beer and you Libby can I get you a white wine?'

'OK that's fine thank you' Libby answered, 'but how was the coffee you made a song and dance about having? How was it?'

'Well since we've been here in Germany I cannot remember such a good tasting coffee so I'll be having one more. The hotel coffee this morning was warm crap. Sorry to be rude but not what I would have chosen had I had the choice. Tomorrow I shall be making my own tea Tony like you did this morning. I saw you so I did.'

Spoken from the heart I knew we had chosen the right bar. Or was Dermot being an extra polite gentleman? We would soon to find out. The bar was so busy you had to see it to believe it, the waitresses were never without an order and thanks to them the punters seldom waited very long for a top up drink. But there we were again and people were smoking in a bar where there was food which was outlawed in Blighty by the EU, supposedly. We tended to forget that in being 'abroad' for some reason we did not understand, not only were there smoking areas on railway platforms, but smoking was allowed in bars and in restaurants as we would find out later when we ate lunch. It was all confusing and we found it rather strange as the French and Germans seemed to have invented most of the rules for the EU, particularly the health and safety rules.

As our conversations began to wane all three of us became people watchers for the last few minutes of our stay inside that room.

'Continental life at its best in here don't you think?' I heard Dermot mutter to Libby who nodded in agreement.

Having finished our drinks we ventured outside back into the cold air of Aachen finding it difficult at first to adjust to the brilliant sunshine that beamed down on everyone. It was past twelve thirty and we had to be back at the Railway station for three forty-five and that after some lunch too. Squinting in the sunshine we headed towards the first of the pretty stalls in the small Market square.

'Not very big is it. I hope this is not all there is because there only seems to be about thirty stalls at most' said a disappointed Libby as she wandered in front of me and Dermot to a stall that was plastered all over with wooden items. 'Can we pay by card here because some of the items I like are expensive?' she squeaked at me without daring to look up at me.

'Pay with anything especially euros' replied Dermot helpfully, I didn't think.

'Hey you two' I said, 'that's only the first stall you've looked at. If this carries on and you buy something every time you stop or pause to look we shall need a whole carriage to ourselves on the way home.'

'This is Christmas' Libby said her eyes boring right through my eyes 'and we are visiting for the first time.'

I could have said some more but didn't and rather played safe by continuing to carry on walking looking at other stalls. Jewellery stalls, toy stalls, wine stalls, food stalls, wurst stalls and 'best' stalls and some stalls with strange metal objects being sold from them. So clean, so busy and so wonderfully Christmassy the whole scene looked. It was sheer bliss for kids and adults alike, unless you were the one spending money of course. I knew my devious ploy had succeeded because Libby followed closely behind at the side of me and in front of me not wanting to get lost in foreign territory, and with a different language. So the wallet stayed in the pocket. Dermot clung on closely too enjoying the company he was with hopefully.

We quickly visited most if not all the stalls that were present in that small market and after looking around and checking our maps to get our bearings once more, we stood back for a minute to see where the crowds were headed, and followed like lemmings. A couple of blocks past beautiful half-timbered houses and shops we came upon the area next to and around the Cathedral. You could smell the medieval atmosphere and in a blink of an eyelid it was possible for the dreamer to transport themselves back in time. But there we were in the Twenty-First century and needless to say there had been interruptions to our progress as we walked. In fact there was a short delay every few yards as Libby paused at first one shop and then another cataloguing in her mind not only the type of product in the shop but their prices and quality of the product displayed. That mental exercise took place at each and every bloody shop I can tell you despite my attempt to gee her along. Dermot also dropped back somewhat and was observing the crowds of people at length as they trooped towards the cathedral's entrance. He was probably counting them in for some obscure reason but why, I have no idea.

When he caught up with us I asked if he'd seen some of our tour group that was perhaps the reason for his delay. His reply stunned me somewhat.

'Tony I just saw the geezer who Libby was rambling on about back at the first set of traffic lights earlier in the day. He was with some old chick or other. I thought I'd let you know. He caught my eye, nothing more. I thought you should know that's all after the way Libby spoke' he whispered in his quiet Irish brogue.

'Yes what are you telling me for?' I asked 'don't say any more I am concentrating on my wife who is looking into the window of a very expensive shop thank you and I am about to drag her away.' I was joking really but he looked equally as surprised by my comment as I had been by his.

'What are you two whispering for I bet it's all lies?' Libby called to us.

'We're just deciding what to do first before we eat as it has gone a quarter to one. Whether we should go inside the cathedral first and take some piccies or go round the market first.' The words stumbled out of my mouth in half truth with Libby wondering what the hell I was talking about. 'What do you fancy?'

'What, in that shop I was looking in? Everything darling and what a lovely anniversary present it would make for tomorrow' she cooed at me taking the 'P'.

'Anniversary, anniversary and which one would that be?' asked Dermot

'Fortieth' I replied with my head bowed down, eyes out of sight of Libby at the thought of what an expensive Saturday it looked like turning out to be. 'Now come on let's go eat. What do you want? Let's not waste time' I blustered unconvincingly.

'I'm easy' she replied.

'Celebratory meal I suggest' blurted our Dermot.

'Ok something special and healthy' said Libby.

'Forget old habits this is Germany and the food is fattening' I said and ducked as a handbag with Libby holding it flashed past my head. 'Only joking, let's go into the cathedral and then go to lunch. How about you Dermot what do you want to do first?'

'Cathedral and then sit and eat I say,' he answered. And that is what we did after first acknowledging Dave and Margie two fellow members of our group who were walking towards us from across the road. They too were looking for somewhere to eat having already been in the cathedral.

However, having seen the lengthy queues waiting to enter the cathedral, organised tours and disorganised tours so to speak, we had a slight problem deciding on which one to join. Both types of queue, from our previous observations of such things, were slow moving. Dermot, on closer surveillance, found they were in fact large parties of tourists or of schoolchildren waiting for official guides to lead them. Cheekily we dodged in between and in front of them which was to save us hours in a queue. Inside that monument to Charlemagne called the Kaiserdom, or Imperial Cathedral as it has become known, the religious importance of the building was overwhelming. Likewise the historical significance attached to it because of all the imperial coronations that were conducted in it. And because of those two prestigious significances subsequent pilgrimages that were made there only served to highlight how important Aachen became for centuries in Germanic life. The fact was not lost on Libby as she photographed as many features in the Palatine Chapel as possible: the ceiling, the huge bronze chandelier, the mosaics and the marble floor really hit her between the eyes. So too did the crowds of people all champing at the bit to see the huge coloured-glass windows behind the altar.

I heard her say several times 'Excuse me please' as people bumped into her or trod on her feet as they too strained every sinew to get pictures. A few minutes later as we stood together by a thick stone column under the octagonal roof, a tired-looking Libby asked me

'What are we still standing here for when we could go out and get some lunch?'

'Because Dermot is somewhere in that scrum taking photographs of the windows like you did and he doesn't want to lose us before he eats' I replied quietly.

'Hey ho let's go' a little Irish voice said from somewhere behind me. 'Can we just pop into this small chapel annex before we leave please, I'm sure Charlemagne's tomb is in there and as he was such a famous Holy Roman Emperor I'd like a picture. Over here' he said and he led us into a corner where a brownish marble sarcophagus type thing was 'inside' one of the walls.

'Is that all it is?' Libby asked 'I thought it would be massive like the one's we have at home in Westminster Abbey type thingy.'

I could saw Dermot squirm looking decidedly unimpressed with Libby's knowledge of British history but then Libby never was into history. A couple more photographs later and we left the cathedral and returned to the brilliant sunlight outside. The call of food superseded a return to a bar and though Libby did like her wine it was well after one o'clock and we hadn't eaten since seven that morning. Therefore before the question of a lunch-time drink arose we went off looking for some grub.

Not wanting to go and sit in a crowded restaurant or bar after our experience of crowds that morning we wandered up a side street looking for a quiet place to rest our tired bones. Not always the best thing to do as we were about to find out. We located an almost empty restaurant rather fortuitously so we thought at that moment, and entered having had a quick glance at the menu.

'What is this place called?' Dermot asked as we were seated at a table by a waiter. 'It's very clean and looks awfully posh.'

Libby had been smarter than either of us and picked up a card with the restaurant's name on it. 'It is the ….. K…….s an exquisite grill by the looks of it. A sort of bistro I think.'

'Very good and what would you like to drink? Oh my good Lord what gorgeous canapés and don't they look the business too?' commented Dermot just as the picturesque plates of canapés landed on the table almost before we were seated.

A wine for Libby, a beer for me and two bottles of still water for Dermot arrived as the waiter remained hovering round us until we ordered some food. I say some food but if we had ordered a whole meal we may have been waiting there now the service was so slow. We actually only managed to order one course which was soup. Two minestrones for Libby and me and a consommé of mushrooms for Dermot that, when it arrived, had taken an age to prepare and from tins I might add. They really took forty-five minutes to arrive and were eaten with such gusto we decided enough was enough. We paid the bill hurriedly and left the restaurant after an hour at about twenty past two, still starving hungry.

Chapter Seven.

'There is less than an hour and a half left before we must leave for the train home and we haven't been to the big Market yet' Libby said grumpily outside the restaurant. Following that remark we quickly headed towards the biggest, loudest and most crowded of the Aachen markets.

The crowds were in fact so huge and so slow moving that despite our wish to walk quickly round without missing any of the stalls, it proved impossible. The stalls came and went as we shuffled by them whether we wanted to or not as we were caught up in what appeared to be the world's largest human crocodile that was both deep and moving so slowly it was almost impossible to get to the front of a stall as we were carried along by the crowd's momentum. Ha Ha I thought what a great cure for Libby's over-active penchant for spending money. Don't you believe a word of it for that woman could have played in the English Rugby Team's front row and been very successful the way she jostled to the front of the stall selling nougat! Though very similar to those lower down in the city that we saw earlier the difference was that there seemed to be hundreds of them.

When you've seen one particular sort of stall and its goods, inhaled the surrounding smells and listened to the whoops of joy as some parent managed to purchase something from it for their children, you've seen them all. But it was impossible to forget the look on the face of the lucky child. To accomplish that feat more than once as a parent would be miraculous such was the volume of people. There were hundreds of stalls and thousands of people I cannot remember such a crush. Products were on display not only in the standard wooden stalls but also in the open-topped gangways at their sides. German sausages, candy floss, burgers, popcorn, sandwiches, beer, gluhwein in celebratory mugs, and a host of other food and drink that was being consumed in such huge quantities it was painful to watch and not be part of it. And believe me the whole moving tableau was conducted in such an orderly manner it was remarkable.

It was whilst shuffling in this human conga that Dermot suddenly grabbed hold of me, a finger to his lips, and pointed towards a jewellery stall as we shuffled past it.

'There Tony in the fur coat and big red anorak it's them I told you about an hour or more ago' Dermot spoke almost in silence so Libby could not hear. 'The bloke Libby saw at the traffic lights earlier that bumped into her last evening you said. Remember?'

'Oh him where is he?' I asked with one of Dermot's fingers almost up my nose, 'I can't see where you are pointing.' And then I saw them and could hardly mistake them from Dermot's description. 'Have they seen us?' I asked 'But I cannot say I recognise them at this distance.'

'Oh definitely they have, but who cares? It is only a coincidence we see them again and again after all because they are obviously visitors like we are surely? But look, they are staring at us now with their hands trying to hide their faces' he replied.

'But why are they so interested in us, do they know us? Come to think of it there is something about them that rings a bell in my head and I'm going to jolly well find out what it is' I countered.

At that moment Libby asked again what we were whispering for as she had finished nougat bar number one. Turning to Dermot I shook my head from side to side hoping he would understand the message. I was not going to carry out my threat of a few seconds earlier and go and speak to the pair who had appeared to be eyeing us up and down and seemed to be following us around Aachen. A backward glance at the nosy couple as we moved on told me they were still intrigued by us for some weird reason that didn't spring to mind. The subject of who the couple might have been was then dropped for the time being between me and Dermot.

Dermot and I were further distracted from answering Libby's question by the passage in front of us of the Knuckle Brothers who floated by complete with a selection of food and drinks that they waved in our direction triumphantly. We waved vigorously back at them hoping they would stop and join us and maybe have a beer, but no such luck. Libby too was waving to some members of our Pineapple group she saw fighting their way through the crowds. They waved and called out asking if we were enjoying ourselves but the constant noise from the crowds camouflaged Libby's reply.

After suffering the crush of the crowd for a time we decided since the stalls were repeated every fifty yards or so that we should head back to the rail station as it was three o'clock and our leader would not be very happy if we were either late or missed the train.

On the way Dermot confessed to us as we broke away from the crowds that he had a fad for collecting fridge magnets. Boy did he enjoy himself as he stopped off and bought a dozen in one gift shop! Outside the shop he asked Libby and me if we collected any knick-knacks or the like. He nearly fell over when she said she was a pocillovist, or egg-cup collector to the uninitiated, and had sixteen hundred egg-cups at the last count.

'Do they all have eggs in them?' he asked with tongue in cheek.

'No more than your fridge magnets have their own fridge!' Libby retorted catching Dermot off guard. We laughed as we walked and talked and soon found out what we all needed. A fresh food shop selling rolls of all kinds stuffed with cheeses and meats from a variety of nationalities. Where, according to a very vocal Libby, we should have visited in the first place for lunch. How spot on she was. Eating on the way back to the station we came across an amazing second hand shop that both Dermot and Libby just had to go and have a sneaky look in, even at that late hour. After handing me their half-eaten rolls to look after, they disappeared into the dusty grotto leaving me to stand alone on the pavement. They were gone for several minutes and with little time left before meeting our leader at the station again I called out loudly to Libby and Dermot in the grotty grotto. Immediately and furtively they ventured out in fits of giggles with Dermot carrying a small parcel. In the parcel which he began to open, and showing me as we walked, was the most gilt laden and tacky watch I had ever seen. It was so big that it was obvious he would fracture his wrist if he ever wore it for any length of time because he even had difficulty carrying the damned ugly thing. We continued walking slowly up the main road with Dermot and Libby finishing their lunch on the hoof. Like spiders returning to the centre of a web to check on their catch, so it was that we caught up with several weary members of our group as they trudged back to the station.

At almost three forty-five the sun had gone from the sky as we crossed the station square and felt the wind on our backs getting up again. In the station concourse many of our party were sat at tables drinking coffee including the ladies we had joined for dinner the night before, along with Dave and Margie, Iris and Richard and Johnson the tour guide. Several others we recognised facially, but not by name, were busily reminiscing about their day in Aachen too. The station was packed with shoppers returning home from a successful day out and Libby and I wondered if we'd get a seat on the return journey.

'Fancy a drink you two?' I asked Libby and Dermot. 'I presume a coffee for both of you and a warming brandy for me?'

'Oh yes? Dream on Buster' was the reply from my wife who told me in no uncertain manner that she too would like a coffee and a brandy. After slowly emptying our glasses and mugs of their liquid the three of us, lemming-like, decided we had need of the toilet before boarding the train home. Decision taken, we left the station café and before setting foot on the platform to go back to Cologne we had made a short detour for the toilet. That toilet visit proved most intriguing because despite clearly having an entry fee, displayed for all to see on the toilet door, no-one appeared to pay the fifty cents necessary. Copying the locals we too waited for someone to exit the toilet so we could hold the door open for them to exit before entering ourselves free of charge. Well I ask you, fifty pence to pee. (50p to pee.)

The train was waiting on the platform and quickly filling with passengers when we arrived and climbed aboard. Again it was a double-decker train due to leave at ten past four. We were upstairs half asleep in the warmth of our carriage when the releasing of the brakes woke me from my reverie at exactly ten past four.

'Why can't Deutches Bahn run the trains in Britain?' I muttered to Libby more than once on the way home.

We were scheduled to arrive in Cologne at ten past five, and guess what? We arrived exactly on time. The journey had been uneventful from what I can remember from behind my eyelids until that was when we tried to vacate the platform at Cologne. It was mayhem and just as crowded as the Markets in Aachen and although Johnson had tried to hold back the human tide at the top of the platform steps, his arms out straight in front of him for a change, he was always on a loser. We poured down the steps as others poured up them and past us with people colliding every now and again in the melee. Turning at the bottom of the steps into the main thoroughfare we found it even more crowded so it was a relief seeing some of the elderly folks safely make it to the station exit. We slowed down walking and talking to Sid who, despite his problems with his walking, had enjoyed himself immensely in Aachen, though he hadn't bought any family presents and felt bad about that. Iris and Richard had a most wonderful lunch in a bar with, as Richard embarrassingly informed all in hearing distance, 'Dead sexy waitresses Tony, you should have joined us.' Iris berated him saying that she was talking about the food but that didn't wipe the smile off his face or the wink he gave Dermot and me as we overtook them.

Arriving back at the hotel across the never-ending road works, the warmth of the hotel lobby was again most welcome. Johnson, waiting alongside the notice-board in the hotel, informed us we had to be back in the lobby ready to leave at seven fifteen if we were not to miss the Rhine Cruise that evening for the Dinner Party as the boat we were travelling on was scheduled to leave its moorings at seven forty-five, and most certainly would.

That set off another scramble towards the lifts and those that arrived opposite them first piled into them and were soon on their way upwards at snail's pace. Some of the unlucky ones had to be content with walking up the seven floors or so to their rooms having first let some of the more elderly folks travel in style up in the lift. Libby was far from amused at having to walk up the steps and more knackered than she thought after a day's walking and took immediate offence as she arrived at our floor. There stood smiling was Sid who asked what had taken her so long to get there. He had of course travelled by hotel lift. Let's just say I was glad to open the door to our room first time with the plastic key and bundle Libby inside quickly before she could reply to Sid's comment that had been made with a smile on his face. Once inside the room she flopped on the bed and was still there when I had finished showering and dressed for dinner.

Ten minutes after I'd showered, shaved, deodorised myself and applied a very expensive après rasage, Libby decided the time had come for her to make an effort and began to prepare herself for the night on the Rhine. It was never a problem waiting for my wife to get ready to go out on a Saturday night on account of being able to catch up with the football scores on the TV. And so it was here when the phone rang in our room.

'Hello?' I asked 'who's speaking please?'

The line went dead, but that didn't stop the phone ringing several more times after that first time as Libby preened herself for the evening. I got the same response each time until I'd had enough of missing the football reports. So, with what was to become the last call to our room that evening, I shouted a piece of Anglo-Saxon language into the phone which had the instant effect I wanted. At least it stopped the calls dead in their tracks.

'Who was that Tony?' Libby asked each time the phone rang and again finally when she appeared in the room after her shower.

'Someone pissing about I suppose,' I replied, 'but it is unusual in a hotel unless it's a mate. I shan't do anything via the switchboard

I think whoever it was got the message with what I shouted down the phone.'

'Perhaps some of the others in the group have had the same calls to their room, it's worth asking don't you think?'

I told her to forget it because I did not think it was anything except someone messing about, maybe Sid seeking to apologise for his joke that backfired with Libby. If it were him I felt sure he would soon mention it to one of us later that night. I intended telling Dermot later but only to keep him informed and to let us know if the same happened to him or indeed others in the group.

'While I think, love,' I said, 'we must get some more luggage labels with the company name on them from our beloved leader. We can't leave luggage around without it being clearly marked not nowadays because some organisations would destroy it. I'll have a word with Johnson sometime tonight or tomorrow and see if he's got any spare labels. I'm sure he must have somewhere knowing him.'

'Listen what time is it because we must have to be in the lobby soon?' Libby enquired hurriedly.

'It's nearly seven o'clock. Fancy a snifter before we return to the cold night air mein liebe?' I thought the request might cheer or wake her up somewhat but I wasn't quite sure at that moment until she said

'Now you're talking babe, a large one to keep the cold away,' Libby smiled and continued 'didn't we pass this way years ago on the river when we sailed to Basle with some company? KD Cruises I seem to remember.'

'That's right and you pronounced Basle correctly. Do you remember the announcer on the boat taking the mickey out of us Brits when he pronounced Basle?' I reminded her.

'How could I forget it was so embarrassing to hear him speak? 'Ladies and gentlemen' he began in all the European languages …. and pronounced the word *Basel*. But for those of you from the UK …. *Barl*. We almost crawled under the table we were so humiliated.' Libby's rendition was spot on and although we suffered greatly with some of the Yanks and European passengers on that boat at the time we had a great holiday.

'Here take this I must tidy up these cans and your empty wine bottle before we go downstairs because the maid will be in for turn down whilst we are out. By the way have you seen my scarf and gloves I can't see them in my drawer? I asked.

'You had a man's look they are in your case on the top of the wardrobe' Libby remarked.

A few minutes later and we had finished our drinks and cleared up the glasses, I had my scarf and gloves, and we were on our way down to the hotel lobby for seven fifteen. Most of the group were already waiting and with Dennis Johnson ticking each person off his list as they assembled we were soon allowed to walk outside and off towards the Rhine and our boat for the night. On the way to the river some people were talking excitedly about what they were about to experience on the trip, whilst others were recalling their time in Aachen and their experiences of the fairy-tale stalls in the Christmas Market.

Walking briskly down towards the river Libby and me we were joined by Johnson and another couple who were commenting on the clear sky and the lights that could be seen all around the riverside buildings. Johnson explained that the tourist industry on the Rhine had always made sure the surrounding area was well lit all year round, but especially at Christmas time when the extra lights added greatly to the whole riverside scene as were shortly to see.

We were not disappointed.

Chapter Eight.

The river Rhine was not more than four hundred yards from the hotel and our floating restaurant, our home for the night, just a half mile further along the promenade. Strolling along the promenade and looking up towards the now floodlit and majestic cathedral only added to the magic of the Christmas scenes around us as we walked along the river. In fact down on the riverside it was an absolute fairyland: the bars, the hotels, private houses and even factories were all decorated with lights and trees making a picture that sadly is missing from home. One of the people in our group likened it to Blackpool and other seaside towns they had visited which did not go down at all well with Elspeth or her friends who I heard quietly ridicule the comparison.

Walking along, taking in the ambience of the occasion I could hear Libby happily reminiscing to someone about the quality and the size of the meals we had experienced with the same company many years ago on our first trip down the Rhine. That year even the Yanks had commented on the size and quality of the portions on their 'trip of a lifetime to see the old country.' Typical of them I thought at the time and hadn't changed my mind since. Libby asked me if we would receive the same type of quality meal and size of portion on the boat that night. I of course said I had no idea, but was hopeful. We were to soon find out.

Standing on the gangplank prior to boarding our boat for the night, aptly named Stolzenfels, the chat amongst the group was both animated and focussed on the voyage to be undertaken despite our being delayed for some unknown reason. It was no fun waiting off the boat and peering through the portholes into the festive laden boat whilst in the freezing cold night air. Johnson did though give a good account of himself as he effectively, but nonetheless diplomatically found out from a member of the ship's staff what the hold-up was. No sooner had he finished his enquiry than the delay was over and we poured onto the ship and into an all round warmth both temperature-wise and with its innards decked out with fairy lights, trees, Christmas gnomes, flowers and paper Christmas decorations. The whole atmosphere onboard spelt out celebration. The hovering waiters and waitresses reflected our anticipation by smiling back at us.

Our tables were all adjacent on the port side of the boat and towards the stern. Our Master of Ceremonies for the evening, none other than that hyperactive, finger-pointing and smiling Dennis Johnson, ably guided us to our seats that we were to occupy for the whole time we were on board. Placing his baseball cap in his faithful rucksack he joined a table near to the bar. Once seated Libby and I found ourselves with six others we had been getting to know from the onset of the trip. They were the three ladies we had dinner with the night before, a rather posh lady from Oxford, a lady from Derby and Sid, who we since learned had worked for the BBC in London. Dermot and the Knuckle Brothers were on a separate table, the brothers having begun sparring with all and sundry, not only on their table but with any person prepared to joust with them as they passed by including a chap who could have been the captain of the boat.

A foghorn sounded only the one in question was to come from the mouth of a fresh faced and very loud lady who was to be our waitress for the night. Collecting orders for drinks as she translated the night's menu for anyone who dared to ask she loudly made her way from table to table. Meanwhile Elspeth had almost completed the menu translation successfully herself, without her glasses, which was a feat in itself. She had lived in Germany before its 'reunification' and could just about remember enough of its language. Libby listened to Elspeth intently before commenting 'Not pork again surely?' But it was so, and this drew a few negative comments from all around the table, particularly from the ladies. Mind you the pork we had in the hotel the previous night was 'soft and tender, melted in one's mouth and tasted really lovely' and would be difficult to beat for quality.

Sitting opposite Mary I discussed with her the starter of beef broth and dumplings that had been identified by Elspeth correctly, just as the drinks arrived along with our over enthusiastic waitress who was shouting out our orders long before she arrived at the table. I arranged a makeshift signalling code to alert Mary early to the maelstrom that was the waitress before she approached our table. It wasn't that Mary didn't hear her when the 'foghorn' approached our table, but I just gave her more time to cover her ears from the loud megaphone-like blast before the lady actually appeared next to us.

When the starter came it halted the conversation fleetingly at our table as we tried to identify its constituent parts, correctly identified by Elspeth in the menu, but that were then being vividly described by the lady from Oxford, and Libby. The meat was sparse and the dumplings spongy like little blobs of tiny congealed lumps of flour. A quick look at the faces around the table clearly awarded 'nil points' from the British jury for that first course. Libby, as did several others, left most of her soup in the bowl and whilst talking with the others decided her wine was far more important. The three female colleagues along with Sid and me were rather pleased with our beer which was helping wash the salty soup down our throats. Sid suggested they had prepared it with water from the Rhine. His comments drew knowing glances from a couple on the table suggesting he was close to the mark.

A quick nod and a wink to Mary saved her from further deafness as the waitress arrived both to clear the soup bowls away and ask if anyone required more 'trinks?' She didn't bat an eyelid as we ordered the same again.

Conversation, despite the disappointing food, was really buzzing as the cruise got underway. It was at a lull in conversation that the lady from Oxford, who really was a Lady, told us she had been an officer-nurse in the Army, taken a degree in the History of Art and worked for a finance company in London, and also used her degree to become a tour guide in some London museums and art galleries. Our jaws dropped to the floor when she also told us she had been camping in Indian Kashmir with four friends and had the time of her life. It came as a surprise then that she had problems at home in her garden with trees that had needed some serious pollarding to create more light. After all she had come across to us at the table as the female equivalent of Indiana Jones. Libby was nodding as the Lady finished talking: what for I had no idea, but the lady from Derby also nodded in agreement at that moment too. Maybe it was something to do with the wine they were drinking.

The Scottish lady - I use that term in the same way as people talk of the Scottish Play – and me nearly came to blows she upset me big-time when we discussed our hobbies. She let it be known that she hated anything to do with cricket. I told her she was typical of her nation. We eventually agreed to a difference of opinion to save scuttling the boat. Due to retire shortly she spoke lovingly of her hoped for return to the west coast of Scotland and a planned for home near her beloved town of Helensburgh.

We sat and waited for our next course. In our feeble attempts speaking 'pigeon-German' to the waitress ordering drinks and food we hadn't even noticed that she was not German but hailed from the Balkans we were to find out later. It was a miracle that our orders arrived as successfully as they did under the circumstance. At least Elspeth had given it her all in trying to speak German correctly but it hadn't always succeeded. Her friend Jenny such a different quiet person, conservative and polite, hardly spoke a word at all during the whole evening. That is not to say Elspeth wasn't some of those things, but quiet she was not.

The enigma sat opposite me: Mary. Mary was a lady career-accountant for a local authority who, in a different guise, was also a seriously talented musician and dancer. Not a professional though and I soon found out why. Both her friends described how she played a whole range of musical instruments with incredible skill, in particular her black trombone. Her passion in music, the reason she had the trombone? Her love of jazz. By the end of the evening I was convinced that on her return to the UK having listened to her reasoning that she would start playing jazz really seriously were she able to hook up and practise with a professional group. There was even more from this talented lady: she could not find a partner good enough to accompany her to dance the Argentinian Tango. When we heard this Sid and I had problems with our breathing as we gasped for air in disbelief.

'Argentinian tango, what on earth is the difference between that and an ordinary tango?' Sid asked.

I felt Mary was about to explain to those of us who were ignorant of even the basic dancing steps when she just laughed and the moment was over and past. She did, however, say she was unable to find a decent experienced male partner to dance with. I couldn't help thinking that it was such a waste of company and talent for some lucky chap.

Our main course of pork eventually arrived interrupting our musical conversation and was again served by 'Miss Foghorn'. It was impossible to compare it with the meal at the hotel the night before. Why? Because this pork was as tough as old boots to eat to say the least whilst the vegetables of swede and duchesse potato were soft and tender. At least there was something to eat.

As we ate and drank so the boat continued its festive journey and a band played in a far off bar on the boat as we cruised down the Rhine past small villages and hamlets bedecked with festive decorations and lights. Every now and again people waved from the shore at the boat engaging various responses from the boat's passengers and diners. At journey's half-way point and the boat's turnaround at Bonn, a new game began amongst the passengers. It consisted of just two questions which were: how far had we travelled and what was the city over on the starboard shore where all the bright white lights were? Guesses ranged from the plausible to the outrageously incorrect. We had travelled for just over an hour and the guesstimated distance travelled ranged from twenty to a hundred kilometres. Guesses about the town or city were even more bizarre and ranged from Frankfurt, to in one case, Berlin. Both would have needed far longer travelling time, Berlin perhaps needing at least several days by boat. Thankfully we would all be home in Cologne and moored alongside the promenade within the next hour having eaten our sweet of tinned plums and 'crumbled sponge-cake'. Well that was Libby's interpretation of what was in her dish anyhow. She was far from being a happy lady food-wise though the wine did help dull the disappointment.

The journey back consisted mainly of people singing Christmas carols in German and English, with accompaniments played out on a nearby piano by our musician, Mary. Back in Cologne on terra firma once we had disembarked, Libby and I decided we'd had enough travelling for one day and just wanted to be home as quickly as possible and in bed at the hotel. Disappointingly for us the meal was not the quality of the previous Rhine trip Libby and I had been on. Unsurprisingly after such a long and busy day some of the more elderly folk amongst us looked really tired and were also ready for bed. It was after all gone eleven o'clock.

Once our leader had accounted for us all we were dismissed go back to the hotel if we so chose. Libby and I after taking several photographs of the boat and quayside, made our way rapidly through a couple of back streets and up the hill towards the cathedral. Cold, dark and with a slight wind blowing in our faces we set off at a fair pace walking, with a bit of a run as my mum used to say, to the base of Cathedral Hill. Cafes and restaurants that we passed were still humming with life that Saturday night as Libby and I arrived, arm in arm, at the foot of the hill below the cathedral. Making the ascent easier for walkers was an arrangement of steps that both went across and up the slope to the cathedral which at its pinnacle seemed almost to be in daylight the lights illuminating the cathedral were so bright.

Climbing higher Libby was alerted to a ringing tone closeby: I thought it was my head after the beer, but no such luck.

'Is that your phone bleeping Tony? Check it because it could be one of the kids calling. They are an hour behind in the UK' Libby said impressing me with her knowledge of my phone's bleeping.

'Hello' I said answering, 'Oh hi Caroline, what are you phoning for at this late hour? Is everything OK at home?'

'Bill and I are just fine dad I just thought I'd wish you and mum a happy anniversary for tomorrow and hope that all goes well and that you have a lovely day together. That was all dad.' Our lovely and thoughtful daughter was talking to her daddy. I thanked her and then I passed the phone to Libby whose first question to Caroline was to ask how her grand-children were. Of course the usual mother-daughter banter continued for several minutes at which point kisses were blown down the small phone to those at the other end. The call over I checked with Libby that all was fine back in Blighty and we continued walking up the hill. Two bodies shot past us running but even in the half-light they were instantly recognisable as a fist punched the air and southern accents rent across the cathedral steps as two people called out to us. Yes, the Knuckle Brothers were in a hurry again, probably to find a bar and have another beer.

I felt Libby's arm inside mine getting tighter as we approached the top of the hill as the bitterly cold wind blew stronger. I hoped we would soon reach the leeward side of the hill and find some much needed form of shelter out of the wind. From the very top of the hill it was possible to view the whole of the Railway Station and appreciate its size and in particular the commanding influence it had on the population of Cologne. But not at that moment on that night. On a warmer day perhaps. What was most surprising to us in that cold wind were the number of people up on that hill at that time of night. Some were lovers clearly experiencing the moment or two; some were friends; some like Libby and me were tourists going from A to B; some were miscreants. It was feasible, with a fertile imagination I supposed, that as we began to descend the path towards the base of the hill, to imagine someone springing out to surprise or attack people there were so many nooks and crannies around the cathedral. Incredibly, as I was thinking it, I became aware of two people walking twenty or so yards behind us, one with their face covered and the other in a red anorak that seemed all the rage in Germany at Christmas time. I wondered if they were following us, stalking us like prey and were about to jump us. Indeed I thought they did hesitate when we slowed to take in the view. Whether or not I was over-reacting on that hill that freezing Saturday night I have no idea. I couldn't remember any of our party in such clothes. For a few seconds, in a foreign country, it would have been easy to have become a bit nervous in that type of the situation. I stopped walking for a split second and turned round to look back at the path we had taken. I saw the couple stand still. I think to hide my own nervousness I whispered quietly, in a deep hesitant voice, pretending that someone was following us just to spook Libby. She took just two or three more steps and turned to me, her face like thunder and asked angrily

'Just what game are you playing and what is going on Tony why do you keep stopping and turning round? Are we being followed? Or are you just being bloody stupid because if you are I shall lobotomise you!'

'I'm not sure, but I think....., don't look now, the couple back there. They stop when we stop' I replied as quiet as a mouse hoping only Libby would hear. 'See what I mean?' as we both slowly turned round that time together. 'Let's call their bluff and walk towards them and see what they do then.'

'There's no-one there you stupid ass. I nearly peed myself for a second, now grow up. You've seen too many James Cagney films. Now pack it in!' Libby was not happy, and I wasn't sure if I'd seen or imagined I'd seen the couple react after quaffing plenty of beer.

'Sorry I thought it would be fun to muck about up here. I didn't mean to scare you and I shan't do it again love,' I replied guiltily.

'Leave it Tony and let's just get back to the hotel pronto please' pleaded Libby.

'Ok' I said 'if they quicken their walk when we do ...' I almost finished.

'Stop it' Libby shouted and we made for the hotel. I peered round several times on the way down the hill and yes, that couple did follow us for a short distance before tailing off. I finally lost sight of them as we jogged down the hill to the roadway tunnel that led underneath the Station. It was around there that we passed lots of people dressed in funny costumes just walking along the road who were either on their way to a party, or they belonged to some strange fetish club. We were in Germany when all was said and done after all.

We headed for the Station entrance as quickly as our legs would take us via the cathedral square and made our way through the Station at a great rate of knots, me tugging Libby along faster than she really wanted to travel. Once we were out the other side of the station, across the road and inside the warmth of the hotel, both of us were out of breath. We paused a second in the lobby then headed straight for the bar. Not one of our fellow cruise passengers had arrived back before us so our drinks were served immediately. Believe it or not we both had hot chocolate to warm us up.

Finishing my drink first I said I thought as we were both very tired and ready for bed we should disappear upstairs immediately. Libby agreed so when she too had drunk her drink we vacated the empty bar and crossed the lobby and were still the only ones waiting for the lift when the hotel front door burst open as several other of our group loudly arrived. We didn't wait to greet them but entered the lift as the doors opened, went straight up to our floor across the corridor, opened the door to our room and entered.

'You were only messing about weren't you Tony, I wouldn't sleep if I thought you had been serious about being followed?' Libby asked.

'No of course my darling I was just messing about.' I replied.

It was eleven forty-five and we were both tired. It had been a long, very tiring and action-packed day. Having been on the train, on the boat, and on the piss it sure had been a long day. It takes it out of you when you enjoy yourself as your years advance and here was the living proof if it were needed. All that was left to do was visit the loo, brush our teeth and fall sleep. After giving the good lady wife a kiss 'Good night' it went without saying that I was soon asleep. On that occasion I even slept without my radio. A whole day had passed and there had been no mention of the accident the previous Thursday and that had to be a good sign that Libby was relaxing.

Chapter Nine.

'Happy Anniversary my gorgeous lady wife' I said leaning across her bed to give her a kiss 'and here's a card and a present for my lady of forty years.'

'Thanks but what time is it please?' Libby asked as I yawned 'it's still dark outside, is it early?' And with that the Tannoy announced an arrival or departure at the Station, I wasn't sure which. 'It is ...... ten past seven' she said 'Jeez they've already started breakfast. Dermot will be on his second cup of Earl Grey tea by now. It's Sunday and if you remember yesterday we said we'd go to a Mass at the cathedral. *Sich erinnern mein goldig?*'

'Hang on my lovely, open your present first it is our anniversary today after all!' I tried to enthuse.

'Not a ruby and don't make me out to be a gold-digger money has never meant anything to me you know that.' she said in a hurry as she ripped off the wrapping paper from the presentation box.

'Aaaah! Wow! That is so lovely thank-you my darling' she gushed as she unfolded the gold chain with a ruby tear-drop on it. 'Where did you find it?' she continued as she wrapped both arms around me and gave me a lovely smacker on the lips.

'I didn't find it but it doesn't matter. Just you make me a coffee please whilst I shower first that's all I want,' and with hardly a noise I skipped straight into the shower without a stitch on. Job done I thought.

A short while later a cup of coffee-looking tea arrived in the shower as she joined me in a 'joint celebration'. Within ten minutes we were both showered and ready to go down to breakfast leaving the family's cards to open later. Libby, with just a dab of make-up on her face, followed me out of our room to join the usual queue for the lift. Old age they say creeps up on you but here we were back in the dining room sitting in the same place at the same table. We had become thoroughly institutionalised after only two days away from home. With the cereals and yoghurt on the table we began to tuck in to our breakfast starter as another couple arrived and asked if they could join us. They were David and Margie when they introduced themselves to us that second morning in Germany. Little did we know the twists and turns that would start to unfold from that very moment on that Sunday. As if by magic, and definitely out of the blue like a stray missile, Dermot pulled up a fifth chair after telling us he was joining us as soon as he entered the room. Having finished eating all we could eat and discussed an action programme for the day that at the table involved the five of us, we decided to meet again in the hotel lobby before going to Mass in the cathedral. Sundays are one of those days when the typical tour brochure tells you that 'today you can be at leisure in your resort. Why not try ......'

It was already after nine o'clock and we had to complete our ablutions upstairs and fix the 'all-day make-up'. Well Libby was to perform that latter task. On the way to the lift area, and as people in our group filed out of the lift going into breakfast, all seemed to be joviality and happiness amongst the various associations within the group that had been forged over the previous forty-six hours. Dennis Johnson had placed on a table for us maps of Cologne's Christmas Markets and as we left the breakfast room he was stood eagerly explaining the map to anyone who needed help. Some folks took the maps with them into breakfast: main course I presumed. Iris and Richard, joviality personified as usual, shouted a 'Hello' to us as they were just disappearing into the breakfast room. There was no sign of Sid, and it made one think some more about the elderly single traveller.

Once in our room we sat and opened our cards, and letters of congratulations would you believe, and then the family presents that we'd taken along for something to do on the actual day. After reading and commenting on some of the verses in the cards we spruced the room up so that before the cleaner arrived she had little to do. Libby later claimed she had deliberately left my present at home as it was too silly to bring a new bicycle with her in a case: had it been wrapped separately I'd perhaps have guessed what was in the package and thus spoil her surprise. Ha bloody Ha I thought. How un-thoughtful of her and after all the time she'd had my joie de vivre to entertain her down the years. Still forty years was a long time.

When the time came to leave the room after nine thirty we were well-wrapped up against the anticipated elements outside Libby saying I looked like the Michelin Man. The cheek of it the little beggar. Better warm than cold I said, not that she was listening she'd had her fun and was at the door waiting to go out. We returned downstairs to wait for our friends to arrive before leaving for the whole day that sunny Sunday. Two of the guests greeted us on their way into breakfast, looking much the worse for wear after being on our table the previous night on the Rhine. We enquired as to their health, particularly after the volume of wine that had been quaffed, and bid them a quiet 'Have a nice day.' The three single ladies who had also been on our table the night before, were also on their way out of the hotel at the same time as we were and were off to the Christmas Markets early.

When David and Margie arrived shortly afterwards Libby had been testing the cold air outside the hotel. Without further ado we joined her and set off again wandering through the now well-trodden path via the road-works to the cathedral and the ten o'clock Mass. It was still bitterly cold even in the blue-sky sunshine as we passed once more through the station, its corridor-like passageways acting like a vortex in the cold wind. We had only been walking a few minutes when Libby made the following comment

'I hope the cathedral is not as cold as this station is. It's no wonder the Germans are always well-wrapped up. Well the adults anyhow.'

'Couldn't agree more Libby, and I am so glad I brought all my warm winter clothes with me.' Margie said, 'The fact remains though we have had things easy at home lately with our mild winters.'

For the next few minutes even Phillip Eden the meteorologist would have been impressed by the conversation that took place between the two ladies as they walked up the steps from the square to a side door of the cathedral. Meanwhile David and I chatted about the crowds heading in our direction for the same reason as us and debated whether or not we would get a seat inside. We entered the cathedral through a side door which we soon found was a mistake. I had thought if we crept quietly like church mice across the small Lady Chapel hoping to remain unseen by the huge congregation that must have been swollen by visiting tourists, we would be OK. We dropped into a pew close by, sliding gingerly along the wooden seat as we went, peering in all directions red-faced with embarrassment as we looked round to see if anyone was watching us since the Mass had begun with the organ bellowing out its cathedral music. When settled like my friends I sat gasping at the height of the roof, the length of the whole church and the sheer size of the place. Next, mind games began in my head as I tried to estimate the number of people in the congregation that Advent Sunday.

'Have you seen how many there are here?' I asked my fellow worshippers 'there has to be nearly fifteen hundred people, or even more. The whole scene is amazing don't you think?'

Looking round him David, who wasn't the tallest chap in the world by any means commented 'Must be a close estimate Tony. Apart from state funerals or royal weddings I can't say I have seen this many in a church before except on the TV. But where are the choir?'

'Expect there'll be a procession along soon with them coming in with the priest' Margie said knowingly. No sooner had she finished talking and a musical chant began to echo throughout the cathedral.

'A disc, tape or choir?' Margie asked quizzically.

'Has to be one or the other' said Libby as the congregation rose and stood waiting for the imaginary procession to come into view.

The sound of the music and singing was louder almost immediately with the words clearly audible, in German naturally.

'That's no disc it's a real choir surely?' Libby ventured further.

Turning round and being much taller than the others I could just make out the choir coming into view down the centre aisle.

'You're not going to believe this' I said, 'but just try and count the number of people in the choir as it passes us on its way to choir stalls, wherever they are.'

David, counting religiously, eventually informed us he had counted ninety-four young choristers and a further forty elders in the choir.

'No wonder they sound perfect like some disc as they all sing' said Libby, 'and look at the priest he has a strange hat on his head.'

'I think he's a bishop in a mitre' Margie remarked 'especially with headgear like that.'

It later turned out Margie was right and the cleric was none other than the Bishop of Cologne. When the choir had snaked into their stalls to our right the service got under way good and proper. We all understood parts of the Mass of course, despite it being wholly in German. In particular we understood when it was time for the offertory: that was when we fiddled in our pockets for some small change for the collection. Shortly afterwards the congregation were invited by the Bishop to visit the rail at the entrance to the nave ready to receive the Eucharist. One could have been forgiven for thinking that it was a rugby scrum such was the melee to gain a place in front of the acolytes. It was at that point in the proceedings we decided it was a good moment to leave the service. And we did, rather hurriedly as it turned out, by a rear door part hidden by at least another couple of hundred folks that could not find a seat for the service. On the way out we caught sight of several of our Pineapple Group in the cathedral but, surprisingly, no sign of our little friend Dermot.

Outside in the sunshine more nose penetrating atmospheric-smells permeated the early morning air very similar to the ones the day before in Aachen. It would have been a mistake to have been led by one's nose to the variety of food stalls – but it could so easily have been a happy option. For instance the smell of freshly made ground coffee, the sound and smell of frying and spitting sausages, the smell of candy floss and the gorgeous smell of freshly made dough nuts intermingled with that wonderful cinnamony smell of gluhwein. We homed in quickly round a stall selling the mulled wine as we were ready to taste a sample. Asked if we wanted to keep the empty mugs as a memento we each nodded like those nodding dogs on the rear of a car shelf. The barman obliged. Drinking gluhwein was a new experience for Libby and not one she would forget as the warming wine and herbs flowed down her gullet. The cinnamon, and I think cloves, increased the pungency of the drink's aroma. It was the longest I'd ever seen Libby with wine in her hand. I was about to mention that fact to her but thought better of it as half of her drink was still in the mug. It was more than my life was worth and better in her than over me! When we'd finished our drinks we dutifully dried the mugs and kept them in a polythene bag for what I hoped would be their further use that day.

Wandering about from then on as the moment took us in that chattering crowd it was obvious that as more visitors crammed into the stall areas it would become even noisier. Though most Germans seemed happy just to stroll through the Weinachtsmarkt they were never happier than when they had in their hand a drink of spiced wine as was plainly obvious to all that Sunday.

The stalls at the Dom Market on the Roncalli Platz, with that fantastic Gothic cathedral as a backdrop was pure fairy-tale material, the stuff made of dreams for both adults and children. Libby and Margie repeatedly commented on the quality of goods on offer in the quaintly decorated stalls. They were not the mass-produced plastic toys or trinkets we were used to in the UK at Christmas-time but were the beautifully hand-crafted varieties many of which were made and painted by the stall-holders themselves. Stalls were selling spiced cake, cinnamon stars, pepper nuts and a host of other intricately made pastries famous in Germany. The baked food smells mingling with the smells of fried sausage also wafting through that late Sunday morning air made for an atmospheric heaven. I thought it possible to have an imaginary feast without swallowing any food there were so many smells around that one could be forgiven for sniffing in so much on such a festive occasion.

'Hi Dennis you made it after all then?' David called to Johnson as he meandered past us with some friends he'd obviously met up with but who immediately melted back into the crowd of people as quickly as they had appeared, seemingly not wanting to acknowledge us. Meanwhile the crowd had grown so much it made walking difficult and appeared to have a mind of its own as it meandered everywhere without being dangerous. We began shuffling along helped by the crowd's momentum just as we had been the day before in Aachen.

Even at our age we were amazed by the elaborate, ornate and fancy goods on offer that must have taken an age to make whoever made them. There were so many and seemed limitless as we spent a great deal of time inspecting their distinctive quality making it impossible to choose presents for our grandchildren. Candles were available in all sizes, colours and shape as well as perfumed smells. Mouth-blown and intrinsically hand-painted glass ornaments, fit to adorn any Christmas tree, we found everywhere. Libby and Margie were particularly interested in wooden toys and puppets some of which looked positively life-like. Alongside those, interesting though they were, David and I found wooden masks of all shapes and sizes that really were scary looking. There were Yule logs with decorative candles inserted into them: some had Father Christmases and reindeers attached to them appearing to pull the logs along as sleighs. Our ladies were more fascinated by the range of puppets and dolls, some tiny and some huge, some almost as big as the children who might play with them. Some of the dolls seemed to come alive when the wind blew and fluttered their clothes as they hung limply in their stall. Their eyes, though probably glass, seemed to penetrate your own eyes as they stared back at you in such a haunting manner, almost challenging you as they did. They had hands that from a couple of yards away looked so real they might perhaps have waved to the watcher. They certainly frightened the pants off Libby they appeared so authentic. Some stalls contained hand-painted glass-mirrors and lambskin shoes or slippers, so soft they would not be felt on the feet they were fitted to. And indeed there were the customary chocolate stalls full of delicately arranged and decorated shapes surrounded by staring children being tantalised by their taste-buds. That was the most outrageous attack on adult and parents' wallets having been well thought out by the Burghermeisters of Cologne. Us? We just loved the chocolate. Watching over all this like some huge green giant was the largest Christmas tree in the Rhineland bedecked with a battery of fairy lights that would have lit up a small factory they were so numerous.

'A hundred and sixty stalls on that market' Libby announced posing for one last photo call with Margie and David next to one of the stalls.

'Did you count them?' I asked.

'Dafty it was on the map Johnson gave us. Of course you didn't bother to read it did you? You had a man's look!' Libby said volleying her response at me.

David and Margie, too polite to take sides during our little discourse, wandered off to a sweet stall to spend mountains of David's cash, not on bars of chocolate but tins of the stuff! Libby, never embarrassed to spend our money, was not far behind suddenly making out all lovey-dovey and holding my hand whilst dragging me along to the same sweet stall even flashing her eyes at me. I think she had really meant to steal my wallet as she followed Margie's bad example and bought some tins of chocolate smiling all over her face like a cat that had literally got the cream, in another form naturally.

'Let's have a change and go have a look at the next market it seems to be quite close on this map' David observed. 'It looks to be less than half a mile away and downhill so should be easily located.'

Margie was impressed with his comments as evidently David was not the world's best map reader, not at that hour anyway. We wandered downhill to where we thought the market ought to be and ten minutes later, hey presto, after several stops and corrections looking at the map, we came to our chosen destination of the Alter Market. It was here amongst the crowd we saw another acquaintance with his new lady friend. I tugged at his arm as we passed them with the simple intention of acknowledging them. The crowded aisles we were in did not allow me that pleasure because when he turned round to see what the tugging was about we had moved on in the opposite direction and were several yards apart by the time he reacted. He assumed that a bulky German woman had performed the wicked deed and gave her such a puzzled look he startled her, and then he carried on walking, probably wondering who the German woman was that knew him in Cologne. I meant to mention it to him later but forgot.

During the half hour that we walked round that market it became obvious it was more suited to children. Many of the stalls were replicas of the previous market but there were differences for instance there was an increased amount of stalls with dolls, toys, and puppets and a wide variety of children's trinkets and balloons that went 'whizz', 'bang' or 'pop'. There was even a Santa's Grotto in one corner that caused consternation for Libby because she thought the Father Christmas looked cross-eyed. At least he looked the part with his long-flowing white beard and in his red and white finery even if he did need an optician. The people that hung around that particular stall looked a strange lot as they peered into the grotto whilst jabbering on in German. It was the adults, not the children who were bad mannered and pushing and shoving to get closer. Closer to who, or what, was debateable.

In another part of the market a puppet theatre was showing Hansel and Gretel as we passed by. But with an admission fee, and a running time of twenty minutes, we did not bother entering. In yet another corner there were play-ground type rides of carousels with trains, boats and planes for the kids to sit on and swings that swung amazingly fast, if not dangerously very high as screaming kids verified. Lastly there was an old and nostalgic children's roundabout with horses bobbing up and down that Libby wanted to try herself but felt better of it. We recalled, standing there, watching our own children at just such a fair back home and the look of glee on their faces each time they went past us smiling. On the edge of the roadside several tourists almost certainly Germans, gave the impression that they were testing a bouncing castle to oblivion. We paused just long enough to watch them perform their version of trampolining while a crowd of onlookers cheered and egged them on. Their gymnastic performances, lacking specific routines, provided a few minutes of hilarity as they hit each other bouncing and tumbling on the way up or the way down. They were unable to prevent the inevitable collisions between themselves and so wallets, purses, glasses and money all flew out of their pockets creating total mayhem in what was a restricted area.

'Should we Brits have a go to see if we can bounce as high?' I enquired.

Libby's response was to be expected but was probingly nearer the mark as she said 'Do you think we've had sufficient gluhwein to be able to bounce as high as the Germans because there is no way you'll get me on that thing unless I have drunk some more?'

'Would that be drunk today or in the past?' I enquired tongue in cheek.

'Piss off!' Libby replied emphatically 'at least I wouldn't have made such a dent in the rubber of the bouncing castle as someone I know' giving me the type of look at that moment that would have burst the rubber toy-thing. I kept low for a few minutes and walked alongside David in case I needed support. We left the market and its revellers and crossed the road to where it was possible to get a good panoramic view of the market. Looking back towards that ancient square with its half-timbered brightly-painted buildings would, David said, make a classic photograph.

After I had taken a few touristy snapshots I noticed that Margie and David had sauntered further down the cobbled road and were looking into a shop window. Catching them up Libby and I were surprised to find the shop was a hunting accessory shop with a huge array of guns and knives displayed in the window.

'Thinking of shooting someone Margie?' Libby asked her friend.

'Not at this moment but sometime soon maybe, how about you?' Margie replied.

'We have lots of squirrels in our garden and a friend I know uses an air-gun to cull them and I just wondered if I could do it. Don't think I've got the heart really' David said 'but then again I lose many bulbs in spring-time and I was having second thoughts looking in this shop.'

With our noses pressed closely to the window we failed to see two other people staring into that same window alongside of us. That was until we turned to walk away and nearly fell over them they were stood so close. Libby did trip over the chap's foot when she turned away from the window and stumbled badly turning her ankle over on the uneven cobbles. When I turned to see what the yelp was Margie was helping Libby who was obviously in some pain.

'That git was laughing when I tripped over him. He was so close to me I could smell his bad garlicky breath.' Libby said clearly far from amused. 'He never even apologised. I should have knocked his woollen hat off his fat head.'

'Shall we stop a moment or do you want to carry on it's no problem?' I asked

No she was OK she said and with a supportive arm from Margie to continue leaning on looked increasingly like an injured pirate. Poor Libby limped along for several hundred yards more until suddenly her ankle appeared to suddenly and miraculously get better.

We carried on walking looking here and there at various shops, or the riverside that had again come into view. Thinking about it I suppose the Alter Markt's setting had been almost as impressive as the previous one at the base of the cathedral. In this instance it was situated in front of the narrow-gabled houses in the oldest part of Cologne and City Hall and had been beautifully restored after being flattened during the last World War.

Our feet began increasingly to ache as we made our way to the Neumarkt a good half mile or more away and lunch-time was fast approaching. Walking along the main road the main topic of conversation after enquiring about the condition of Libby's ankle duly turned to food. Where would we eat, what would we eat and how would we eat it? Margie alone then decided we would walk to the next market and not take a bus or tram, damn it. Carefully avoiding falling into the foundations of what was to be a new U-Bahn we meandered slowly towards the oldest of the markets. Standing at some traffic lights waiting to cross a main road opposite the market David brought our attention to a car that was also waiting at the lights. It was the most perfectly preserved dark blue Jaguar XK 140. Saluting the driver who returned our salutes with a smile David pointed to its UK number plate which promoted sentimental talks of envy as we reminisced about our own cars we had bought down the years.

Over in the new market square it was so obviously different from the others because the stalls were painted grey and white and all the surrounding trees were fully decked out with a variety of Christmas lights and twinkling stars. It was then long after one o'clock and the smell of food intensified our desire to eat as soon as possible. As if by magic, and with little resistance, David succumbed like a little boy and joined a queue of what he thought led to a hot potato stall. Wrong. The queue turned out to be for some other German delicacy unknown to us. Not understanding German he had joined the 'wusrt' queue he could find! He soon backtracked, found the potato fritters' stall which when they arrived tasted divinely even if they were a little oily. At least the apple sauce helped them go down sweetly.

When refreshed and fed David and Margie needed to locate an ATM machine to make use of the traveller's bank card they had brought with them from England. They located one across the road directly opposite from where we were stood by the potato fritter van, and went to claim their prize. The quest was to find if it would accept their 'special' card? After a few tries the mission was successful so much so they both arrived back with smiling faces and a wallet with more notes in it.

Back in the market the variety of leather goods particularly purses, wallets, bags and shoes were all of exceptional quality the stalls also displaying a far wider range than in previous markets. The Christmas tree decorations sold on stalls were so intricate that to touch them one could easily have broken them particularly with my clumsy hands. But it was a whiff in the air of a totally different sort from anything we had previously experienced that teased our nostrils as it drifted between the stalls. Locating it we found it was salmon being smoked in the open air on a blazing log fire that gave off such a gorgeous smell we just had to stand and take in the fumes, watch the smoke rise and take in the flavour of the surrounds before moving on yet again.

It was shortly after that David took me to one side quietly mentioning that whilst at the ATM he had seen Johnson walking past with a couple of people who he didn't recognise as being in our group. He said the bloke looked remarkably like the chap Libby fell over when she hurt her ankle earlier in the day, and like the one in the red anorak in Aachen the day before. Thanking him for that nugget of information I asked him not to mention it to Libby as she would freak out. I reminded him that Johnson had had a German father so perhaps the people he saw him with were relatives. He didn't look impressed with my reasoning, but smiled politely.

By half past one we'd seen enough of the markets for one day and began to tire of seeing so many stalls and though the stalls on the Neumarkt were excellent we decided we were going to leave without seeing them all. Maybe it was the call of nature that intervened to remind us of our age. It was certainly the time when the fun started again if looking for a toilet in Germany was fun. Following our instincts for what we thought were the correct signs for a toilet we descended, via escalator, into an underground precinct below the actual market. Just as we thought we'd been successful in following the signs to the toilet we suddenly found ourselves back upstairs and outside on the opposite side of the subway without having been able to find either the loos or an English-speaking person to help us. It reminded of my student days and a visit to Soho in London with some fellow PE students. Thinking we had entered a door taking us into a 'Ladies Club' after paying an entrance fee we quickly found we had walked through the building and ended on the pavement outside another door that closed behind us heavily and was locked. We didn't get our money back of course. A similar situation began to unfold in Cologne with Libby and Margie seeing the funny side as David and I walked ever more quickly around that subway looking for the toilets without success. On the point of giving up the chase and looking for a lonely tree instead, we reluctantly returned to the area where we had started looking for the loos in the first place, and guess what? Libby spotted on the other side of the square a toilet sign hung above an entrance to .... underground toilets. Though the ladies could see the funny side David and I didn't find anything to laugh at in case we had a plumbing accident. We bolted at great speed to the toilet's entrance fumbling in our pockets for the regulation fifty-cent piece necessary to gain entry past the door to the blasted toilet.

Relieved and refreshed we re-surfaced and joined the ladies back in the sunshine who were discussing how we would travel back down to the river Rhine and closer to home. A comforting and relaxing ride on a tram that saved our feet from further damage it had to be, at least that was our intention. But further merriment and frustration was round the corner as we tried to buy a tram ticket. Were it not for an English-speaking German who sorted out our problem we would probably still be there trying to find a ticket with the regulation fifty-cent piece!

It didn't take long to our tram-stop on the Rhine and we arrived without further incident next to the promenade. A very leisurely stroll down the promenade in glorious sunshine found us heading, along with huge crowds of people, towards the Medieval Christmas Market which was next door to the Chocolate Factory. Hence the smile on the faces of our wives! Clowns and jugglers around the market whilst they displayed remarkable skills were unable to hold the attention of our wives as much as the call of chocolate. We found the chocolate shop absolutely packed with women who were all full of smiles whilst their men, for the most part, were quite sullen. I wondered why but was to soon find out as Libby and I approached the check-out tills. So little chocolate for so much money, aargh!

Chapter  Ten.

With that part of the day and the chocolate-buying duty completed our next priority was to find some food, so I thought. Strolling back towards our hotel we studiously checked out several restaurants we passed before finally deciding to stop at an attractive looking restaurant that had a large and colourful canopy over the outside tables. Once seated, and hearing the loud banter from an adjacent table, we recognised the voices and laughter as coming from where sat Sid, Dermot and coincidentally Dennis Johnson putting the world to rights. They were complimented by two ladies from our group who were clearly enjoying the repartee with them. When they eventually had time to acknowledge us four interlopers it was clear that alcohol accounted for their ostentatious flurry of hand waving and rosy grins that greeted us. They were, to quote an oft used phrase, 'well on the way'. Libby and Margie went over to speak to them whilst David and I looked through our menu and drinks list on our table. Riotous laughter exploded regularly from the other table and I was pleased to see Libby laughing and giggling with her new acquaintances.

'Have they been there long, or are they well on the way not having eaten yet? You know how it is with wine on an empty stomach' I said naughtily as Libby and Margie returned to our table.

'So what?' said Libby turning round, 'it is Christmas next week and if you can't let your hair down at Christmas when can you let your hair down?'

'Quite' said Margie with quiet approval of what Libby had said.

'Bitte, guten tag' said a German waiter 'Vier beer or something-else?'

'Two beers, an orange juice and a dry white wine Libby?' asked David as if he'd been there before. And with nods all round the drinks were ordered and the waiter turned on his heels and disappeared through a small entrance to the main insides of the restaurant. When he returned it was only seconds before

'Thanks David that is lovely' Libby said and continued 'I don't think I want anything to eat yet though Tony, that potato fritter isn't sitting easily with me at the moment. The others had been there for about twenty minutes when they met up with Johnson near the boat market. He had said it wasn't much cop, but they all went in anyway and he just tagged along. Lonely I suspect.'

'He gets around though but I agree it must be lonely on the trips for the reps, but he did stare at you Libby for quite a few seconds' chimed in Margie, 'as if he knew you somehow.'

It didn't take Johnson long before he arrived at our table in time to say to Libby, and anyone-else who was listening,

'I think I have remembered where I know you from. Weren't you a teacher or something to do with education? You did say you started teaching in London nearly forty years ago.'

'Well?' said Libby.

'That's it. London. I worked there too and I reckon, no I'm certain, you lived close by which is how I come to know your face. That's where I know you from. I told you I never forget faces, only names. In fact you were not living nearby me? No, I remember now, it's coming back to me slowly. You were in the same block of flats, but you were two floors below me in a block in Islington, remember?' he said more hopefully than sure of himself.

'Events all that time ago are only foggy memories for me so forgive me if I appear flummoxed.' Libby made out. 'Were you the one with the strange girlfriend that was always in trouble with the police all that time back?'

'Not half. Surprised you remembered her. Became my wife, but as I said earlier in St Pancras, we divorced after a short while. I could not tolerate her moods, her temper and her jealousy particularly if I spoke or even looked at another woman. Weirdo she was right put me off marriage for the rest of my life however long I live. I know she married and divorced some foreigner or other after me. Poor bloke didn't know what he let himself in for I suppose.' Johnson had really unloaded himself onto Libby as if by remote control whilst we others were bit parts to the conversation just listening on.

Our drinks came with Libby and Johnson still reminiscing. Libby asked him if he ever saw his ex-wife.

'Only very rarely these days thank God. Evil that one, you never knew what she was thinking or what she was capable of. Her sister lives near my sister Louise. They were at school together and occasionally when I visit Louise I see my Ex with her sister. She still spits venom at me when we pass by each other. Still it takes all sorts. I'm glad to be rid of her. Strangely, I saw her today with some other weirdo bloke tagging onto her apron-strings in Cologne. Visiting for Christmas she said. Only a passing Hello that's all I could manage. Couldn't get away quick enough from her, such a horrid woman. She'll do someone an injury if I'm not mistaken you wait and see.'

Johnson was again emotional as he spoke for the second time in two days the previous occasion had been when he told us about his late father on the train to Aachen.

After his conversation with Libby he quickly upped and left our table returning to the people he'd been with on the other side of the restaurant leaving Libby in a state of semi-shock at the amount of information he had informed her of. It was also noticeable when he spoke to Libby that her brain kept ticking away attempting to try and remember the meetings and relationships he had recalled from all those years ago. But even so she still appeared bemused by it all.

After he left us our conversation again turned to food as we tried to make sense of the menu, not that it wasn't in English, it was just a discussion about the way the food was put together in certain combinations. So different from our English food because we wouldn't be so bold as to put gherkins with everything now would we?

'I must admit to feeling the same as you Libby. Much as I enjoyed the fritter a couple of beers will be enough to see me through.' I explained.

David, who decided he wanted a German toastie or something, conned Margie into having the same. Safety in numbers I thought: if one goes down .... The waiter having returned with yet more drinks took an order for two lots of warme speisoneise. We waited in anticipation and when the food arrived at the table a few moments later it looked to be the German equivalent of croque-monsieur without the ham, but with camembert cheese, and a couple of croquette potatoes instead from what we could make out. It was also noticeable that David did not speak from the moment his plate of food arrived in front of him until he had finished eating every last crumb. Margie said it had been the same from the first day they met. After yet another round of drinks I insisted on David having a chaser of slivovitch. It was a real good tot too when it arrived which went down in one mouthful, German-style. At least mine did to the annoyance of Libby who was by then twiddling her empty glass, a habit over the years that signalled her need for another drink.

We settled the bill after a short argument about payment, which I won, and so David paid! Leaving the restaurant and waving goodbye to our fellow travellers who were still at their table we found ourselves following the same route we had taken after last night's dinner on the boat. Once more, before we arrived back at the hotel we would break off the journey and take a break for a drink. You see David was aware and had seen next to the cathedral a coffee shop that reputedly sold the best drinking chocolate in Cologne, so he claimed. Allegedly so did most of our hotel colleagues who had also, coincidentally to strengthen David's defence, visited the said café. That reference was good enough for Libby who was only too pleased to assess the beverages. After the walk up and down the cathedral hill and steps Libby led the way by entering the welcoming Café

Raphael. It was very nearly dusk when we arrived at the cafe not that you'd have noticed around the cathedral's streets where it did not seem to matter with Christmas just days away. Children and adults were still to be found everywhere in the increasingly cold night air carrying their balloons and mementos after having had a good day out. Christmas-lights flickered, twinkling and shining brightly; car horns could be heard honking at people who stepped off pavements into the road; and music continued to play carols across the sky. Old folks present just stood and smiled looking skywards towards the cathedral that was lit up in all its majesty. Were they perhaps thinking of former years when they were young or simply soaking up the atmosphere of Christmas?

Inside the café having squeezed into our chairs and around a table for four people, who should we spot in one dark and secluded corner but the Knuckle Brothers in lively conversation with each other as per usual.

'What will you have?' David asked looking firstly at Margie and then Libby, 'chocolate or coffee and perhaps a cake or something?'

'Oh yes' said Libby winking at Margie, 'chocolate for me please and 'er a ….. '

'Which cake would you like, or even something sticky and gooey in a pastry?' I interjected, 'go on tell him I know what you're like. No room to finish a main meal because you are full up, but room for a pudding every time.'

'How on earth did you guess?' Libby laughed at me. 'Yes David two plain chocolate drinks and an apple strudel with cream ice-cream please' Libby replied coming over all business-like and dominatrix all of a sudden.

'Well I never that's exactly what I shall have too' David sighed having scanned the menu and looked towards Margie for approval.

A passing waiter was all but hauled to our table to take the orders before he could disappear. At the same moment as if they were following the waiter the Knuckle Brothers, John and Kevin, came over and spoke to us. They told us without explaining why that they were upset that the brewery trip was still going ahead that evening. Then they too disappeared out into the crowded streets leaving the four of us on our table with puzzled looks on our faces at the strange comment that had just been made. We took it with a pinch of salt not knowing what he was on about.

'They had a real go at Johnson on the way home from the boat trip last night. Said what a waste of time and money the meal was and were berating Johnson who was trying to exonerate the tour company from any blame. At one stage I thought John was going to hit him' David said. 'It was becoming embarrassing in front of everyone. They were so loud.'

'They had a point don't you think' Margie said 'but just went about it wrongly.'

'They passed us on the cathedral hill just below the summit, running as usual' I said, 'but they never stopped to talk.'

The conversation stalled when the drinks and cakes arrived totally justifying the reputation that had gone before making the evening a really warm and satisfying end to a long walk. No sooner had I drained the last drops of chocolate out of my mug when I noticed through the café window as he strolled along outside our mate Dennis Johnson. Having seen him only fleetingly a couple of times during the day since breakfast, there he was chatting away animatedly to a couple of people he seemed to know and I seemed to recognise from somewhere in the back of my mind. I glanced at David who shook his head as if he were saying leave well alone. I did, but was witness to plenty of finger-pointing going on outside as they all spoke, the pair who had their hoods up presumably shielding their faces having a right old go at our tour rep. The taller of the two, whom I took to be a bloke, was wearing a red anorak I thought I seen on several occasions those last two days.

'Did you see who just walked past?' I asked the others who were idling and savouring each and every mouthful of the strudel treat. 'That was our leader with two other folks, but I couldn't see if they were from our group, because their hoods were up. They really were arguing with him. It looked quite nasty.'

'Could've been the Knuckle Brothers, you know how keen they were at getting money back after last night. If they have any issues over this trip they are right in his face every time. I wouldn't want to get on the wrong side of either of them particularly involving money' Libby pointed out.

'What in a red anorak?' I countered but was ignored.

'Bet he's been bored out of his tree today' said Margie, 'he has hardly been seen at all since we arrived except at the start and end of each day when he meets and greets us. Today's sightings were more luck than judgement I think.'

'Still it's his choice. At least he must get to see lots of Europe both now at Christmas and in the summer season. And let's not forget he is living on his own, he is fluent in German as he has demonstrated these few days and comes and goes as he pleases whilst he is here.' David's comments came across as somewhat envious of our tour guide I thought. It was true though that Johnson was good at his job when he was around and you engaged him one to one, but his modus operandi involving the whole group, I thought from observation on our trip, was more like 'organised ad hoc'. I meant by that you could do as you liked and come and go as you pleased most of the time, but there were sessions when we had to meet together. The Brewery trip scheduled to take place that night in Cologne was just such and example.

'Better get back to the hotel and freshen up' David said, 'look at the time it's now gone five-thirty and we are out tonight for seven-forty five aren't we?'

'You're right' Libby added 'and I will definitely need a shower after being out all day.'

We paid another bill for food and drink albeit non-alcoholic for a change and left the cafe making our way back through the lit up and still very busy Cathedral Christmas Market towards our hotel.

Once in the hotel, who was there waiting to meet us but that all-round good egg of a tour guide Dennis Johnson. Conversing with all and sundry as they passed through the hotel lobby I could hear him giving out a reminder of time for us to meet later and the name of the brewery we were visiting for the evening.

'We shall leave here at seven forty five for a brewery.' Johnson enthusiastically informed several ladies including Elspeth, Mary and Jenny and buried amongst them who else but Dermot? Calling across the lobby for all to hear Johnson suddenly beckoned to Libby who was at the time reading one of his company notices regarding the train times for our journey home the following day.

'Libby, can you spare me a couple of moments to talk please, if it's OK with you Tony?' He remembered my name too. I was surprised. Anyway I replied it was not a problem and told Libby I was going upstairs in the lift with David and Margie and left her talking with Johnson.

I was in the shower when she entered our room with her own plastic key for a change. She came in laughing loudly and sat on the loo seat opposite the shower and began spouting out the following:

'You won't believe this Tony. Old Johnson apologised for babbling on to me as he did at that restaurant where we met him this afternoon. And he reminded me again of how our paths had crossed all those years ago. He says he remembers the smile I always greeted him with when we passed each other on the stairs at the flats. Ha Ha. Moreover he repeated he found it a strange coincidence after so long that we met here in Germany on the same rail tour. He apologised if I thought he was staring at me these last few days but he was trying to figure out from where he knew me. But that was nearly forty years ago. How about that? He repeated that he never forgets a face, only names and when he heard you call my name out, things clicked in his brain and bingo he remembered me because he'd only ever known one Libby he said. However, whilst we were talking one or two of the others in our group gave us both funny looks as they tried to listen in to our conversation, particularly when Johnson spoke, which was most of the time. Couldn't believe what they were overhearing I suppose because his arms were going and he was smiling all the time. And look here what he gave me. I asked for some luggage labels like you said to replace those we'd lost.'

'Still no harm done, eh lovely, and a little reminder that we are going out in under an hour. Well remembered about the luggage labels too believe me they are important' I said trying to allay any fears or doubts she had talking with Johnson. 'This type of thing, remembering faces, does happen from time to time but often it really is pure coincidence believe you me' I added. Libby didn't seem to be able to make her mind up whether she was glad or worried about her latest encounter with Johnson. I told her not to worry, for what it was worth, as she sauntered out of the bathroom and started to place her 'going out' clothes on her bed packing away all that she had worn that Sunday.

After showering and replacing her make-up it was nearly time for us to depart for the Brewery and what was labelled as the highlight of our trip on the hotel's information board. Libby appeared to have forgotten the conversation with Johnson completely until we arrived downstairs in the hotel lobby and bumped into Dermot. He had been close by when Johnson beckoned Libby over to speak to her and, thinking he was being helpful, greeted her by saying out loud for all to hear

'How about this for coincidence then folks, Libby here used to share a flat with our tour guide years ago in London. Can you believe it?'

'For God's sake Dermot steady on that's far from correct and bloody untrue. I lived in the same block of flats, he, Johnson says and I suppose I do remember him if I start to think about it' Libby responded defiantly.

'Who's the lucky lady?' John of the Knuckle brothers asked cheekily after overhearing that last riposte. Libby red-faced, like the best cooked lobsters, was not interested in replying and moved outside into the cold night air to fume some more and collect her thoughts.

Seven forty-five came and went with all guests vocally anticipating a good night's drinking as we waited for our leader. Eight o'clock approached accompanied by much fidgeting, shuffling of feet and murmuring and still there was no sign of our leader.

'You've not locked him in your room have you Libby' called out Kevin of Knuckle Brother fame. Though for how much longer he would call out after the look he received from Libby I wasn't sure, but you could see Kevin was suitably chastised as he received Libby's eye-ball to eye-ball lobotomising stare.

'That's it' Elspeth said, 'I ain't waiting any longer. I know where the brewery is and I'm going there now. If Johnson wants to give me a bollocking later so be it. That's his call. Call me a surrogate tour guide if you like and follow me if you want folks but I'm off, and now.'

With that she left with her two colleagues and with about ninety-nine point nine percent of our group who followed quickly in her wake. Libby and I ended up slightly separated from the main group as we walked with Sid whose legs did not allow Formula One walking at eighty years plus, particularly on some of the cobbled streets close to the brewery. On our arrival and at the entrance to the brewery, having caught up with the rest of the party who had waited patiently outside for us, there was still no sign of our tour guide which strangely did not provoke any sense of loss from either Knuckle Brother. I found out later one member of our party had popped into the brewery and explained our predicament re' the absence of Johnson at that juncture.

'No problem' was the reply of the brewery staff and we all paraded in expectantly for what we hoped would be a memorable last night. We would not be disappointed for several reasons as the night would prove.

Chapter Eleven.

Libby and I sat at a table with Dermot who drank only water and ate even less; our 'posh' lady friend from Oxford and her pal; old Sid from the BBC; David and Margie; Ruth, the Esme Cannon lookalike and a lady all the way from New Zealand, not that night of course. We were a collection of 'fruit-balls' who just happened to come together that night at the dinner table and enjoyed having fun and being very loud.

The drink's waiter got ever closer to us as our collective thirst increased. But ordering the drinks for all at the table became a problem for me. It should not have been, but then we did not reckon for the likes of the drinks waiter. He had obviously taken all his week's quota of 'grumpy pills' that night so that when the drinks eventually arrived and were handed to all of us except for one. You got it, it was mine that was missing and despite the comments from the others that I couldn't organise a round of drinks in a brewery the evidence was on my beer mat and told a different story. Igor, for that became his name for the evening, had missed just the one drink off his tray, the one I was gagging for, but could I get Igor's attention to explain about the missing beer? Could I attract his attention to put right his mistake? Could I as hell and I could have killed him at that moment. He kept himself away from my waving hands despite me replicating the missing Johnson in my attempts to attract his eyes and attention. I really could have been mistaken for our tour guide, he also of the windmill-waving arms, as my arms whirled and my gesticulations all came to nothing. I even stood up at the table to make myself more visible to him, but no such luck. When he did pass me he said he was busy serving meals and too busy to order drinks. I ask you and in a brewery, the home of serious beer drinking too!

When the first course arrived the soup resembled a similar soup we experienced on the boat the night before and so was easily recognisable. Libby left hers in the bowl again, untouched, as did several others at our table. Not surprisingly there were no other takers, so in the interim conversation once again turned to our missing tour guide and any possible fate that might have befallen him. We assumed there and then, and rightly or wrongly, that he had fallen asleep in his room or as someone commented mischievously, probably one of the brothers, that he was perhaps drunk from his afternoon's exertions. But both of these assumptions were scotched when Mavis, the 'posh' lady from Oxford, sitting in all her majesty at the top of the table, said she had seen him in a heated discussion at the far end of the bar of our hotel only twenty minutes before we were scheduled to meet in the hotel lobby that night. Firstly, he was in trouble with the angry-looking Knuckle Brothers who were after his blood yet again followed immediately after when he was confronted by another couple she hadn't recognised.

Further comments about Johnson were brought to a halt when the main course of chicken, accompanied by mashed potatoes and tinned carrots and peas, arrived that only served to flummox everyone further. Tinned vegetables? What next?

I had said, with Libby's permission that the soup was too salty and appeared to have had a previous life on the sea-bed similar to shrimps. But that was nothing compared with the gravy when tasted that was so salty it could have been prepared from the Bonneville Salt Flats in good old US of A! That is not to say that the atmosphere at the table was not without interest and reward regardless of those epicurean failings. Despite politeness ruling the roost when we arrived in the place at first, when it came to a discourse on the salt in the meals there was no shortage of culinary discussion as to why it should have been so. Libby said it was to make people drink more by making them thirsty: Mavis said it was probably because we'd upset the big fat chef with our noise; little Ruth said it was because they could not cook properly in Germany and pulled her cardigan over her face and produced an hysterical bout of giggling just like the actress Esme Cannon would have done. David said it was because the Germans still did not like the Brits. Dermot, who of course was from the Emerald Isle, thought the meal was lovely as long as you drank plenty of still water with it. He, like me, had run out of bottled water because his main meal was almost untouched bless him. When the blancmange and fruits of the forest arrived they were devoured ravenously and such was our hunger that people began looking to see if anyone had leftovers. That meal really did get the thumbs down that night and again through no fault of the tour operators. I imagined the Knuckle Brothers giving a good earful to Johnson when they found him later that night and demanding money back for another botched meal. That was if they had not done him in themselves already and therefore the reason for his absence. They stood for nothing less than good value and would not tolerate poor service. I hoped they would be lenient with him when they found him.

As we prepared to leave the brewery Libby's mobile phone rang and I could tell by the look on her face that it was one of our children: she was smiling. When talking or listening longer than a minute I knew that she was always speaking to Caroline's kids. On that occasion they had remembered our anniversary, and where Libby was concerned that phone call would help her forget the awful brewery meal. She would be happy and smiling all the way home, her day complete, her accident before we set off, at the back of her mind.

It was somehow typical of that never to be forgotten evening that a party of Germans came and went after eating and drinking in the same restaurant room that we'd been in and left long before us. Now I am not saying they received favouritism in the form of Formula One waiters but I couldn't help wonder what that said about us Brits? Not a lot I suppose really. However, by ten o'clock it appeared we'd all had enough, had finished eating and finished talking about our tour guide and were ready to return to the hotel. It was then time to begin the customary shuffling about on seats for some people, just like naughty schoolchildren at their school desks before dismissal at the end of the school day. Some collected their coats prior to leaving the restaurant and of course there were the ritual visits to the toilet by so many of our party that heralded the final preparations before departure and our journey back to the hotel. We waited as a group before we left together all drifting out into the cold night air for what was supposed to be our last night in Cologne. The night had been a complete disaster for me and Libby and many others in the group too who probably anticipated much more from the actual dinner than it had provided. Had it not been for the phone call from our daughter it would have been a sad end to a great Christmas break, and a sad end to our special day. We hadn't let on to the others that it had been a special day for us, well we hadn't reminded them, but apart from the meal it was memorable for the markets and the cathedral service, and that's what we hoped for before we set off expectantly from home.

On the way back we walked with Sid, David and Margie through the Cathedral Market by then left to the mercy of stray and hungry dogs running around the cathedral. We soon passed through the station and back to the hotel in record time even with Sid. Approaching the road-works from the railway station the first thing that struck us was all the blue flashing lights parked at the side of our hotel.

'You can bet your bottom Euro it'll be British drunks again' said Sid.

'Why an ambulance then, and in our hotel, look I can see police everywhere?' David said his voice rising, 'Police maybe, but the medics?'

'It is the weekend after all' Libby said which ended any further conversation on the subject.

At ten thirty we entered the hotel to see the place crawling with police who were everywhere either standing still or moving quickly in all directions and shouting out what were obviously orders to colleagues. It gave an air of complete and utter chaos and confusion for anyone entering the hotel at such an hour let alone us being mystified by what we saw. Not wishing to embroil ourselves in any distraction we headed immediately to the lift, by-passing the bar where Martha and John were 'entertaining' each other. We were so knackered after all the walking we'd done that day with David and Margie we got to our room, packed a few things ready for the next day's travel home and then finished eating the most gorgeous bar of chocolate between us. Slumping on to our beds for a few minutes whilst mumbling about the super day out we had had and the visits we had crammed into those sixteen hours, we reminisced about some of the impressions the markets had made on us. So much that day was positive. In particular we had enjoyed the company of newly made friends. Even the night out was enjoyable company-wise and the conversation stimulating, despite the meal, but I couldn't wait to get into my bed and go to sleep regardless of the ongoing bedlam and mayhem somewhere in the hotel. A peck on the cheek from Libby followed by a warm embrace and an acknowledgement that the anniversary had not turned out as we would have wanted that evening, meal-wise, but the rest of the day had been well worth the trip. The day had flown by and Libby was really chuffed with the call to her mobile from Caroline our younger child and of course the chat with the grand children.

The bed finally felt my weight at about eleven fifteen and since we hadn't even switched the TV on when we returned we were so shattered, it was utter and total bliss. The next day, Monday, our train was scheduled to leave Cologne for Brussels quite early at eight forty-four, not eight forty-five. That required us to be in the queue for breakfast earlier than was usual. A good night's sleep would do the trick and a night without the radio would help that wish.

Nothing and no-one could have prepared us for what would happen next.

Chapter Twelve.

We were awakened at precisely one o'clock in the morning, a time that will be forever etched in my mind. I know it was one o'clock because my eyes were absolutely wide open with fright and horror at the bedlam I thought was close to our door on the Monday we were due to leave Cologne. There was such an almighty hammering on a door, somewhere very close, enough to wake the dead it seemed. I sat up in bed alarmed by such pandemonium and looked across at a confused and very sleepy Libby who was struggling to wake up. My still drowsy brain told me the banging hadn't been on a door close by but that it was our door being smashed so vigorously it was about to burst open having been hit with such awesome ferocity that a sledgehammer broke through the door again and again splintering wood or plastic all over the room. It was no dream but a real nightmare.

'Schnell, schnell offen die Tur, diese ist die polizei!' shouted a voice several times, as though the earth had erupted and split open to reveal some demon who had found our door. Gingerly moving from my bed towards the door I didn't need to open it because I was immediately knocked over, thrown backwards and trampled on by several uninvited and uniformed guests as they entered our room. In a micro-second I knew these were not party goers in the wrong room but were police officers. Out of the corner of one eye I glimpsed a couple of women police officers who had moved towards Libby quite menacingly gesticulating to her to get out of bed, fast! Once removed from her bed Libby began screaming. As long as I live I hope I never hear anyone scream so loud, so long and with such anguish. Libby never stopped screaming or howling until later when we had been ushered outside the hotel.

I too was lifted from where I had fallen on the floor with a little 'boisterous and enthusiastic help', grappled from behind, my arms almost being torn off as they were pulled behind me into a position they had never before been in before being hand-cuffed. Libby and I were totally unable to move both of us being held by two police officers. I could not believe my eyes when they eventually focussed. There seemed to be about ten or twelve police in our room: no wonder it seemed crowded. An officer not in uniform, probably a detective and more senior than the others in the room, read from a piece of paper that must have been an arrest warrant or something. I had a vague idea it was a warrant because I vaguely heard our names read out. But we didn't hear all of it as we were still utterly confused and Libby was still screaming at that moment so if they read us our rights I wouldn't have known ...... It then seemed that charges were read to us in German which we obviously didn't understand it was only that the officer assumed the regulation pose of such circumstances. What the hell was going on and why, or what was being said was a blur. All I could see was that the officer kept flicking the paper with his hand as he spoke.

And then a modicum of dignity as we were 'assisted' in getting a 'little more dressed'. I say a little more dressed because it was a somewhat difficult manoeuvre as my arms were still held by police officers at the time, so another kindly pulled up my trousers. How Libby coped I've no idea as she was still screaming her head off. It was blindingly obvious that those police meant business so the charges against us, if that is what they were, must have been serious. When dressed and handcuffed we were hustled out of the room through our busted door and towards the back stairs of the hotel at a rate of knots missing since the age of steam engines.

Back in the hotel, those who had been asleep must have been woken by the up by the racket because the hotel lit up like a Christmas tree as lights were switched on everywhere. Some residents awakened by the noise opened their room doors or threw open their curtains at windows as they attempted to locate where the rumpus was coming from. As we were moved past what remained of our door to the back staircase, Libby's screaming increased in even more loudly like some banshee. She called out asking anyone who might have heard her to tell her what the hell was going on. Several tugs to her slight frame by her minders nearly caused an accident on the stairs as she tripped when losing her balance almost taking her minders down with her. I managed to catch sight of the look in her eyes a couple of times as we were swung round the stairs: she was understandably petrified and panic-stricken like I'd never seen her before. We both were, and could do absolutely nothing about it.

Once downstairs and having been frog marched quickly outside the front door of the hotel with what few clothes we had on we shivered like never before in the freezing early morning air. We would have been shivering in our coats, but without our coats we were numb. I might add we were deposited, no dumped, unceremoniously and firmly in the German equivalent of a Black Maria which had been conveniently parked outside the hotel's main door. One of the vehicles no doubt we had been aware of but taken little notice of a couple of hours earlier when returning from our night out. Inside the vehicle we were abruptly lifted from our knees high enough so we could actually sit on a small bench seat in the back of the vehicle. I could see the tears rolling down Libby's cheeks as she sat perched opposite me.

Looking through a small window in the van and up at the hotel as we moved off it was, needless to say, apparent that residents were awakened by the racket because the hotel was lit up like a Christmas tree. Some were at their windows wondering what the rumpus had been in the hotel to wake them up. I so wanted them to help us but it was all too late. Thunderstruck and with both of us in a trancelike state I was trying to unravel what had happened in the last few minutes when a more senior looking officer tried to explain in broken English more about our arrest. Believe it or not it was somewhat of a relief because with all the commotion in our

room earlier, when I presumed they had cautioned us before, neither
of us had a clue about of any of the charges read out, and certainly
not Libby who was still apoplectic.

'We are arresting you both and holding you both in custody
for your involvement in the disappearance of, and or the suspected
murder of Herr Dennis Johnson. You may not wish to ......' the
Kommissar or German detective read out to us. I didn't hear anymore
following 'You may not wish to ....' as my mind became even more
paralysed by the situation we found ourselves in. Libby stopped
screaming for an instant and turned ashen grey in a split second
the blood having appeared to have drained completely from her
face. If the commotion in the bedroom had not struck home to us
then those charges against us certainly did. Libby began perspiring
rapidly and I could see the blood vessels in her neck throbbing and
pulsating vigorously. I thought she was about to explode and have
a seizure she was so unsettled. I tried to tell the senior officer that
the arrests were all some big mistake, that they had arrested the
wrong people and that they should be looking for someone with
grievances against Johnson. Why had they arrested us I asked? The
police women handcuffed to Libby told me in broken English to
'Belt up!' I didn't argue. They then tightened their grip on Libby who
flinched and squirmed in pain as they did, the bitches. I could do
nothing, I could not move myself and as an overwhelming feeling of
inadequacy spread through my body I wanted to be sick as I could
not help my wife. I needed to say something, shout out loud and
scream the city down but one glance at those women officer attached
to my wife was enough to silence anyone, even a coward like me.

The vehicle we were seated in, as it raced away through the streets
of Cologne with only its blue lights flashing, was very uncomfortable
seated as we were on bench seats that were of little use as we swung
round corners without seat belts. The crying and sniffling, the
complete feeling of impotence and inferiority in that situation, the
shaking of the body, the hot sweats followed by the cold sweats
and the horrific fore-boding that descended on both of us did not
diminish when the police van pulled to a halt at some traffic lights.
Thoughts of any attempt at an escape were a waste of time such was

the overpowering police strength in numbers sat around us. They weren't there for our safety that was obvious. I looked at the officers sat amongst us, their anonymous faces all looking at the floor of the vehicle as we sat there, and couldn't help wonder if they really enjoyed their job.

How long after we left the hotel I had no idea but with a last act of bravado that had been missing since our arrest, I told the police detective accompanying us in no uncertain terms we wanted a lawyer when we arrived wherever we had being taken to. Even the British Ambassador to Germany, or one of his henchmen, if he could fix it. To this day I don't know if he understood my demands or thought I was nuts but he just laughed at my impertinence. The look of disdain on his face indicated to me that I should immediately shut up or else. I sat back against a pillar in the van, gazed at the floor again and looked over towards Libby, and went quiet.

Just when it seemed that another lifetime had flown past the police van slowed to a crawl before stopping with a jolt. Both Libby and I slid sideways into those immovable objects that were our temporary jailers. Libby who was still crying her heart out and utterly despondent at our situation, looked up from the floor and over towards me for the first time since we had left the hotel. Before she could speak, outside there was a burst of an official-sounding conversation in German that broke the silence. I gathered from that conversation we had entered a building of some sort. We would find out afterwards that it was the Central Cologne Police Station or Polizeiprasidium. It hadn't been on our tourist route when we chose to visit the city's markets all those weeks ago!

Bundled out of the police van separately it would be some time before I was allowed to see Libby again, though I did not to know it at the time. As we were led away I could hear Libby still sobbing for all she was worth and I knew in those circumstances that she would be straining every muscle to turn round to see or speak to me. I called to her, telling her to stay strong because she had nothing to fear as we were totally innocent of the spurious charge that had been concocted and laid against us.

I heard her call out to me faintly 'First the accident and now this ......'

I called back to her 'We'll soon be together again, I promise.' The words seemed to fall on deaf ears as she was already out of sight.

It was then those bastards tugged really hard on me, and being handcuffed as I was to my 'chaperone' I didn't want to have a broken wrist, so I followed closely. I was forcibly frogmarched along a dim corridor, dragged through a large wooden door which clunked loudly behind me as it closed because it was so heavy and into and down another corridor. Passing through several more doors I was finally released from the 'chaperone' I had been handcuffed to and placed, or rather pushed, into an empty, smelly little cell. No words were spoken to me by any police officer from the van to that cell. It was if I didn't exist, except on said 'chaperone's' arm of course. In that cold, dank and unheated cell, I shivered like I'd seldom done before. With tears in my eyes all I could do was think of Libby knowing that she felt the cold more than anyone I'd ever met. She was only happy with the temperature when it was high enough to make me sweat which was normally when it was above sixty degrees Fahrenheit. How she was to withstand the cold and conditions in her cell if they were like mine and with her being half-undressed, simply beggared belief. I hoped they had they would provide her with some blankets to keep her warm at least that would have been a humane start.

I paced around my cell and began to wonder what sort of evidence was available to the police for them to accuse and incriminate both me and Libby with any kidnap or murder. They had not placed any such facts before us at all. Well not that we had fully understood or been aware of I mean. They had only arrested us on suspicion of having committed a crime, so far. I could not think of any reason why we would be held for any length of time without some form of evidence and felt they had to bail us both fairly quickly. I wondered if they had they found Johnson's body? And what did they mean when they said he'd been abducted, and it was us that had done it? When? How? We had been together all night in the company of others in our tour group which we could prove. So why arrest us? Libby had spent a short time with Johnson in the hotel for sure when we arrived back from the cafe, but was never alone and always there were others looking on, and as far as I knew in the half hour they were talking together they never left the hotel, did they? But they said Johnson was missing. Maybe he was, maybe God forbid he was dead but I couldn't believe it. I began to wonder if I was dreaming but knew I wasn't when there was a rattling of keys in the lock at my cell door and some goon in uniform having unlocked the door and threw me a blanket with not one word spoken.

'Thank you. Have you taken one to my wife?' I asked as the door was closing but I was just as rudely ignored. I didn't use the blanket immediately I was so hung up on how Libby would be coping without me. I began pacing the tiny stinking cell again, scratching my head, trying to think of just one good reason, even a miniscule reason why were in that situation. I began shivering again, only this time badly; huge goose bumps appeared on my naked arms. I relented and put the blanket round my shoulders, sat down on a cold stone bench-like bed-seat and carried on trying to work out what had happened in the last hour or so that we had arrived back at the hotel. Over and over I wracked my brains for any answers but the thoughts that were going through my head were making me more and more angry. Some thoughts regarded the possibility that other people at the hotel had far more reason to be implicated with his absence than me and Libby. Not that we had any reason to be involved at all with Johnson's disappearance. I only knew of the bloke because of the trip we were on, so why me, why Libby? Libby's association with him was years ago and very tenuous. No, arresting us didn't make any sense at all to me. Bloody wedding anniversary trip to Cologne? We'd been set up I thought, I'd never set eyes on the chap at least not knowingly. And even though he professed to know Libby when they were both younger in London, it was after all nearly forty years ago.

In a cell on another wing of the police station Libby was still under incredible strain, had no idea why we had been arrested and was freezing to death in her cell. An officer had given her a blanket but it was so thin she continued shivering with it wrapped around her not that anyone-else cared but me. Eventually a female officer took her a warm drink in an unbreakable beaker. It was the type of beaker that could not be broken and so enable a prisoner to make a mess of their body. How thoughtful. When the time arrived for Libby to be escorted from her cell for questioning, only then did she begin to stop shivering as her interrogation took place in a warmer room. They were to ask her questions that simply passed over her head as she was totally freaked out by the aggressive nature of them. No she didn't have any idea where Johnson was, alive or dead.

'So, he may be dead, you say?' some hostile police woman detective jumped in quickly.

Few if any of the questions made sense to Libby throughout her sobbing, which brought a premature end to the interrogation sooner than her questioners would have liked, and so Libby was returned to her cell.

I must have been left undisturbed in my cell for what seemed over an hour, probably the time Libby was being questioned, when suddenly my cell door was flung open and in excellent English I was commanded to stand and follow the senior officer in front of me to wherever he was going. He was a Hauptkommissar or senior detective. I asked the other policeman who had me in an arm-lock if he had any news of how my wife was. His look gave nothing away, his mouth never moved, and his eyes on contact with mine melted any further thoughts of me asking questions as I lurched around on my journey to my interview room. I didn't speak again until I was told to sit at a table opposite the Hauptkommissar who was clearly ranked very senior in police hierarchy and was about to demonstrate it by his questioning of me.

'Name?' he asked. I told him.

'Date of birth?' he asked firmly. I answered.

'Why are you in Cologne?' he barked. I told him. 'Why are you really in Cologne?' he shouted at me. I gave the same answer to him again but this only made him thump the table and stand up straight at the table hauling himself fully up to his five feet six inches I guessed. What is it with these little blokes who seem to want power so badly? I thought he was about to hit me as he was just about higher than me when I was sitting. I could see him going extremely red in the face, his cheeks beginning to blow when he asked me

'What is' and he corrected himself, 'was, the relationship between your wife and Herr Dennis Johnson?'

'I don't have a clue what you are on about she hardly knew the chap. What is going on?' I pleaded with him. 'Where is my lawyer? I want a lawyer and so does my wife. Has she got a lawyer? Be careful with her as she was in an accident before we came.' I was in deep 'dodo' at that moment for speaking out when his response came full blast.

'*You* are not asking the questions. *I* am asking the questions. What was the relationship between your wife and Herr Johnson?' the Hauptkommissar of police was then so red-faced and his voice at screaming pitch just as I was just thinking that I'd heard those very same lines before. In some black and white war film I think it was that I saw with my dad when I was a teenager when my thoughts were interrupted as the other two policemen in the room moved nearer the table. I felt threatened. I sensed they were not happy with my replies. I was all of a sweat, my shirt literally soaking and I was desperate for the toilet but I was going to get nowhere unless I told them that Libby had been vaguely aware of Johnson when she began teaching in London.

So I told the Hauptkommissar what I knew and I also told him of the encounter that Johnson had instigated earlier that last evening with Libby in the hotel. He wasn't impressed. He asked me if I knew where Johnson was. I told him I presumed him to be in his room where else would he be at the time of night the police barged into our room? A sort of pained grin covered his face for a few seconds, the type that appears on a dog's face before it bites you.

The Hauptkommissar sat down in his chair again slowly taking the grin off his face and replacing it with a scowl before saying

'Don't get funny with me Englishman! I will ask you one more time. Where is Johnson?' and he thumped the table in front of me so hard I thought with strength like that he would win the World Karate Championship at his weight, or height, I forget which.

My head was thumping, not only because of the stupid unnecessary pressure I had been placed under, but also because I knew if Libby was under the same questioning routine she would fall silent, or completely crack up. I gave him the same answer as before.

'I have no idea where Johnson was, who he is, who he was with and I don't care,' I rattled off and continued 'Why are you holding me and my wife without any evidence or reason at all? If you had a body perhaps you would have a case, albeit flimsy, not that it would have anything to do with my wife or me. But you haven't. So where is my lawyer?' I blurted out my reply so quickly he didn't have time to interrupt me.

He was not happy with my comments but immediately the first chink of light in why we were being held, or more to the point, what was going on, came to light. But it was not good news.

'Why do you say if we had a body? Do you know where his body is? We have no idea of where Herr Johnson is, except he is missing from his blood-stained room. Do you know where he is? What relationship did he have with your wife? We are aware of the connection that you and your wife had previously with him. We can prove this by conversations at your hotel that your wife had with Johnson last night, overheard by British guests, yes British guests, last night in a quiet corner of the bar. Some of my officers have already spoken, at this early hour, to some of the hotel's guests who were only too willing to come forward to talk to my officers and confirm those facts. They said Johnson told several of the guests he had been quite fond of your wife before you met her. What do you say now Englishman?'

I said nothing except I put my head in my hands and stared at the table. Libby could be trusted I knew that and she had told me that crap about Johnson only the other day. So what was the Hauptkommissar implying, if he was implying anything at all? But blood in Johnson's room and lots of it seemingly from what this guy said and no evidence of Johnson, that was different. Why was this policeman in front of me questioning me and then giving me information about Johnson's room? It did seem rather cockeyed. I knew that neither Libby nor I had anything to do with any crime here or in England, with or without Johnson. He was trying to trick me of course that was it. Libby too I bet. I hoped she remained silent like in America, the Fifth Amendment or something. That's right say nothing I thought.

In the end my silence didn't help me and so I was led back to the cold cell I had been in previously. A bucket had been placed in one corner of the cell: was it for my urine or my head I asked myself? Could I hear sobbing nearby at that moment or was my mind playing tricks? Was I dreaming it all in some nightmare? I would soon know.

After a few minutes alone enabling me to begin thinking again and I heard a key turning and unlocking my cell door again. I stood back wondering 'What next?' and my jailer stood by the open door inviting another person to join me in my cell who immediately offered me his hand that gripped mine firmly and began shaking my hand energetically. I pulled away from him wondering what the hell was going on. He introduced himself as Boris Holloway a criminal defence lawyer who had been notified by the British Embassy, and our tour company, of the predicament Libby and I had found ourselves in and of course the charges laid against us. I apologised for my reaction to him and said he had not taken long to get to us. He said that we were in Germany after all, and they were efficient. I knew what he meant but it was still dark outside even so and he had arrived within a couple of hours of our being arrested. Perhaps an acquaintance of ours at the hotel had rung through to the tour company in England and set things in motion. If so then they had been very helpful. I hoped it was someone from the hotel because it meant that we at least had some support there.

The cell door squeaked to a close and was noisily locked again as my jailer, who I hadn't noticed standing in the doorway, left the cell so just me and the lawyer were left alone.

'I am English, although I live in Germany, and have German roots on my mother's side. I speak fluent German and English. Pleased to meet you I am sure. I am here to help you and your wife. I have spent a little time with her already.' He reached forward with his hand and shook mine again firmly. I liked firm handshakes so I warmed to him straight away after all he was a bonus.

'How is she?' I asked. 'Was she more relaxed after you saw her? Tell me please, I need to know?'

'Relaxed? No, she is still somewhat, 'er how can I say, 'erm, unstable. I am afraid she did not interview very well in that state of mind. However, when I told her who I was and what I was there for, and that I said I would be speaking with you too, she said to tell you she loved you and for you to be strong and hang on in there.

He glanced at his watch before saying

'Look the time is flying past and I only have a short time alone with you so I need to ascertain some facts about the situation you find yourself in as quickly as possible.'

It seemed strange talking to an English-speaking lawyer in Germany but so what if he cleared our names? And pretty damned fast I hoped! We spoke only for a few minutes during which time he seemed to ask me hundreds of questions. I tried to clarify in my own mind our movements the previous evening, what had happened and in some form of order for him. It took several minutes because of the mess my mind was in. I asked him what Libby had said to him but he declined to tell me. I even asked him if we needed consular help at this time. He refused my suggestion saying he could help me himself better but could not rule out consular help for Libby since she was the one accused of a more serious crime whereas I was charged with being an accomplice. I told him it was news to me and asked him what he meant by his statement. He said that one of the facts in the case against us was that Libby had admitted to the police that she had purchased some travel pills for me back in Birmingham. So what I asked? He said coincidentally a bottle of pills from the same chemist had been discovered in Johnson's room and the police had put two and two together assuming Libby had been in Johnson's room at sometime earlier. That shaky fact, according to the lawyer from his interview with the police, was why Libby and I were both arrested the link being that we were from Birmingham, and so the cap must fit. At the very instant he finished his last sentence, as if it had been deliberately planned, a key turned again in the cell door lock and I knew our interview time was up when an officer asked him, in German, to leave my cell. Holloway left saying he would see me and Libby again soon, but how soon he didn't know. As he disappeared from view I asked him to give her my love next time he spoke with her. The door was then locked and bolted and I was again left alone with my thoughts.

The sweat on my shirt had hardly cooled and dried after what seemed hours despite the cold atmosphere in my cell. It was in fact only seventy-five minutes and by then nearly five o'clock in the morning when again my cell door opened and two burly police officers beckoned me to follow them. I thought 'No handcuffs?' and withdrew my wrists. I was led to the same room I had been questioned in earlier and beckoned to sit down. Just me and those two burly officers of the Rhineland-Palatinate police force. They stood over me watching my every move with me seated on the same plastic chair at the same table I'd sat at uncomfortably earlier. Five, ten, fifteen minutes maybe passed but I had no accurate way of knowing as I sat and stared at the table in front of me. The police had my watch and belongings and the clock on the wall clearly needed new batteries because it had shown ten to eleven when I was last in the room hours before.

Then the Hauptkommissar entered the room in his personal flurry of activity still with a face like thunder. I knew it was him before looking at him because of the way he walked. He had a slight limp which would have been far worse if I'd had my way those last few hours. His mood was instantly picked up by the other officers who, recognising the look on his face eased back their shoulders and stood bolt upright. Boris Holloway my lawyer also entered the room so unobtrusively I failed at first to notice him. I was glad he was present because he seemed more relaxed than when I saw him earlier when he had appeared very uptight and tense, and he was the lawyer.

'So,' the senior policeman said as he began talking abruptly, 'we are going to caution you and bail you to return to your hotel where you must stay until I release you at a later time.'

Before he could say anything further I asked 'What about my wife is she being released too?'

'No!' he growled, 'we have many more questions to ask of her as she is very uncooperative and maybe I need to see you again too. For now, no more questions. You will be escorted back to your hotel where you will wait for me. In the meantime, as I have said, you must not leave the hotel. We will begin questioning other guests after breakfast at the hotel sometime later today. You will find many officers around the hotel and maybe if the Met Police, whom we have contacted today, and who have been very cooperative and are able to spare the staff, it is possible some of their officers may arrive later today from London and escort your wife back to the UK tomorrow Tuesday to be questioned further in England. So long as she cooperates with us first that is. You may now go.'

'Can I see my wife please before I leave here?' I said, tears streaming down my cheeks.

'Absolutely not and until we are satisfied with her you will not be allowed anywhere near her until we say so!' he shouted back at me. 'Now go with my officer to a waiting car. We have more interviews to conduct with your wife and you are delaying us. Now please go. See him out please.' He spoke to another officer abruptly commanding him to deal with me. I hoped that would be the last encounter I would have with Hauptkommissar Schmidt until Tuesday morning. I called back over my shoulder to thank the lawyer to say thanks for getting me released. He had not said a word in getting me released but was somewhat amazed when I was hurriedly removed from the interview room by my burly minder. The confusion in my mind that followed as I was bundled out of the building had me thinking 'Why me why am I released? Why is not Libby released too?' Fat chance I had of getting any answers at that moment.

I wanted to ask someone where and how Libby was at that moment. Could I see her? Why Libby in the first place? What was she doing? Why couldn't I see her? When would she be released? Why were they continuing to hold her? What further charges had been used against her by the authorities so that she remained behind and I was released? And many more questions that only served to bewilder me even further. Pity that time did not allow me to get some of those answers from the lawyer Boris Holloway.

With no answers forthcoming from anyone in the police station and having been dispatched abruptly from the interview room, I was ushered along to the front desk of the police station by one of the burly policemen who had been 'minding' me. I signed for my valuables and they were returned to me, everything that was, except my mobile phone for some reason and my passport. As if I would leave Cologne without Libby. With my head spinning fast I was becoming dizzy, and whilst I was ushered out of the building my head was still buzzing with a million questions I wanted to ask my minder as I exited through the front door. Turning to ask him a question at the top of the steps by the front door I managed to catch sight of him melting back into the main building behind me, on the other side of the door. I had, without noticing it with all the haste of being escorted outside the police station, been passed on to another officer who quite cleverly steered me into a waiting police car at the bottom of the steps. The confusion continued with me being shoved inside the car next to another officer who had set the child locks so I wasn't able to escape as I was returned to my hotel.

It was still dark and icy outside and from the back of the car I could just about make out the clock on the car's dashboard. It read twenty two minutes past five. My own watch was still in my pocket in the police bag it was returned in. We'd been gone from the hotel just over four hours which wasn't so bad for me I suppose as I'd been released quite quickly. But Libby, she couldn't have known anything about Johnson's reputed sudden demise, could she? I thought not then and still do to this day. But that awful Monday had only just begun and over eighteen hours remained when I arrived back at the hotel exhausted, cold, dishevelled and needing a clean-up. Of far more importance I needed to know why Libby was still being held.

I decided I had to phone Caroline our daughter and explain that we would be delayed home by at least one day, and that her mum could be even later getting home which is why I was in the hotel and her mother in the nick. It would not be an easy call to make and so I had to be certain in my own mind of the facts as I knew them.

Firstly I had to get by the police officers both uniformed ones and those in civvies who were still crawling all over the hotel like some rash. There appeared to be no guests up and about the hotel when I arrived back when a strange thought suddenly struck me. Which guests had been only too happy to be questioned by the police in the hotel, after we had been arrested, at such an unsocial hour? I was unsure momentarily, and then the penny dropped. Some of our group could have been spoken to as they were returning home from the brewery, after all Libby and I were among some of the first back. But that must have been long before we were arrested later that night or the early morning because we went straight to bed after saying goodnight to our friends. We had come home with Sid who was a slow walker, and David and Margie, but still arrived well in advance of the majority of revellers. Enough time for some preliminary questioning I bet, the devious bastards. And of course only John and Martha were in the bar when we shot off upstairs in the lift and to bed. That was it. By the time we were arrested some of the guests would have already been subject to questioning by the police. Some would have been only too happy to be questioned I figured.

Around the hotel the police manned all the doors back and front not allowing any of the Pineapple Tour party to leave at all and only other guests, not in our party after having had their papers thoroughly scrutinised, were allowed out. There were many guests in the hotel that had come from all parts of the EU and further afield, but apart from a nod of the head we had not had anything to with then.

Walking through the main door of the hotel I was stopped by an officer with a very good knowledge of English. He clearly knew who I was and where I had been having seen me get out of the police car in the few clothes I was wearing. He led me to my room via the backstairs where another two officers were present at my newly replaced door, to keep an eye on me in case I tried to do a runner and break out I supposed. The English-speaking cop opened my door for me and gave me the new key to it. Before leaving he told me, again in perfect English, that the two officers would be stationed outside my room at all hours until further notice. He said as the room was fairly high above the pavement outside they didn't expect me to leave via the window in the room! It was good to know they have a sense of humour and that taxes are being spent wisely on public relations in Germany!

I went immediately across the room to use the hotel telephone as my mobile phone was still 'in custody'. I dialled nine for an outside line listened and waited for the dialling tone, and then dialled the number of our daughter in England. Just what use mine and Libby's phones were to the police I had no idea at all as I stood waiting for my daughter to respond at the other end of the phone. I heard a different and ghostly click on the line, not the one that meant I could talk to our daughter Caroline, but loud enough for me to differentiate between the two types. It was clear my phone was being tapped and that some spook downstairs, or at a police station, was listening in. I knew Caroline would not be pleased at my phoning at such an ungodly hour and was soon proved right when someone answered at the other end of the line.

'Who the hell's phoning at this time of the morning?' my son in law William asked 'do you know what the freaking time is?'

'It's dad' I said quickly and quietly, 'Mum and I are in the shit. Mum's in jail and I've just got out.'

'Hang on dad is this a wind-up or what?' William asked very un-amused. 'Would you like to talk to Caroline? She's awake now although I'm not surprised.'

'Dad what the hell is going on?' I recognised the screeching tone and voice of my daughter and tried to interrupt and give her my news before she could say too much but was too late.

'Dad what are you going on about are you drunk or something? Not one of those late nights or, should I say, early bloody mornings is it? Do you know what the time is?' Caroline's blast was not the first I'd suffered from her but then perhaps I needed it occasionally if only to be reminded she was a woman and not my 'Little Princess' anymore.

I tried to explain briefly and as lucidly as possible what had been going on during those last few hours but without much success. Her tears and sobbing told me she knew I was not bluffing and she handed the phone back to William. He offered to fly over to help there and then. I said I hoped the problem would clear up pretty quickly as there was no substance to their charges and he should stay where he was and I'd keep them informed. Just as I was apologising for having had to phone at such an ungodly hour there was another loud click on the phone line heard by both of us.

'Where are you dad' he asked 'in Russia, I know what that was, it ....?'

'Speak soon' I replied cutting him off and put the phone down.

I could hear some animated talking in German outside my door, then the unmistakable rustle of paper and finally someone's mobile phone ringing. I went to the toilet in disgust before showering and getting changed. It was after six o'clock when I'd finished. I had thawed out but wondered how Libby was coping.

What should have been the last day in Cologne for our trip was not to be. The hotel resembled a prison with the heavy police presence everywhere. I would find later there were as many police present as guests at breakfast that Monday morning, maybe more. I decided I had to face the other guests sooner rather than later after all I had been scheduled to travel on the same train as them back to England that very morning. That likelihood was to prove impossible for all of us as we were to find out.

Leaving my room and crossing the corridor to the lift my police escorts followed on my heels insisting at the last moment we didn't use the lift but should descend by the back-staircase. Perhaps they thought I had some mad escape plan that involved me overpowering them in the lift, escaping from the hotel and rescuing Libby from the main police station via ropes and ladders whilst carrying a box of dark chocolates. As it was when we arrived in the hotel lobby members of our group who were going in or out of the breakfast bar just stood and gawped with incredulity as I walked into breakfast not with Libby, but with my two burly chaperones in uniform.

Some guests obviously had an inkling of what the commotion was all about in the early hours that morning even if they hadn't been interrogated last night because they were either up at their windows watching, or down in the bar. Let's face it if they had looked out of their windows they would have seen both Libby and me leaving the hotel under protest in a police van with flashing blue lights, half-dressed and clearly under arrest. At that time in the morning they were bound to wonder what all the commotion was. When I thought of all that had taken place in and around our room that morning, the sledge-hammer smashing our door down, it was understandable why some of our party were frightened, or very reluctant, to speak to me. Others, who may have been oblivious to the goings on, thinking of Ruth in particular, had probably heard the Chinese whispers that do the rounds in such situations. It was obvious that something similar happened with Mavis and Elizabeth who smiled a weak smile of support in my direction without looking me in the eye. That's what I thought then in my sensitive state of mind so I tried to return the smile but failed utterly. They left the breakfast room and headed for the lift to go upstairs. I was annoyed with myself that I never spoke to them and I think they knew it.

I wandered slowly into breakfast where David met me at the coffee vending machine and told me

'The police have called a meeting for ten o'clock. Information about it is on the notice-board in the reception area. It explains that our departure from Cologne will be delayed and will not now go ahead today as planned. The guests are far from happy, well those who have already heard the news. However, I just wanted you to know that Margie and I are on your side no matter what happens. As if you both need to know that. Come and join us for coffee if your 'guards' will let you.'

A friendly voice and face was very welcome at that moment because the strain of the charges made by the police, let alone Libby's continued incarceration, was beginning to tell on me. Dermot was sat with Margie munching his way through his cornflakes when David and I walked over to their table. I sat down next to Dermot. He fidgeted about uncomfortably for a few seconds and then said

'How's Libby is she bearing up? All sorts of rumour are flying round the hotel about what has happened to Libby, and Johnson the tour rep as well you need to know. What's going on? Is it OK for me to ask?'

'I think it is better to wait and see what the police say at ten o'clock this morning rather than for to me give out any incorrect information' I replied. 'Besides' I continued, 'I have absolutely no idea what will be said by the police, or how much detail they will want to share with people.'

Dermot was gentleman enough to drop any further questioning, but not Margie who persisted politely in asking how Libby was coping with her ordeal she found herself in, particularly within the confines of the Police Station cell.

'Where is she Tony? Was she with you all the time you were gone with the police last night?' she enquired, 'I mean what has caused this situation that involves Libby? There do seem to be a few hasty presumptions made by the police with regard to the situation. What evidence have they got against her for starters? Did they speak to the Knuckle brothers? I've seen them on more than one occasion having a right old go at Johnson threatening what they would do to him if he didn't sort things out in their favour. Particularly after some of the meals we've had. Some of the guests in our party have already been questioned by the police, did you know that? Look, as we speak people are at it again talking behind their hands. Presumably the police questioning was about Libby.'

So many questions from my friend left my head buzzing. I replied as I had to Dermot adding there was no way Libby could have been involved in anything suspicious as she had been with me all the time except when she had the conversation with Johnson in the bar area last night. I said I was only too glad that so many of our group saw them talking together before he went missing. Who was involved in his disappearance, if indeed he had disappeared and I repeated that neither me nor Libby were involved, we hadn't the faintest idea irrespective of the police's charges and speculation that Libby was somehow implicated. After about fifteen to twenty minutes with those friends I'd had enough of being sociable and certainly had little time for others in our group. With all the thoughts I had running round my head about Libby's imprisonment I just needed to get out and away from that dining area.

I returned to my room followed by my minders having managed to dodge any further encounters with members of our party on the stairs or lift. The two 'guards' re-positioned themselves outside my door. Inside I tried to get some rest as best I could but found I couldn't settle for more than a few seconds at a time so decided I'd make notes of the last time Libby and I saw Johnson alive. Who had he been with and who were they? Anything that might help the plight of my wife or the situation we found ourselves in. My list included amongst others the Knuckle Brothers, Sid, Mavis, David and Margie, Elizabeth and Dermot, and the couple we were unable to positively identify at the time. So why did the police choose Libby and me? All the people I'd listed I had seen in the company of Johnson that day. Why was it then that they were not pulled in for questioning I asked myself? I wondered if perhaps they had been questioned whilst I was away from the hotel anything to help me calm down. The possibilities were endless and gave me such a headache meaning there was no way I could get my head round it all at that moment in my lonely room.

Chapter Thirteen.

A knock on my door woke me from an unpremeditated half an hour's doze. The noise really brought me to my senses quickly, the officer reminding me that the meeting in the dining area downstairs with the police commandant was about to begin and I had to be present. It was almost ten o'clock and I was not late, but with the usual German precision the meeting had to start on time. On entering the meeting-room with my chaperones I greeted immediately with only silence and stares. At the front of the room, and the whole tour group faced him when I was seated, sat the burly figure of Hauptkommissar Schmidt who had on either side of him two other plain-clothed officers. He had said previously he would next see me on the Tuesday, but there he was leading the meeting. Uniformed police with revolvers by their side were stationed around the room at regular intervals. After I sat down a buzz of conversation and supposition as to mine and Libby's crime filled the room at least that what I thought. The room's atmosphere began to worry me as it seemed to change, and negatively towards me as Schmidt launched into his talk.

'May I please introduce myself and my staff to you people? I am Hauptkommissar Schmidt and these two detectives are Uberkommissar Skidelski and Kommissar Johannes and we are all based at the central police station in Cologne. The purpose of my visit is to tell you that your return home to the UK has been delayed by at least twenty four hours.'

Moans and groans accompanied that last sentence as the assembled group of guests proceeded to discuss the potential knock-on effect of that decision both for themselves and their families. The noise in the room grew ever more loudly until

'Please, however,' Hauptkommissar Schmidt continued 'if I may be permitted to continue, I must inform you of two further pieces of information. Your Pineapple Tours guide, Herr Dennis Johnson, is missing and his room is currently at the centre of our investigation as we search for clues as to his whereabouts and disappearance this very moment. Secondly, I wish my officers to interview each and every one of you before I allow you to travel home, maybe tomorrow, back to the United Kingdom as we are treating the whole of this hotel as a potential crime scene. That is why we have armed police inside the hotel. It is the way we conduct such proceedings. When you are interviewed English-speaking lawyers will be available should you need their services. There will also be interpreters available should there be any problems of translation. When you have been questioned you will stay separate from the others who will not have been questioned. This must be so. If you need any service in the hotel you must be escorted by one of my officers. If Herr Johnson is not found, or I declare the interviews terminated, another of the company's guides will escort you back to London. She will arrive soon. Her name is Adele Simone. For now though you will not be allowed to leave the hotel until I say so. Is that understood?'

A reluctant nodding of heads by those to be questioned was followed by some better news at least as Schmidt continued

'All meals will be provided free of charge as will non-alcoholic drinks. There will be no questions. Thank you.'

And with that he stood and left the room taking his two fellow officers with him. The room then erupted into a form of controlled disorder as everyone tried to talk at once. What no questions? What is this? What sort of country are we in? We have rights you know. Stay here another day? To be individually questioned by the police? And so on and so on. I looked for David to help me escape from the verbal carnage I thought I was about to experience and undergo if I stayed in the room, but he was engaged in deep conversation with Margie. I tried, unsuccessfully, to leave the room. I wasn't allowed to get very far and was sent back because the hotel's exits were completely sealed off. I'd forgotten a policeman was guarding every door. Even trying to enter a lift proved difficult as no-one was allowed off the ground floor of the hotel. Some adjacent downstairs rooms had already, or were being, converted into mini-interviewing rooms for the police to question all guests individually. Needless to say the toilets were a haven in such strange circumstances as I tried to avoid fellow travellers!

After a few minutes of my self-imposed isolation I saw the arrival at the main door of the English-speaking German lawyers that had been brought in to sit with the guests as they were interviewed. And strange as it seems, from what I gathered later, I was the only person not to be interviewed in the hotel by the police that day.

I sought out Herr Schmidt later when he appeared near the lobby to ask if Libby was OK but he would only say that she was still being interviewed by female Kommissar detectives. The day dragged on, interviews were started and finished, some drawn out some short but time to me seemed to stand still. Some of the guests enjoyed the attention they were getting but others were obviously and understandably disgruntled about the situation they innocently found themselves in. I wondered what they might be saying about my lovely, and to me, totally innocent wife. What would those people who had overheard her conversation with the missing tour guide tell the police about her supposed liaison with Johnson? Just how long would the questioning last?

Lunch approached and at one o'clock all questioning ceased for an hour resuming again at two o'clock. Guests were divided into two clear sections: those who had been questioned were in the Dining Room whilst the others were placed in a side annexe. During lunch I could overhear those guests who had already been questioned by the police recalling all too vividly the questions they had been asked. How did they know my wife? What had they seen of Libby and Johnson? Had they overheard any conversations between Libby and

Johnson? By lunch-time over half of the party had been interviewed by the police and seemed to be tucking into their lunches more eagerly than those who were waiting to be questioned after lunch. The latter, in fairness, seemed disinterested in the food before them. Perhaps it was the anticipation of the situation that was shortly to befall them.

After lunch it was impossible for anyone present in the hotel not to notice that, when summoned to be interviewed the Knuckle Brothers were held and questioned much longer than any of the other folks. My hopes rose temporarily. Could they have been involved in the disappearance? Or was it because of John's looks that the police kept him and interviewed him longer than the rest? Or maybe Libby's hunch about him from the moment she first set eyes on him at St. Pancras Station that he looked an out and out thug had come back to bite him. Suspicion grew even more when he was actually taken out of the building to be questioned. Where he was taken to of course I had no idea but he was gone for some time. John's anger in particular had been noticed by several members of the group, but younger Kevin was no slouch in that department either. He was almost as truculent on being released himself which manifested itself in a barrage of swearwords that would have made a sailor blush. Certainly from the puzzled looks on the faces of some the more elderly ladies they knew nothing of his Anglo-Saxon vocabulary, nor had they ever heard of some of the rhetoric he hurled at the German police! When John eventually reappeared the similar linguistic gymnastics displayed by Kevin were repeated for all to hear all over again.

By mid-afternoon guests were asking if they could go to their rooms for a lie down after all the tension and the tea and coffee they had consumed since the start of questioning. All but a few had not been questioned at that stage, so permission was given to the majority as long as they re-assembled once more in the dining area at four thirty for a further meeting with Herr Schmidt.

I too was given leave to go to my room where I fell asleep in an armchair in the corner of my room only to be awakened at four fifteen by one of my 'chaperones' banging on my door to see if I was still in there and alive. I tried again to compile a list of all the happenings of the last fifteen or so hours since Libby and I were arrested before I fell asleep but with little success. It was as I was clearing my sore eyes and placing my notepad on the table by the window that I could vaguely see some people in plastic suits leaving the hotel below. Clearly they were part of a forensic team. It was obvious they had been in our room whilst I had been 'away' because my radio had been moved, the tea-pot, cups and saucers we'd used Sunday were re-arranged and one of our cases was open, something Libby would never have allowed to happen because of the moths! I sat wondering what they found to take away from Johnson's room and felt they would have had to take his room apart bit by bit. They'd have gone through it like a dose of salts searching for vital clues that would lead to them solving his disappearance or that would perhaps convict his kidnapper. But what did I know of such things? My only concern was for my wife, and currently the only person who had anything good to say about her was me. Herr Schmidt would later confirm my suspicions, when asked, that the forensic team had been through mine and Libby's room. Nothing was being left to chance so it seemed and shouldn't. I then dozed off worrying about Libby.

Another loud bang on the door, when it came at four fifteen, woke me with a start. I opened the door knowing it would be one my chaperones, which it was, asking me to follow him down the stairs and back into the company of Hauptkommissar Schmidt who was then stationed in what was the main hotel office. Schmidt explained to me that all the questioning of the guests had proceeded painlessly for the police at least and that all the guests would be free to come and go as they wished in the hotel after the next meeting which was imminent. He also confirmed that further developments had come to light in the case without explaining what they were and that Libby would to be held overnight again at the police station. However, he did go on to say that, the next day Tuesday, she might be allowed to travel back to London on the same train as the rest of us, but in the custody of Met Police officers who should have arrived before midnight Monday to take her back. The possibility of her travelling back at the same time as me hinged completely upon the safe arrival of the officers from London, and nothing else. I must say he looked pleased with himself that he was off-loading her onto someone-else which I thought quite strange at the time.

At the four thirty meeting he told the rest of the group everything that he had told me privately ten minutes or so before. He also reminded people of the imminent arrival of the lady Adele Simone of Pineapple Tours who had been directed by the tour operators to accompany our group back to London the following morning Tuesday. At the same time he confirmed the arrangements for travel would be identical to the schedule that we should have taken that day Monday. Further, Adele would be available from dinner that night at seven o'clock to answer any questions guests felt they needed to ask about the travel arrangements or about meals. Elspeth asked him who was responsible for the extra expenses incurred because of the delay, for instance, dinner that night. Another questioner asked about the people who should have been in work next day Tuesday. Who, she asked, would attest and certify to their bosses back in the UK that they had been legitimately delayed?

In answer to the first question he replied that the tour company would pay for all the hotel meals and secondly the Met Police had received a list of people delayed with their telephone numbers and addresses from the tour operator that would help in that direction. With the meeting finished people were dismissed which sparked a rush for the main door, for even after such an arduous day there was a need for fresh air despite the cold and ever darkening German evening.

Me, I decided to call it a day and went to my room to phone Caroline our daughter and give her the latest information about her mother from what I had been told. As had become the custom when I made a phone call from the hotel there was a 'click' on the phone line when I lifted the receiver to dial the UK. That told me the 'listeners' were still listening. Caroline was surprised that I had been released before her mum, even though I was unable to tell her why. I told her neither of us should have been accused and that the police or someone had over-reacted. I said that her mum and I should have arrived home by the time of our phone call, certainly be together in a police-station somewhere in London, and said again that I felt the German authorities had jumped before they should have and would be found to be wrong in their judgements of her mum and me.

'Have you been able to speak with your brother Miles and tell him what's happened to mum, or is he still out of reach? I don't want to call him on his mobile if he's out of the country, not from a hotel room with other people listening in.'

'What are you going on about dad?' Caroline began. 'Listening in? Who's listening in? I thought you said mum was in the nick still. You've not been on the sauce again have you? I told mum that Miles has gone to New Zealand to visit a lady-friend for the summer over there and won't be back till March at the earliest.'

'OK then, now listen to me as I'm off in a minute. Mum is still in the nick and hopefully will be on her way to London tomorrow albeit accompanied by police officers, if they arrive here in time. I have not seen her for over twelve hours and things here are moving quickly. Our schedule remains the same, but a day late. I only wanted to update you with some of the facts as I know them. I'll talk to you again soon I'm sorry this is a short call. OK?' She blew me a kiss and was gone. I waited a little longer with the hotel line still open and sure enough there was another 'click' as the listener replaced their receiver.

I was unable to eat that night, my stomach being so tied up in knots at being separated from Libby again, and fretting and wondering how she was managing in her cramped, crappy little cell. I even spurned the help of our new friends' offer to take me out for a walk and at least talk with me. I was so unresponsive it bordered on the rude. I hoped they would understand that I wanted to be left alone and I would explain to them the reason why some other time. The police had by then left the hotel except for the ones searching the top floor where Johnson's room had apparently been. That floor was still sealed off apparently and as luck would have it there were none of our group members on that floor.

The sudden ringing of the phone in my room startled me when it rang because my room was so quiet.

'Hello' the voice at the other end said and carried on before I could question who it was. 'Hello is that Tony Russell, this is Boris Holloway the lawyer, remember me?'

'Sorry I was caught napping what can I say or do for you?' I stumbled in reply.

'No problem. I thought I'd let you know I have just returned from the police station having interviewed your wife again.' The lawyer continued 'She was able to talk to me much easier this time. However, the police still believe she is guilty as charged but for now are unable to be clear what the crime is without a body. But the bad news is that she will stay under arrest for her journey home which will hopefully be tomorrow. The Met Officers should arrive by tonight to escort her back to London tomorrow probably to Paddington Green Police Station. OK Mr Russell, are you still there?'

'Yes, yes, thank you for the call. It's good of you to let me know that Libby has improved even if she is still under arrest. It is just that it has been a long and tiring day, but nothing like anything what Libby will have had to endure. I really appreciate your call. Has she been given any more clothes? Will you be travelling with her tomorrow? Can I see her tonight?'

'She now has some warmer clothes despite the fact that they are ill-fitting. No sadly I will not be travelling with her. When she is in the hands of UK police she becomes their responsibility, I only work for the State system here in Germany. The answer to your other question is that no-one will be allowed near her until she is in London I'm afraid. And that does mean you too Mr Russell. That's the way it is in these circumstances. OK Mr Russell? I wish both you and your wife well and hope this case is concluded in your favour for you both very soon. I'm sure it will be. My work is done now in Cologne and your wife's statement to me and my report will travel back to London with her. Goodbye Mr Russell.'

I thanked him once more for the support and kindness that he had demonstrated to me and Libby and for letting me know that Libby had calmed down a little. I could not though sit and contemplate her fate again that night and decided at that instant, as we were free to come and go as we liked, even me, to return to the

Police Station where Libby would be held captive a further cold and lonely night. What type of husband was I if I did not at least try to see her irrespective of any inhibiting regulations?

I knew there were plenty of taxis over by the railway station so I grabbed a coat, opened my door and ran across the corridor with my 'chaperones' following in disbelief and out of breath in my wake as I easily out-ran them. Down several flights of stairs and out into the night I ran leaving the two policeman way behind. My ruse had worked and on collaring a taxi jumped in slamming the door and told the driver 'Schnell, Schnell die Polizeiprsidium bitte!' And with that the taxi driver left the station rapidly passing my out of breath 'chaperones' who had tried to follow me without success.

On arrival at the police station I told the taxi driver to wait at the front of the main entrance as we would never be allowed to drive into the restricted area that Libby and I had been taken to in the early hours of that morning. I ran up the steps, through the main door and speaking slowly asked if I could speak to someone in English and see Herr Schmidt who had interviewed both Libby and me earlier that morning. Phew, I was so out of puff. The officer in front of me just stared blankly back at me but I was told by another cocky police-woman in Pigeon English that there was little chance of seeing Herr Schmidt as he was off duty.

'Well anyone then, I'll see anyone. I just want to see my wife.' I was shouting loudly and mainly out of frustration and anger at her shilly-shallying as well as the potential fear of not being able to see my wife. Other officers arrived out of the woodwork wondering what the noise was about and ushered me forcibly away from the counter. In an adjoining room I explained my position and put forward more politely the request to see my wife. I was turned down flat, led away from the main entrance and put out through the front door with me telling everyone who cared to, or could listen, that the Third World War was about to break out if I could not see my wife and it was against the bloody Germans again. I'm afraid I lost what little self-control I had been born with as I stumbled down the steps at the front of the police station. At least I had tried to see Libby.

I could see the taxi driver watching me from where he had parked in the car park after even he had been moved on. He must have been unable to believe what he saw and heard from me as I stumbled down the steps when I heard him start his car engine. I walked slouching slowly across the car park towards his car, occasionally looking back over my shoulder and cussing the watching police officers who had 'removed' me from their workplace. I had only been in the place ten minutes for heaven's sake. I slumped into the taxi and murmured 'Hotel' to the driver and we set off. Although my 'chaperones' back at the hotel when they knew that I had returned did not hinder my progress towards my room or, surprisingly, even question me. I presumed someone at Head Office had contacted them to tell them of the failed exploits of the crazy Englishman.

Having calmed down and trying to reflect on the day's events, I began to understand and sympathise with the thoughts of the other guests who had appeared a little unhappy with me and Libby to say the least. But what could I say or do to alleviate their problems when I could not even solve my own? I started to write a letter to Libby on hotel writing paper that was in the desk draw in the room. After several failed attempts to construct meaningful sentences, the only thing I really achieved was a full up litter bin of scrunched-up paper in the corner of the room as I struggled to write my letter.

Later, with the curtains still open and the lights of Cologne my only illumination, I heard someone knocking on my door again only this time with much less ferocity than I heard in the early hours the previous morning. Pulling myself together and off the bed, I turned on the bedside light before opening the door somewhat tentatively. I was surprised to see David and Margie stood there. Bleary-eyed I asked them in but they refused saying they just called in passing to see if I was OK and had any news of Libby. I told them I was fine and about the phone call from the lawyer. I then thanked them for their concern and having wished me some sleep they returned to their room. After they had gone I looked in the mirror but didn't like what I saw in that tired, old and wrinkled reflection and went and lay down on the bed again. I set the alarm clock to ring at six o'clock. As if I would need it. I lay awake a while thinking of Libby and trying to imagine what she was thinking and before too long fell asleep. In and out of sleep for what seemed hours in the end I cried myself to sleep trying to picture Libby who I hoped would be able to sleep herself despite being in her cell.

Chapter Fourteen.

As is usual with advancing age you can be awake with your eyes shut for no earthly reason most of the night. It's what we Seniors call 'resting ones eyes' apparently. Sod's Law normally dictates you then fall into a deep sleep just before the alarm goes off and so one alarm clock is not enough to wake you. Fortunately, on the night in question I had also set the radio alarm and this did the trick on what would be my last morning in Cologne. Consequently I was wide awake at six o'clock. Knowing Libby I did not think she would have slept a wink that Monday night locked in her cell after having been told there was a chance that she could be travelling back to the UK. The 'gruel' for dinner would have been left untouched and her clothes only 'slept on' and creased. I too remained hopeful that she would be travelling back to London even if it would be in company of two Met Police-women detectives.

Once out of bed I was still so tired after a mainly sleepless night I only just managed to stagger across the room, eyes nearly open, to the kettle to make a coffee before I attempted anything else. I was still numb from the previous day's events that I drank my coffee very slowly before taking a much needed shower, shaved carefully to avoid nicking my chin, and toileted all within half an hour of surfacing from my bed. Finally, before I had any breakfast I searched for my travel pills to avoid any further problems on the journey home. I looked in my toilet bag but couldn't find them. I looked in Libby's toilet bag but there was no sign of them there either. That's funny I thought, I had taken them before we travelled to Aachen and then before the return, so where were they? I remembered seeing them each time I'd shaved or cleaned my teeth because, for obvious reasons, I had to take out my deodorant and the like out of my toilet bag. Surely, I thought, I could not have lost them from the room because they stayed in the toilet so never left our room in their container. Unless …… no, police-men never get travel sick do they? I recalled a conversation I'd had with Hauptkommissar Schmidt. He had told me the police had made some link or other with a bottle of pills found in Johnson's room that had the gravest of implications for me and Libby. No amount of searching for them turned them up though that morning and I still had certain tasks to complete or I wouldn't have been on the train. Nonetheless I would have to purchase some from a chemist before we travelled.

I set about packing our cases slowly. Never an easy task to perform by oneself let alone in the circumstances I found myself that morning. My case was straight-forward: pants, shirts, socks and toiletries. In they went folded tidily and neatly and arranged as Libby would have packed them. I also remembered to attach the replacement luggage label correctly addressed on Libby's case and then did the same to mine. Packing her case though was a much more difficult proposition. Placing her clothes as neatly as I could in the case was a constant reminder to me of what she had been dressed like in Germany. It cut me up something horrible proving to be a much more difficult task than I could have imagined. Even worse was the thought that I might not see her perhaps until we reached London, if then. I placed our anniversary cards and the present I had bought her especially, the one she had been so pleased to receive and open, into her case bringing more tears to my eyes. Having to close and lock it had the same effect on me. I was distraught that she had not been with me at that time.

With the job done, much more slowly than it took to complete my packing, I placed the cases outside the door ready to be taken downstairs in the lift. My minders had long since disappeared from their post outside my door and, come to think of it, they were not there last night when David and Margie popped round. I caught a glimpse of Iris and Richard going down to breakfast, they waved to me and smiled. It was seven o'clock. There was another hour and a quarter to go before we left the hotel and began the journey back to the UK. Adele our new tour guide had said we should make our own way to the station before departure to Brussels. It was made easier because our cases were clearly labelled ready for collection from the hotel lobby at seven thirty. Porters were to collect them and take them to our platform and leave them directly opposite where our carriage, number twenty seven, would come to a halt. I had learnt more about German organisation that week before Christmas, particularly their railway system that I would never forget. It truly amazed me.

Time fast approached the point when I would again have to face the group without Libby, an ordeal, the thought of which caused me to perspire abnormally. I felt the sweat trickling down my back even before I even left our room it was unreal. There was no way I could go into breakfast feeling and looking like I did. I tried to sneak down by the back staircase for the last but one time, creep out of the hotel and get a breath of fresh air, maybe go and get some travel pills and so hope to cool down. Not a chance! As I was about to exit the front door of the hotel I was snaffled by Sid who called over to me and began asking questions. Our conversation alerted one or two other sharp-eared members of our group who stood and stared wide-eyed at us. Sid moved closer to me on account of his marginalised hearing to talk some more. He spoke very quietly asking

'How are you Tony and how is Libby? I cannot believe what I have been listening to from some folk who jolly well ought to know better speculating about this and that where Libby and you are concerned. I admit I told some of them they had no right to talk about you both in the manner they were because they did not know any facts and they were indulging in hearsay most of which was libellous. I hope you don't mind me having said as much. So my friend tell me how is your wife she must be absolutely distraught in her surroundings?'

I spoke very slowly and quietly hoping only Sid would hear what I said. At least that was my intention. It didn't help that I had got him on his wrong side where his hearing was at its most challenging. In the end I explained to him that I had not seen Libby since about half past one the previous morning. It was no good though because I had to keep repeating myself so he got the gist of what I was saying, most of it at normal volume which meant the nosey parkers who were trying to ear-hole opposite, heard every word.

'I suppose she will be glad to return to London just as we are. But if I know her, she will not have slept a wink of sleep these last two nights. The first night we were both isolated and questioned separately and because I was released I was hoping, naturally, she would be released with me. I can only surmise they think they have some other evidence they will have used against her, or have accused her of. I don't know what that evidence could be Sid but thanks for asking' I replied hoping that it would satisfy that grand old man who had, over the last few days, become a real chum.

'She'll be alright just you wait and see. They have added two and two together and got three I am pretty sure.' And with that he bid me farewell and went towards the dining room after I had I told him I would not be joining him for breakfast that morning. It was comforting to have the support of friends like Sid. He, for instance, had seen a lot of the world, travelled widely with the BBC and worked for them first in London as a programme editor and later as a producer of radio programmes. His experience came out in some of the conversations we'd had with him on the trip and his stories of celebrities he'd met, and their behaviour at times was most revealing and informative, enough to make anyone blush.

David and Margie appeared just as I was leaving the hotel lobby and asked if I was going into breakfast. I waved back indicating I was going outside of the hotel hoping they would know what I meant. I also pointedly waved, apologetically I suppose, to the two ladies who I knew by sight but not by name, who had been nosing in on my conversation with Sid waiting for some salacious comment or other. Being outside the hotel in bitterly cold weather soon brought me back to my senses and woke me up as I walked past the road-works outside the hotel on my way to find a chemist in the station. I caught Elizabeth and Mavis returning to the hotel fully laden with their rations for the journey home. The Knuckle Brothers too waved at me smiling again as they shot past on the other side of the concourse loaded with food and drinks again for the journey presumably, though that was not necessarily the case knowing those two chaps. Finally, taking a last stroll together in Cologne were John and Martha oblivious to the chap waving to them as they walked on by in their own world. Dermot had not seen me either as he too was collecting enough food for half the party. In the chemist I thought it ironic that back home Libby bought my travel pills without me being present, and there I was without her doing the same. How I wanted to be with her. What would those next few hours present?

At bang on eight o'clock after one last close look and a few prayers said in the direction of cathedral I crossed the threshold back into the hotel for what was to be my last time. The cases had been collected and taken long before and some of the guests were already standing around waiting, wrapped-up warm, ready to take their last short walk to the station. I went up in the lift to my room and before my last visit to the loo checked to see if anything may have escaped both my attention and my packing. It was what Libby always did before vacating any establishment we had frequented for the last time. She had never trusted me to complete the check always casting her eyes around the place even if I had had a man's look first. I found the situation different. I took one last lingering look around the room I had shared with my wife for two and a half nights, switched off the lights, opened the door and let it close by itself before disappearing down the back staircase also for the last time. In the hotel lobby I checked out returning my room keys at reception. It was eight fourteen and I had made it with one minute to spare. The Germans would have been impressed. We set off for the station.

A niggling thought occurred to me as I paused, turning round to take a final look back at the hotel. I became agitated wondering whether Libby really would be travelling on the same trains as us back to Brussels and London. I would soon find out that was for sure.

There filling most of the scene in front of us was the huge monolith that was the railway station. Pulsating, dynamic and extensive on its own, it dispatched passengers and their luggage into the bosom of Cologne, transported them to other towns and cities all over Germany and Europe and sat dominating the city it served so well much the same as the cathedral. It always created in me a child-like fantasy and invention that held my imagination when I stood and looked at it in total awe. On my final journey towards it I felt like some dignitary, not that I was of course but with my new trusted chaperones around me I certainly felt like one. My newly formed and very concerned loyal acquaintances had formed a circle of support round me from the moment we all left the hotel. Dermot and Sid walked in front, David and Margie on one side and Elspeth bless her on the other. Lastly Mary and Jenny walked closely behind and the whole formation and support of those people gave me a warm glow inside that cold Tuesday morning. I only wished Libby had been able to see the support that was given to me on her behalf. I wept openly as that demonstration of support for Libby edged ever nearer the station for the last time. Platform five was on the hotel side of the station. As we approached it my heart beat faster in anticipation that I may have got the faintest glimpse of Libby on the platform with her 'minders'. The time will be forever etched in my memory. I could see on the large clock above us it was eight twenty-five when we set foot on the platform and, despite having peered into every space, doorway, lift-shaft and shop on the way up to it, I had not seen a glimmer of Libby or her police escorts. Not that was until we as a group gathered by our cases, left at the precise point where carriage number twenty seven would come to a halt, just like Adele said it would. Waiting, talking and shuffling about on the platform we watched a stopping train on its way to Mainz arrive and leave just before ours was due to arrive. At eight forty-two, I was still monitoring the clock above us when David who had stopped off earlier to find a British newspaper to read on the journey home, arrived breathlessly in front of me. He spoke far too quickly for me to understand what he was trying to say his words tumbling out of his mouth incoherently.

'I've just seen her' he said puffing and blowing, 'I've just seen Libby walk out of a lift at the end of this platform with two Met Police officers at least that's what I think they were.'

I froze rigid on hearing those words. Words that I had wanted to hear for over twenty four hours. Why the stiffening in my body? Because I didn't know what to do, which way to turn or what to say at that instant I was both happy and angry. I suppose I wanted to run off and see Libby, hold her, cuddle her, kiss her but that was impossible because the train to Brussels breezed in bang on time and I knew with two cases to load on the train I would not get to see Libby and place my luggage on the train as well. Incredibly and simultaneously Boris Holloway, our German lawyer appeared from out of nowhere, shook my hand, and wished both Libby and me good luck with our case before departing the platform as quickly as he'd emerged in front of me. It was too much for me to take in at once and, distracted temporarily from David's comments, I looked down the platform towards where I believed Libby to be. Though tall enough to see over most people's heads all I was able to see were several German Police in uniform around the point where David had seen Libby. But there was no sign of Libby herself. I realised too that I wouldn't see her either if I didn't get on the train and stop dithering about instead of ignoring the shouts of friends imploring me to get on the train. At least Libby was travelling with me though we were separated by several carriages. All of that activity and excitement had lasted less than sixty seconds which was why the train began pulling out of the station, as usual, on time. The majority of the group had barely sat in their correct seats and with me having only just closed the carriage door, there was the usual chaos as the train gathered speed. The commotion, always present I learnt in such a situation, escalated as the ceremony of lifting cases onto overhead luggage racks began all over again. With that task completed, and being as there were spare seats in our carriage, I moved away from the rest of the group and sat on my own to contemplate any next move I might make.

No sooner had I sat down than Dermot came over and asked me to move back and sit with him. I refused politely. I told him not to be offended it was just that I needed to be alone for some time whilst I mulled one or two things over in my head. I knew what I was about to try and do and wanted to be on my own when I set off to do it. I didn't want any distractions. Our new guide Adele came and asked if I was ok as, surprisingly, did John of the Knuckle Brothers on his way to the bar as usual before nine o'clock in the morning. Selfish of me I knew but I could not erase the thought of Libby from my mind and how and what she must have been feeling now she was on our train. In the plight she was in I knew she would be distraught and with all that grief constantly gnawing away at her she would become completely hysterical. How she was coping without me because we'd never been separated since we married I could not imagine. What she must have been thinking if she had been informed of any news of her change of circumstances and impending journey was anybody's guess. Just thinking of her in that continued predicament left me totally neurotic too. Crucially I knew only too well that when problems had occurred in our life together they were always best sorted when we both put our minds to them, not one or the other. That was impossible but I hoped she would be able to keep her spirits up long enough until we were together again whenever that was to be.

Chapter Fifteen.

Conversations I had with other group members regarding my self-imposed segregation concluded with me expressing the same comments: 'Thanks, but no thanks. Please don't think me rude I just wish to be on my own.' What they couldn't know was that I was poised ready to sneak off from them through the door to the next compartment behind me and continue walking through the train stopping only when I found my wife. Try as I might to begin my clandestine journey I was hindered at every turn. First there was Sid who came and asked me why I was sitting by myself. Again without being rude I said I just wanted to be on my own because I was too tired to socialise with others. It may have looked odd sitting away from the others and being on my own, but I hoped it wasn't misinterpreted as being anti-social.

Adele our new guide on the journey home asked me more than once to join in with the rest of the group. Each time I told her a little white lie that I didn't want to sit with the rest of the party because I needed to get some rest. In fairness to her she would leave me on each occasion without appearing to be offended as she returned to sit with Elizabeth and Mavis who were never without a coffee at their table courtesy of German Railways. When I did at last stand up and pretend to have a good stretch next to my aisle seat, readying myself to go walkabout along the carriages behind me, my mobile phone rang. It was my daughter Caroline wanting to know if there was news of any progress with her mum. I told her all that had happened and what I'd seen or been told that morning hoping she would be happy with my explanation particularly as her mum was on the same train travelling to Brussels. She seemed content that some progress had been made no matter how small and asked to be kept in touch with any further news when I was back in London.

The phone call over, and with the coast clear, I was ready to hatch my plan. I tried to make my first move but would you believe a steward arrived from behind me and unknowingly blocking my exit asked if I would like any drinks. I declined his offer rather brusquely and followed behind him out of our carriage and into the adjoining one as the train began slowing down. It was about to come to a halt in Aachen. Out of the blue, and even now I cannot believe what possessed me, another crazy idea popped into my head. I knew the train would stop in the station for a minute or two to offload or take on new passengers. Thinking I was clever I thought I could maybe get off too, run along the platform to the rear end of the train where I assumed Libby to be and see if I could see her. So that is what I did. That brainstorm almost ended in total disaster for me. I had forgotten how long German trains could be with their endless carriages as I jumped onto the platform before the train came to a halt. The platform was jammed tight with passengers. Bumping into several waiting to board the train it seemed I was thwarted in every way as I dodged in and out of bodies along the platform. And then it happened, the moment my brain turned to jelly. Loud enough for me to hear, but ignore, those little bleeps rang out that signal the carriage doors were about to close. Shit! And where was I when doors began to close? Still wandering about on the platform that's what nowhere near Libby's carriage and with no chance of seeing her especially as it looked like I was about to become stranded on the platform and miss the train. I watched as the doors began to close and panicked.

I hadn't wanted to sit with the rest of the party when the cases were loaded onto the train and so, whilst alone on that platform the penny dropped at the predicament I could perhaps shortly find myself in. No Libby, no train, no clothes and alone in Aachen. In a flash I wished I had stayed on the train and not been so crazy as to believe I could see Libby. All seemed lost in a moment of stupidity. But wait, relief was at hand. The only reason that I got back on the train at all was because my little Irish mate Dermot had been taking a breath of Aachen fresh air himself. Getting back onto the train he was casually looking around the platform when he caught a glimpse of me looking marooned as the bleeps sounded to close the doors. Summing up my predicament from five carriages away in seconds he bravely left his foot in the carriage doorway so the doors would not close but remain open when the door hit his foot. Dermot called my name alerting me to what he'd done and, realising what was about to occur, I succeeded in jumping into the nearest carriage and once inside gratefully made my way back to the group to thank a smiling Dermot as he waited for me before giving me the king of all bollockings.

Alone again I could think more clearly after my near calamity. I again found myself thinking of Libby and coping, or not coping with her dilemma. Her arrest, supposedly based on suspicion of kidnap and murder, had made me really ill with worry for her. I felt totally inadequate being unable to help her let alone see her to talk to. Of course there was categorically no way she could have done the deeds she had been accused of, I knew that. I took great comfort from the fact that Dermot, David and Margie were towers of strength and support for me at that difficult time. I needed though to clarify one or two few issues about our arrest whilst I was alone and began making a mental list. For instance I knew Dennis Johnson had been with our group throughout the holiday until Sunday night when he was missing from the brewery; he had regularly taken drinks in the bar with members of our group; he had chatted away amiably with all and sundry at any time of day or night he was required to and had sat at our breakfast table albeit briefly to hand out notes, information and maps; he had walked for a while round the Christmas Market in Aachen with us but for all that had later simply disappeared into thin air. That had nothing to do with my wife or me, yet somehow I had to try and prove Libby was innocent. But how and where would I start? All I'd done up to then was shout at people in authority after I had been released and that got me no-where.

I hadn't envied the position Johnson found himself in with some people over problems with food in Cologne. It cannot have been easy with what many of us thought was the loud and unnecessary argument he entered into with the 'Knuckle Brothers', John and Kevin, after the Dinner on the Rhine. So why hadn't they been arrested over Johnson's disappearance? Admittedly John had been taken away for a lengthy interview but that was all. Even so everybody and their neighbour must have heard the shouting that went on after that Saturday night on the Rhine. It looked like coming to blows at one point during the fracas so there must have been aspersions cast in their direction. If not, why not? However, that came with the territory and was part of Johnson's job to sort out tourists' problems and grievances, albeit not the violent bit. He had though chosen to be a tour rep hadn't he? No doubt he had taken stick from other trippers in our hotel too especially when the hotel's central heating and air conditioning failed on the first evening we arrived, in the middle of winter and on the fourth floor.

My head was spinning with the traffic that was passing through it and my thinking was muddled again. I began to lose sight of my main objective and my mind blanked as we continued at speed through the Belgian countryside towards Brussels. All I wanted was to get a glimpse Libby somehow, anyhow. I had been foiled at every turn I ventured as stewards came and went serving drinks and breakfast to passengers in the carriage. I couldn't face either. I wanted to get cracking and move along the carriages and find Libby. I stood aside to let another steward through the door of our carriage and following a quick glance towards the breakfast-munching group, I left through the same door he had gone through. The train left Aachen some fifteen minutes before I was able to put my plan into action and so was moving very fast when I began. Nevertheless it was so smooth and therefore made my passage through the train that much easier. Carriage after carriage came and went in my search and I genuinely lost track of the number I passed through. It must have been twelve or thirteen carriages before I came upon a door that would not open. Despite lots of pulling and pushing really hard and giving it a good kicking, the damn door would not open or shift.

My progress had terminated at what I realised was the train's and as such Libby's temporary 'black Maria'. I slumped down dejectedly on the arm of a seat nearby staring blankly at the locked door. It was when I gradually turned round and slowly raised my head I noticed out of the corner of one eye that I was being watched by a speechless and goggle-eyed group of people. They were passengers in the open carriage all of whom watched terrified at what I had been trying to achieve in front of them and what I may have looked like doing next.

I had to get out of that carriage fast and away from those poor souls. I was so embarrassed that I stood and moved gingerly off my seat at first before walking quickly back down the carriage becoming redder in the face and repeating over and over as I walked

'Sorry, I am so sorry, please forgive me.' Whether they understood me or not I have no idea. What I do know is that they were not happy and smiling at me as I walked past many of them backing away from me in their seats perhaps expecting me to lash out and hit or kick them like I had done to the door in front of them. The wonder to me was that nobody on the other side of the door I attacked and assaulted tried to open the flaming thing from the other side to see what the commotion and noise was about.

Arriving back in what had been the relative tranquillity and sanctuary of the group it seemed my arrival in such an apparently distressed state disturbed the equilibrium of peace and calm that had always been a factor of the trip so far that morning. That was until I went walkabout. Adele our new petite and brunette guide wandered over to me and asked where I had been for that last half hour. I told her my stomach had been dodgy and that she would be silly to use the toilet on the right hand side through the connecting door of our carriage. She said she had just returned from it, had used it before I returned to my seat and that I couldn't have been in the toilet. Had I made some mistake? I stared at her not quite understanding why she persisted in questioning me about a toilet. Clearly aware of the situation that had arisen over her missing colleague Dennis Johnson she had tried hard to smooth out some of the problems our group had experienced following his supposed disappearance. She had gone from table to table in an effort to keep people abreast of company policy in such a situation which cannot have been easy for a young tour guide. Her excellent communication skills eased what could have been a tricky situation for Pineapple Rail Tours. She had also spent time phoning a variety of companies in the UK attempting to allay people's fears over not only the money needed for our extra day's emergency living expenses, but also phoned some of the employers and relatives of the group explaining the problem for our delay. Give her credit though, she never questioned me from Cologne to London about Libby's arrest and treated me the same as any other Pineapple Tours' traveller. I respected her for that.

The train slowed and eventually came to a full-stop in Liege station as Dermot popped across the aisle and came and sat opposite me politely asking me in his own inimitable way

'You're not about to repeat that trick you played on us earlier at Aachen are you Tony?'

I said I certainly would not repeat any more stupidity at my age, not that kind anyhow and asked him how long it would be before we arrived at Brussels my next chance to get a possible sighting of Libby. He said it would take an hour if we were to arrive on time. I asked him if he'd heard members of the party discussing anything about Libby during the journey. My guilt showing I suppose for not having been sociable enough or talking fifteen to the dozen as usual to anyone since leaving Cologne.

'Not really some of them thought it unnecessary to delay them getting home and back to work, some have enjoyed the extra day's holiday. Apparently Elspeth should've had a meeting with some chaps in the government today and her phone has been going twenty-five to the dozen. The brothers should have been back at work too but they are so laid back they nearly fall over. I find it strange though after they had their little upsets with Johnson. I don't think they seem too worried either. Though I must say that in my interview with the police I said I thought the brothers might have had something to do with Johnson's disappearance. Especially after the way they spoke to him and threatened him on the Saturday night. I know it's always wise after the horse has bolted so to say but I feared for Johnson's life back then, I really did. Of the rest most are pensioners and when the boss copper last night let them call home to their families for free they thought he was great. Do you know Tony some of them were still up well after midnight phoning so they were? Adele has been a real sweetie helping out too she's a good kid, I like her so I do.'

I thanked him for his kindness and sympathy just before I dozed off his last few words echoing in my ears and it was only when the train seemingly jerked to a halt in a station some time later that I awoke.

'Just outside the main Brussels Midi station,' one of the anoraks called out loudly so everyone in the carriage could hear.

My thoughts returned to Dermot and I couldn't help but think that he had been so kind throughout the whole weekend to me and Libby and noticeably to me after Libby was 'removed' from the tour party. It was difficult not to be touched by his kindness and generosity. I thought he had such a big heart which more than made up for his lack of height. My daydreaming came to an abrupt halt as the train pulled into the main Brussels railway station and stopped sharply. Slowly disgorging its passengers and their luggage as they waited patiently to leave the train, when my turn came to leave I collected my two cases and placed them next to David and Margie's on the platform. I asked them to keep an eye on them I ran towards the back end of the train. I approached the very last carriage and stood on tiptoe and began jumping a few extra inches off the floor. I could just about make out, at the top of my jump above most of the crowd of passengers, the back of a small figure disappearing into a darkened lift area at the end of the platform. Two very large people, one who was very close to the smaller person, appeared to be escorting the smaller figure towards the darker area and into the lift. I recognised the smaller figure as Libby presumably still handcuffed and uncomfortable. I just knew from her body position, with her rounded shoulders and her head hanging down that she was uncomfortable and her mind in turmoil. Had she been afforded any dignity on the journey I asked myself? A drink or two maybe, or perhaps a visit to the toilet, doubtless all the time handcuffed to a police officer.

'Libby, Libby' I screamed at the top of my voice, 'It's me Tony. Call back if you can hear me.' They could well have heard my shouts back in the UK but my shouting and screaming was all to no avail because as I reached the top of the lift shaft the incumbents had vacated the lift which by the time I had got to it was empty below me. I looked at my watch. It showed five past eleven. Oh my God I thought only another three and a half hours to wait around before our next train left for London. I thought about dumping my cases in a left luggage office which would enable me to move about the station and even stroll in the lunchtime air. I walked about slowly wondering how I would really occupy my time. My God I suddenly remembered I had forgotten about David and Margie who were waiting patiently for me to return to them to collect my two cases. I apologised profusely for having left them so long hanging about when all the others in our group had disappeared off the platform. I asked them how they would spend their three hours before departure to London.

'Adele explained to us how to get into central Brussels by underground train and David and I thought we'd go visit and have a meal in a Brussels bistro. You are more than welcome to come with us Tony,' Margie offered kindly as was her usual way.

'I don't think I will under the circumstances, but thanks for the offer. I'd rather sit around and contemplate a few things and maybe have a beer. I'll be OK you go ahead' I replied and walked with them down the stairs to where they left me as they made their way to the underground station.

'See you later,' I said and they waved back heading into the city of Brussels whilst I carried on and into the huge concourse of Brussels Midi Station. Now what was it I was going to do for the next three hours prior to the connection to London I asked myself by which time Libby and all the rest of the Pineapple Tours Group were conspicuous by their absence several of them having preceded David and Margie and gone into Brussels for a couple of hours. I wandered around the station's shopping malls, idly peering into shop windows and taking in the smell of fried onions and burgers, or the whiff of beer at the bars I passed. The constant waft of tobacco smells and other sweeter noxious substances couldn't hide the fact that we were in a foreign country. Passengers from all over the world walked or sprinted past me searching for their rail connections to who knows where. Europeans, Asians and Africans came and went and yet nothing could remove from my mind, not even for one second, what I considered to be the unmitigated, false and unjustified arrest of my wife Libby Russell.

I sat on bench somewhere once more trying to compile a list of some of the occurrences over the last forty eight hours. Who I thought might be involved; what had been said in my company; had I noticed anything unusual in the hotel or during any of our journeys from Cologne to Brussels? I'd compiled so many of those lists in my mind particularly one listing the people we had befriended, had spoken to, waved to, sat near to or eaten with. The list was so long it mashed up my brain again so all the information was scrambled and I was unable make any sense of it. Another lost list.

After ten minutes contemplating my navel, the continual announcements of train arrivals and departures over the loudspeakers began to get on my nerves so I took a walk outside the station for a change of scenery and some hoped for peace and quiet. What a mistake that was. It was even colder than in Cologne even though surrounded by tall office buildings on all sides and with a straight road that ran down the middle between them. Thereby lay another problem. Walking along the path between the buildings the gap between them had created ideal vortex-like conditions as if it were a wind tunnel with the wind really pressing and contorting one's facial features. I walked for what must have been half an hour not that I can really remember. Unable to get Libby's face out of my mind or the situation she was still in only served to sew more confusion and that feeling of inadequacy in my mind. I knew for certain she wouldn't be eating or drinking not with only one leg of the journey to go. Without me to support her Libby would have undoubtedly come across as truculent to the police officers she was with because of her stubborn refusal to communicate with anyone in a situation that was beyond her control. Scorpio she was born you see, and they are the most stubborn in the whole of the universe when they want to be, or have to be.

I wandered into a bar and spent some time slowly drinking coffee whilst continuing to trawl through the list of notes I'd compiled checking to see if any one of them would trigger some inspirational breakthrough and help for Libby. Nothing like that happened so I upped and left both the coffee and the bar.

Chapter Sixteen.

I looked again at my watch. It was one forty four and there was less than an hour before our train left for London. I made my way back to the station and joined the queue at the passport control ready for the now usual security inspection. I had forgotten for a moment that Libby's passport had been confiscated by the German police so it was only when I had to produce mine that I remembered about Libby's. I presumed the Met Police would have it and deal with the Custom's procedures in such a situation.

At precisely two o'clock the gates to the Eurostar Lounge opened and the waiting queue, that was then quite lengthy, pressed forward. Passports were checked as the queue moved forward constantly until the bag check began and that preceded a scramble for seats in the lounge. Some passengers were pulled to one side out of the queue and questioned further for some reason or other by the security people before they were allowed through. When my turn came a lady checked my passport and waved me through without making any mention of my wife's situation, but then I thought, why would she? I sauntered slowly through the gate and into the cavernous and anonymous lounge and waiting area that preceded the last section of my journey only to be greeted by the sight of several of our tour party who coincidentally just happened to have perched themselves as close as possible to the bar and were already enjoying some liquid refreshment before their journey. Irrespective of my refusal to join them because I still had little or no desire to socialise with people, and despite people being very friendly towards me, I felt like a real old grump but couldn't help it. I thought too deep down that they were unsure of me let alone Libby.

It was while I was seated, waiting in a sort of in-between never-land frame of mind and contemplating what the next few hours of self-imposed solitude would bring that Adele came over and sat by me, enquired as to my well-being and whether or not anyone had contacted me on my mobile about Libby. I told her politely no-one had phoned so far, that I was knackered and very worried about Libby's state of mind chiefly because I hadn't seen her to speak to for ages. I also mentioned that I was still trying to fathom out what had happened to us these last couple of days since Libby's arrest as it all seemed like a bad dream.

'As a matter of interest, have either of the two police forces involved been in touch with you or your company about Libby Adele?' I asked sounding rather like a sheepish schoolboy.

'All I know for certain is that Libby is being held in a police holding-cell somewhere in this station and should be escorted to the train at the very last moment by the Belgian Police as well as the escort from the Met. And probably as before, she'll be held towards the rear of the train. Other than that I'm sorry I've neither heard nor know of anything further.' Adele confirmed my own thinking that a security screen had been placed around Libby making any contact with her impossible. Adele left me to attend to other passenger's needs and I settled back on my bench and composed myself before the final leg of the journey.

When the announcer informed the waiting passengers that they could begin boarding the train to London, the rush towards the ticket barriers began. For the umpteenth time we had to show our tickets causing the customary obstruction as the melee of people charged towards the platform on escalators. Further panic and anguish came over me: what would happen when the train terminated at St Pancras. It was predictable Libby would be carted off and be taken away again for questioning. The German police had mentioned that the day before. I hadn't an inkling of where that would be but would make it my priority to find out in London.

Coach sixteen waited on the platform for us like some beached whale. Our home-going tour party, minus one, was busy getting on board the train for the last time on that holiday. Routinely our cases were neatly arranged on the platform adjacent to one of the coach's doors ready for us to collect. Inside, having stacked my two cases on the rack, I sat at window seat number forty seven opposite Mavis and Elizabeth. The vacant seat next to me was obviously that allocated to Libby and it too was laid ready for afternoon tea like the others were. When peace and calm at last descended into the compartment, meaning all the other cases had been placed onto the overhead racks, I looked around and noticed that Iris and Richard were comfortably seated behind me. I left my seat to go and chat to them. They'd been very good to me and Libby and I was grateful for their support these last couple of days.

'This is how we first met you Tony on the outward journey, do you remember?' Iris slipped her little nugget into the conversation as easily as she slipped into her seat.

'How could I possibly forget that moment Iris? It was a good trip too to begin with' I replied, 'not like the last few days.'

I returned to my own seat again for a moment before craning my neck looking about the carriage hoping to locate spare seats. I spotted some near the rear of the compartment. I would make my move.

'Excuse me ladies and don't think me rude I just need to be on my own for some time yet' I quietly informed Mavis and Elizabeth as I went and sat alone one more time.

The train pulled out of Brussels slowly at first creaking and clanking as it went leaving the station behind. I stared out of the window without really seeing any of the images that passed by as the train began to pick up speed. That sort of void outside my window kind of helped me concentrate as I started to ponder once more how Libby must have felt on the last leg of her journey. I assumed she was still handcuffed to a Met police woman somewhere at the rear of the train at least twenty coaches or so behind me. I could not begin to sum up my feeling of utter inadequacy so close to her. The German police, I was to find out later, had requested personal information from the Met police about Libby. It was only when they found out she had no police record that they agreed for the Met Police to escort Libby through to London where I believed she would be questioned further. What difference it would have made if she'd had a record I failed to understand, but then that is how I'd felt all night and day.

Over and over again in my mind I kept asking myself what Libby must have been thinking of me. I had been so inept having just stood by without protest when the police arrested us in the early hours that previous Monday morning. It was so totally out of character for me and yet I kept returning to the same thoughts that numbed me to the bone increasing my guilt. Had Libby slept at all that last night in her inhospitable, smelly and cold cell? Had she eaten? Did she answer her questions or clam up despite what the lawyer said? I had stared at her bed in the hotel for several minutes before I left that morning, sure I could see the indentation her body would have made had she laid on it. Mind games I know but it does play tricks on you at moments like that. That was nearly twelve hours before and now it was Tuesday evening. The trip to Cologne had been to celebrate our ruby wedding anniversary not spend the time behind bars, not prison bars anyhow. The anniversary, coincidentally the name of our grand-daughter Ruby now almost four years old, had turned out to be a complete disaster and utter shambles at the end.

There I was sat in a first class compartment ruminating on what should have been the last day of the holiday with Libby with waitresses walking by bringing complimentary drinks to the tables. I ordered a large brandy and when it came it really was a double-double. Drinking it certainly warmed me up. Funny then that as I wondered if there would there be a glass of wine for Libby, a sort of gesture of kindness to her in her current dilemma, when someone caught my attention at the far end of the compartment. Not from our group, but didn't I know them? Yes, I was sure I recognised them from somewhere, sure I recognised the person as a 'her', or was it a 'him'? Then again my sureness began to decline as I became drowsy, the brandy influencing my brain, and all thought of them disappeared from my mind.

The compartment was full mostly of our holiday group who were about to start munching their afternoon tea before arriving back in London when I deliberately moved to another of the spare seats to avoid people asking questions about Libby's arrest, and 'how was she', or 'we know she's not guilty' type of comment. All well meant of course but I found it very hard to be polite all the time when even I had little idea of how she was coping at that hour never mind that minute. I had no wish to be discourteous to the others whilst in my own turmoil at events so it made sense to move further away from them. In the meantime I hoped if I was lucky to stay awake that I might note down some of the issues concerning me before we arrived back in London. I felt I had to put it on record, because some people on the trip were taken aback by Libby's arrest the day before, she had been such a bright light in their company. Another reason I told myself for me to keep out of their way as much as possible and write some notes about what I felt, something that I'd failed to do so far. I started from the beginning that morning by tracing the start of the journey home from the hotel.

My mind began darting from one idea or thought to the next. There was no pattern only confusion. For instance I wasn't sure if any of the group had seen the police take Libby to the station in Cologne or when we changed trains in Brussels. Neither had I in truth, but I had tried to find where she was on both of the trains but was eventually deterred, for my own good, despite knowing she was seated in the last carriage on each train. Another example of my muddled thinking was that I remembered later getting off the train in Aachen to walk down the platform looking for her. How could I forget? It was only when the doors began to close, and down to the quick thinking of Dermot, that I even came to be on the train going home. Then my thoughts changed again as I recalled that even the 'Knuckle Brothers' asked if they could be of any assistance at breakfast back at the hotel. What they could have done I had no idea but it was, I suppose, an offer made out of kindness. I had thanked them and declined their help which turned out to be foolish because

I could have asked them to help me with my two heavy suit cases. I was feeling sorry for myself all of a sudden when I should have been dwelling on the plight of Libby. Selfishly I had been wrapped up in my own world when I should have counted my blessings that the German police had allowed her to travel to England that Tuesday with the Met police in tow.

Contemplating what little evidence the police had disclosed to me, or what had come out in conversation on the return trip, didn't leave me with much to go on. I had forgotten years ago that Libby had been very loosely acquainted with Johnson when she first started teaching in London. I remember him saying on the trip he had lived in the same block of flats as Libby until he married and moved to a small housing estate in Hounslow or somewhere. He said he had worked for London Transport on the Underground until he retired and then, for pocket money, became a tour rep for Pineapple Tours based in Greenwich. He reminisced with us on the journey to Aachen how good it felt to be back in the Rhineland city of his father's birth. Even going so far as to tell us of how his father had escaped to London via Russia as World War Two was breaking out. Being bilingual he was in his element for it had allowed him to indulge his passion of speaking fluent German at every opportunity especially enabling him to help and assist travellers by smoothing out hiccups on his rail trips around Germany. But just when I needed him to help me, where was he? He'd been missing since Sunday night after he failed to turn up for the visit to the Brewery. He was missing from the hotel bar and lobby when we returned that Sunday evening, something that was unusual for him, though it didn't register at the time.

Some guests said they had not seen Johnson since the Saturday evening trip on the Rhine which came as a surprise to me. Yet according to one or two guests, how they knew I have no idea, his hotel room had apparently been 'vacuumed' by forensic scientists on the Monday in the search for clues. What little evidence officer Schmidt was able to divulge to me about that bedroom search, providing them with the only clue that the police had found by that stage enabling them to detain Libby, concerned the bottle of travel pills bought from the chemist before we travelled. The Germans had queried the data on the bottle with the Met police I was to find out later following their checks with the West Midlands police. But the evidence found in Johnson's room, and the main reason Libby was under arrest, was the discovery of some hallucinatory tablets in a pill bottle. The small brown bottle was clearly labelled and dated showing it been purchased from a chemist's in Birmingham which just happened to be the one Libby had visited before the trip. Who were the only people from Birmingham on the trip? Libby and me, that's who it was. It was Libby eventually who, regardless of several persistent attempts by Johnson in asking her, was to give in eventually saying 'Yes perhaps maybe' she had vaguely recognised him earlier. The attempt to talk to her before dinner on Sunday when he called her over to speak to him was to be the last time he was seen by most of our group. I also learnt later from police in London that Libby had admitted she vaguely remembered Johnson when questioned by Schmidt on the Monday morning after our arrest. There were so many twists and turns creating further confusion as I looked for a chink of light in the police's evidence that could perhaps get Libby released.

The train picked up momentum rapidly as we left Belgium behind and began hurtling through Northern France at speeds that meant the remaining journey was less than an hour before we were due to arrive at St Pancras. Waitresses began applying their sommelier skills once more and members of our group, only too happy to comply, were the beneficiaries as more drinks and more food arrived in front of them. A short stop at Lille was over in a flash and we were on our way again. I had the feeling as I sat and watched them eat that some in the group were becoming less amicable to me as the journey elapsed. Yet only a few hours earlier nearly all of them were sympathetic to Libby's plight and supportive and friendly towards me. I am always reminded in such circumstances of a saying my dad often used to quote to me which was 'there's nowt so queer as folk'. The words seemed so relevant at that stage of the journey. Folk that had been friends seemed to avoid eye contact with me or were always in too much of a hurry when they visited the toilets at the end of each carriage whereas before they had stopped to talk asking many questions and offering support. I hadn't helped the situation having isolated myself more and more on the way home having felt less able to socialise like I had done with them when Libby was by my side. Had I imagined it or was I just being oversensitive? I don't think so. Tired yes, angry yes and annoyed that I could not be with my wife all of which contributed to deepen my malaise. Amazing how you can be so lonely with people all around you.

Those selfish thoughts I know which were forgotten and over-shadowed by a click and swoosh of the compartment door as it opened distracting my attention as another person visited the toilet. Hold on, don't I know the face of the person who just went into the toilet? I sat bolt upright, rubbing my eyes as if to confirm what I'd seen. Though not in our group, I had seen them before, of that I was certain.

At that infernal moment the train swept into the Channel Tunnel's darkness and I was caught in two minds whether to stand and wait for the mystery person's return, or forget it. We would stop at Ebbsfleet minutes later and perhaps the person was getting off the train and not visiting the toilet. That's all it was, I was too sensitive. Being in two minds I hadn't noticed the waitress by my shoulder asking if there was anything else I needed, another drink perhaps? I did order a drink after an embarrassing pause. What I needed was a large brandy. When my drink arrived in what seemed a fraction of a second I found myself completely distracted from taking a closer look at the face of the bloke I thought I recognised as he passed round the waitress who was serving me. He seized his chance when he left the toilet, seeing me talking to the waitress. Or maybe I was just fantasising and I hadn't recognised him after all and it was my imagination running riot. I felt the brandy beginning to help me to relax, or maybe it was my brain playing tricks with me again. Either way I was knackered and worn out and fell asleep. When I woke up we were well into bright winter sunshine and beginning to slow down as we approached to stop briefly at Ebbsfleet. I had fallen asleep with the brandy glass wedged in my right hand. Fortunately the contents were well gone and my trousers dry.

The last leg of the journey into London had begun when our new rep Adele decided to come and pay me a visit sitting in the spare seat next to me to ask a few questions. She began by saying she was glad I hadn't tried to reach Libby since Brussels and then asked how I was. Did I think Libby would have coped with her isolation on the train and how did I think she would cope in a London police cell? Would I be going as support with her to attend further sessions of questioning and lots of other silly questions that frankly at that stage began to irritate. I think she realised she had picked the wrong moment because she wished me and Libby the best of luck as she returned to her seat. Luck, bloody luck I asked myself. Who was she kidding? It was only a complete coincidence she was arrested in the first place by my reckoning. The only link was the bottle of pills that I presumed sad old Dennis Johnson had taken at some point in his room allegedly bought from a Birmingham chemist. There was no way that they could link them to Libby of that I was certain. She had known Johnson years ago but wouldn't have recognised him again on the street in a million years let alone hold a conversation with him for God's sake.

The train slowed right down to a crawl as it entered St. Pancras station and once again passengers throughout the carriages began preparing to disembark before it had stopped. I was surprised even members of our party stood and put their coats on in readiness to retrieve their cases before the train finally pulled to a stop. Others in our group busied themselves swapping addresses and telephone numbers promising to write and phone one another once they reached home. That end of holiday ritual was soon forgotten when the people arrived home and returned to their daily routines. Some I swear, as I sat amongst them, began muttering about Libby and her arrest deliberately loud enough for me to hear now the journey was almost over. Others approached me asking me what I thought would happen next to Libby. A couple asked if she would be in the papers or on the TV. I tried hard to back off and understand their views but found it impossible. I just became angrier with folk who had been friends only hours before. However, I shook hands with David and Margie and said I really hoped when all the kerfuffle was over that we could meet again and I stood and gave Dermot a hug and said I'd write to him and let him know what happened from there on in. All three then joined the queue their cases trailing behind and moved towards the door. I was saddened to see them go because I realised what good support they had been throughout the last couple of arduous days.

The train lurched gently to a halt on the platform and passengers were thrown forwards, then backwards and sideways. Doors, though still locked for safety, were tampered with by passengers in a hurry to leave long before the locks were lifted. Once opened passengers jumped off the train to start running, walking and carrying or trailing their cases behind them. I just sat and watched all the hustle and bustle from my seat.

Chapter Seventeen.

Looking out of the window contemplating what my next move on behalf of Libby ought to be when the wake up call I'd been waiting for hit me like a bolt of lightening, so obvious it was untrue. Two people who had kept popping up all over the place those last four days, in England or Germany I wasn't sure, came floating past my window walking very quickly and acting sheepishly their faces mostly hidden. Most peculiarly they walked without any luggage, except for the woman who had a small hand-bag round her neck. Something not quite right there I thought. I knew I wasn't imagining things: we'd been aware of them and had sightings of them in a variety of places, round corners or on trains, at several markets throughout Germany and now outside my carriage. I'd have instantly recognised the bastards anywhere because they had been up to no good most of the time we saw them, staring at us and then moving off when we espied them. But there they were, but where was their luggage because there were no porters with them? Why were they not carrying any luggage? I jumped up quickly out of my seat and excusing myself for pushing into people, headed for the luggage area of the carriage where all the cases had been stored. I began to rapidly lift the cases off the luggage racks and move those by the floor near to the door just to try and get to mine.

With adrenalin surging through my veins the cases I lifted up and placed on the platform were like featherweights. Reaching for Libby's case and my own I was about to remove them when I was distracted by a horrible and putrid smell which certainly did not come from the nearby toilets. Someone pointed to the floor in disgust. What was the liquid leaking out from one of the cases next to my foot? Ugh the stink! The liquid was a reddish colour or reddish brown and looked as if it was congealed too. Someone screamed that it was blood. Pandemonium broke out.

'Oh my God' I blurted out, 'those cases have got our old luggage labels on them. Look, see the writing on my cases here, it's the same' I said as people were still trying to get past and behind me to get off the train.

'How the hell has that happened because these are my cases next to me? There's something wrong here I know because those are not my cases. I bet the labels were stolen not lost back in Cologne.' I was yelling loudly at anyone listening close by. Many had a frightened look on their face staring at me as if I was mad, but holding their noses as I spoke. The smell was so nauseating and awful that the remaining few people near me were stuck, like me, amongst the mountain of cases I had not yet been able to sort out and place out onto the platform.

Something was seriously wrong in that luggage area and I had to act and think quickly or I was back in the doodoo. I stood up for a breather, the stench being overpowering, just as Libby and two burly Met police-women walked past our coach with Libby still handcuffed to an officer. I could do nothing but stand and watch as I gasped for breath with those two gruesome cases at my feet. Simultaneously, several passengers pushed past and left with their case in one hand and their other hand over their faces to get away from the smell while they were still able. I was left with a queue of elderly people waiting for their cases, unable to move forward or backwards without injuring themselves. Even I became stuck and the more I tried the more I was hindered each time. My pleas to move past people were completely ignored. However I did manage to break free and get back into the compartment by a window that I banged and knocked on so hard I almost broke it. The whole caper had taken but a micro-second but I was trapped. I called out Libby's name loudly, and I mean loudly. Her head swivelled round as if she recognised my voice but didn't know where it came from and the moment was lost.

Again I felt hopeless. I had a dozen or so nervous faces all watching me and wondering what had become of the mad man in front of them. I shouted again, even louder, still hoping to attract her attention but all I did was to arouse the interest of two police officers fairly close by. They arrived by the door of the carriage as the last passenger apart from me left the train. They asked what all the commotion was about and why I was shouting. Forgetting Libby for a moment I pointed out to the officers the two cases on the floor particularly the one with the liquid seeping from it. The officers too began holding their noses and asking what the smell was. One of the officers got off the train after studying the scene in front of him for a few seconds, took out his radio and radioed for help whilst the other officer asked if I knew who they belonged too. I told him I didn't know who they belonged to but that for some unknown reason that I could not explain they had my name on them both. The puzzled look he gave me meant I was going to have some serious explaining to do.

Looking totally puzzled at what they saw one of them who gave me a curious look asked if I knew how long the cases had been there. I told him presumably from Brussels but could not confirm it, how could I? With passengers from other parts of the train walking past gawping at the sight of two police officers standing inside the carriage door, and with several of the train's stewards looking on, police reinforcements arrived on the platform and stood around the door to the carriage our group had been in.

I was still shaking with shock next to the two policemen still observing the cases where the smell came from when I became surrounded by more police officers than I was comfortable to share space with. Sirens that screamed and echoed deafeningly in the enclosed space of the station got closer to us. By now all disembarked passengers had left the platform and when the sirens eventually fell silent all I could hear was a senior police officer somewhere bellowing orders out to his team. Station staff and I were all that remained on the platform apart from the police and my own genuine cases, and of course the putrid ones. I had wondered if the train and its passengers would be isolated or put into a form of police quarantine in order to facilitate the questioning of the passengers. But it was too late because the train was empty and the passengers gone. I was the lone civilian left behind on the platform and I was about to be questioned by an enormous police sergeant who had clearly seen better days. He asked what was my association with the train was; how had I come across those putrid and suspect cases? How come the labels on them had my name and address on them? He was not too happy when I explained about Libby which, when he confirmed my version of events via his police radio, seemed satisfied I was being honest with him and became more easygoing after that.

Passengers who had congregated on adjacent platforms stood and stared across at what was unfolding in front of their eyes. All became a blank to them when another express pulled onto their platform obscuring the view. Even me the police sergeant and a couple of other officers were moved off the platform and out of the way as forensic officers arrived. My only observation of that scene, though short, was long enough for me to see that a tent-like fixture had already been erected around the door to what had been our carriage.

No sooner had I begun walking again towards the exit, a case of mine in each hand, than I found myself being escorted away from the upstairs platform by a pair of female officers.

I was thinking more clearly then and asked one of the female officers if she had any idea which was the most likely police station they might have taken Libby too after I had explained the situation. After making a call from her radio to some control room in another police station I presumed she told me that Libby had been taken to Paddington Green Police Station.

I said my farewell to the WPC's before entering the lift to descend to the shopping area below with my cases. I couldn't just leave that platform though with my luggage without turning round and having one last glance back towards the carriage. I caught a glimpse of two people in white spacemen-like coats lifting each of the suspect cases very gingerly one at a time into a waiting police van. The last recollection I have as the lift descended was the van then driving off along the platform and out of the station precinct with its cargo. Downstairs I continued walking to the taxi rank. It was my intention to hail a taxi immediately: some hope. The queue was ridiculously long and even with the volume of taxis in London took several minutes before I was able to set off for Paddington Green Police Station. Once inside the taxi, and after instructing the driver where to go, my brain was tormented by the two unknowns that I'd seen plenty of but did not know. I kept getting flashbacks of instances that had occurred at various times whether in the presence of Libby, David or Margie and particularly Dermot. Throughout that taxi journey I got reminders and prompts of seeing that odd and unidentified couple in the most offbeat places in Germany. I was fairly sure I had seen them hanging around when I was with Libby, in or near some of our hotels we had stayed in, even the one in London the night before we left. They must have been travelling on the same trains we travelled on from city to city. Come to think of it I remembered seeing them at the Aachen Christmas Fair last Saturday but I never saw them close enough or had a clear view of their faces. Even so there were features I'd recognise enough to place them in a police line-up. They always seemed to be somewhere in the background, behind a stall, at the end of a street, in an alleyway or simply blending into the crowds whilst we were in Germany I'd swear to it.

I wondered if they had been with us along every step of the way on our break. But who the hell were they? The question preyed on my mind so much I started fidgeting in my taxi seat moving from side to side, crossing my legs, uncrossing my legs, cupping my head in my hands, scratching my head with thumb and forefinger and pressing on my eyes I was that desperate searching for answers. I never looked out of the taxi window once during the whole of the journey. Over and over again I asked myself what type of person would involve Libby and me in such awful circumstances the like of which we had found ourselves these last two days.

While I struggled in the back of the taxi to slot those two mystery persons somewhere in our life the taxi driver tried every way he could to winkle his way quickly through the London rush hour traffic. In the end he had to settle for second best and join the crawl like every-one else. It was considerably darker when he stopped suddenly to allow some kids on a crossing on their way home from school at the end of term, put their lives at risk in front of his cab. The looks and language that came from the children was symptomatic of what our country had become – needless to say the expletives aimed towards the taxi were far from poetic. Traffic was at a standstill all over the place: horns blared, drivers shouted obscenities from their vehicle windows at some poor lorry driver, or a pedestrian putting their life on the line crossing the road. Only the pedestrians seemed to be moving. I asked myself why anyone would consider living with such congestion. The crawl speeded up and we soon headed out on the West Way, or A40 road, that would take us to the police station. Eventually that became so grid-locked because of a shunt between a pair of vans but it was still possible to see my concrete police station long before I arrived there, its sixteen stories of lights visible for miles around like some gigantic Christmas tree.

It was half an hour after leaving St. Pancras that I arrived at Paddington Green Police Station. I paid off the taxi driver, waved him farewell as he headed for more gridlock and then lugged my cases into the police station. After clambering up so many steps I was only too glad to have a rest at the top of them. Inside I had difficulty at first looking for somewhere I should check in. Help was not far away. Unfortunately Mr Grumpy was on security that evening. Who was I and what did I want asked Mr Grumpy the surly security guard? Why guards in a police station? Had I proof of identity? Fortunately I remembered my passport in my pocket having just returned from abroad and showed it to him. He directed me to a civilian in uniform at a high desk nearby. Told to take a seat I found myself waiting around once more. Frustrated further because not one police officer came to attend me or even spoke to me, I thought it possible that I was invisible even to police radar. They must have thought I was staying next to my cases to keep an eye on them. But this was no hotel it was the most secure police station in the country and had held some of the worst villains in our recent history in its walls and my wife was inside it somewhere.

After another half hour a woman officer came over to where I was sitting and introduced herself to me as Detective Superintendent Richards and asked me again to confirm who I was. After shaking hands she asked me to follow her and check in my cases securely at another desk. Using plastic cards to enable her to open doors along corridors and up stairs she led me to a small interview room where another police officer stood guard. No sign of my wife in the room which was who I thought I was being taken to see. So where was my wife? Where was Libby?

I became restless, agitated and annoyed at being left wondering where my beloved was and what had happened to her when the silence was abruptly disturbed from behind me as yet another door opened in the small interview room. And in she came. There stood Libby distraught, dishevelled, her eyes red from all the crying she had noticeably done and looking thoroughly exhausted and distressed, still handcuffed to a female police officer. She tried, without success, to tug the officer along with her as she made a beeline towards me her free arm pulling on an imaginary rope as she reached out as if to gather me to her. She hardly moved an inch towards me though such was the power of the 'anchor' at her side.

'What the hell is going on Tony?' she asked looking incredibly shaken by her ordeal. 'Why am I in this mess? What can you ....we do about it?'

'Listen' I muttered through closed teeth, all the time hoping that her 'anchor' would not hear me from across the table that was between us. 'There have been a few developments. Firstly, the police took two cases off the train after its arrival in London that I suspect must have been left there deliberately to implicate you or me. What was in them I have no idea but there was a putrid smell about them. I further suspect, and I must remember to inform the police about this, that they were left by a couple who were not in our rail group but that we had seen numerous times in Germany for starters.'

'What are you going on about?' Libby asked.

'Look we saw or caught glimpses of them on several occasions, and so did Dermot, and David and Margie. Those two seem to have been around or on every other corner we have been on from the time we left London, all through Germany and back here to London.'

'What the blazes are you talking about?' she asked both loudly and impatiently, 'do you know those people or not? Why didn't you tell me about them in Cologne? All this might never have happened then.'

I looked at Libby and shook my head because I knew if I recalled to her how many times I'd seen those people whilst we were away there would be all Hell let loose. All I wanted to do was to place my arms around her but there was no way I would chance it knowing that I would also have to cuddle that big woman police officer at the opposite end of the handcuffs Libby was wearing. Sitting opposite my wife in that room I was numb with anger at the way she had been, to me anyhow, mistakenly treated and I felt inextricably impotent that I was unable to help. Such spurious and trivial reasons for her being held in custody, so groundless and unreliable I just knew the evidence against her would never stack up in court. Thinking I only had to convince someone with a semblance of nous and she would be free I asked her

'Have you been interviewed here yet?'

'No not yet. Just stood and watched as my 'appendage' handed in my passport at the main desk here along with my other valuables like money and false teeth. You know how it is, like the sort of thing that we've seen on TV. And then I tried to sign a form registering them in, bound like this. Anyway, forget that. Why did you mention some strange couple we supposedly kept seeing? Have you spoken to them?' she asked.

'It's something we spoke about earlier on in the trip but dismissed as some figment of our over-active imaginations. However, the fact is they got off the same train we travelled back on empty handed except for the woman carrying a handbag. And that set alarm bells ringing in my head. You said that when we were in the Cathedral at Mass in Cologne before we took our seat with David and Margie, you thought someone had deliberately bumped into you not once but twice, on the station wasn't it, or was it in the Cathedral? Can you recall that incident and can you think of any more that may have come to light that you now might think were not an accident but a deliberate assault on you? Can you for instance remember what the bloke looked like? Was he the same one each time? If it was the bloke in the Cathedral for instance had you seen him before? Was he the chap with the bad breath at one of the markets that caused you to stumble?' I asked despite Libby's increasing and understandable hysteria.

'Well I didn't think much of it at first. Just thought it was an accident it happened so quickly. You think it a one off don't you? That first occasion I only caught a vague sketchy-type of glimpse of his face and I apologised thinking the collision was my fault. But the second time I knew it must have been a deliberate collision because there was only me and him in front of the book-stall at that precise moment. He looked so damned maniacal. In fact I'd say he looked insane now I have thought about it. All I did was swing round with my mouth open ready to speak and apologise to whoever was in collision with me. I never thought for a moment that ...... It was when his nostrils seemed to flare and he snarled at me. His eyes narrowed, his mouth and lips turned down at the edges, I thought he was going to start frothing at the mouth. I remember thinking what was he doing acting like that, it was a house of God we were stood in after all.' She paused still sobbing and sniffling. I gave her some tissues before saying

'Carry on' I said 'you're doing great.'

'Thinking about it now he must have been the same person that made me trip up at the gunsmiths when we were David and Margie. Then later at the one of the Christmas Fairs, the Neumarkt I think it was, I'm sure I saw him with a woman appearing to be looking at some trinkets on a stall. I tried to attract your attention thinking you'd recognise him from somewhere, or at least get a good look at him in case he was the same guy. You were though unavailable shall we say at that moment. That woman he was with, she looked familiar too from what little bit I could see of her. Maybe it is all wishful thinking, we'll soon find out. But why am I so, so, so ….in this mess?'

I had longed so much to see and hear Libby talking again and just listening to her talk in that room made me realise that she was increasing in confidence judging by her whole demeanour.

The police-woman in the room coughed several times as if indicating that we should really be sitting quietly waiting for someone more senior to interview Libby, but we politely ignored her. Perhaps I should have offered her a Fisherman's Friend!

There then followed one of those precious moments in life that we've all had at some time or other. Such a moment when one pauses in mid-conversation to suddenly realise the bleeding obvious has entered your head. Well that's what happened to Libby at that precise moment and in that room.

'Bloody hell fire I think I know who she is. Wait a minute I think know …… yes it's coming to me now. Why on earth didn't I connect with this earlier?' Libby shouted. The police woman was aghast and quite shaken as Libby swiftly stood up dragging the police woman upwards too. An Olympic feat in itself as her adrenalin began flowing and all the time they were still hand-cuffed together. Strange chemical adrenalin when it curses through ones veins.

'Go on Libby say what you know, right now and perhaps we can get some officer in to listen to your story.' It was all I could do stop cheering after what she had been through this last thirty six hours. She sounded really upbeat for the first time in ages. Almost as if a load were off her shoulders she looked more relaxed than she had been since our arrest.

'She's the woman in the bloody chemists back home. She was the beggar who served me when I went to buy the travel sickness pills you had to have for the journey. She asked me why I wanted them, where I was going, who with? I told her like everyone else everything Tony, even the places and a couple of the hotels we were staying at I was that pleased someone else seemed interested in where we were going and for why. I recognised the scar below her eye, that's it, the scar. I never gave it a second thought till now. You don't think? No, no, no-one would do such a thing. Would they?' Libby was speaking as I was thinking exactly the same thing at the same time. My brain was sweating it moved so quickly round my thoughts.

'Officer, could you ask for someone to come and to interview my wife, perhaps someone more senior. I think we might have stumbled on something, a firmer lead perhaps and more vital and relevant information re' the disappearance of Pineapple Rail Tours rep Dennis Johnson' I said firmly raising my voice to her. I was so convinced we were at last in possession of concrete evidence. Raising my voice brought other officers into to the room to find out what the commotion was all about, making sure their colleague was safe, and tell us to calm down.

Dragging Libby with her the policewoman disappeared for several seconds returning with Libby free of the handcuffs. The other two officers left when they could see all was calm and when the door closed again Libby was ushered back across the floor to her chair to sit down again next to the police-officer. We talked endlessly checking and comparing our verbal notes almost shrieking with joy as we pieced together what we thought was meaningful evidence across the table separating us. It all began to make sense and drop into place for us at least. All we had to do was convince somebody likewise. If only someone other than us could see it too. Of course, it must have been the woman Libby remembered from Birmingham with that nasty looking bloke who also drove his sports-car crazily cutting Libby up and forcing her into a lamp-post. Was he the very same person we had seen staring at us at various places on our trip?

Though we had found it difficult to talk at first we managed quietly and increasingly with more conviction even though Libby was still mentally wounded by all her recent experience. Libby leant forward across the table her hands free and held mine tightly with renewed strength irrespective of the close attentions of her minder. I had waited longingly to feel the touch of her skin again and though I wanted more over the next few minutes we needed to deal with and discuss the sequence in which possible leads and evidence fitted together that we thought might be useful to the police. We felt it was imperative that we share our thoughts as quickly as possible with another more senior officer and secure her freedom and so get out of the damned place.

'You know Libby,' I said looking into her big blue bloodshot eyes, 'either or both the two people we've discussed could have planted that incriminating bottle of tablets in Johnson's room. I was told it had a Birmingham chemists' address on the label stuck on the bottle. And that was the prime reason the German police had tried to pin the crime on you, who with me, came from Birmingham. They had also found some way to link the albeit very tenuous connection you had with Johnson years ago.' I continued to stare into her eyes and though they were still horribly bloodshot they were at last beginning to smile and light up.

Other bits of the jigsaw began dropping into place giving us both a belief that the situation she was in might, when all our information was presented, maybe lead to her quick release if indeed it did lead to others being arrested and charged. That evidence, so far as we were concerned, included information of our trip's full itinerary that Libby had divulged to, amongst others, the lady assistant in the chemist's shop. Then there were the poisonous tablets, possibly from the same chemist because the woman assistant must have had access to poisons. And then there was the label on the bottle that could be more evidence. There was also the crash involving the injury to the dog and the death of the pedestrian too that Libby was sure involved the same bloke. Finally there was evidence that the pair of them had at times appeared to shadow us and our acquaintances we had socialised with throughout our whole time in Germany. Facts that to me and Libby, when they were placed together, convinced us that the pair we suspected of committing some heinous misdeed to Denis Johnson were also trying to get across some weird message to us, or about us. There was too the small matter of them leaving the train without any luggage at St. Pancras that had set the ball rolling with me. We would soon find out if our little jigsaw of evidence and facts was valuable to the police.

Chapter Eighteen.

The interview room door opened with a flourish and in came a smart looking guy in a light grey Marks and Spencer suit who introduced himself as Detective Chief Inspector Richard call me 'Dickie' O'Mara of the Met Police's murder squad. He nodded to and acknowledged the officer next to Libby, sat down, opened his brief case and took out a file with Libby's name and a long number on it.

When he had paused for breath I asked if I could stay for the interview to support my wife with her having not slept for three nights and with her still in such a distressed state. No joy there, only the duty solicitor would be allowed to stay and of course the woman police officer. I left immediately after giving Libby a gentle kiss on her cheek and, reluctant as I was when I saw the look in her eyes, did as I was commanded. In the corridor outside I began worrying again about Libby's state of mind and health that had fluctuated wildly under intense pressure and when she felt alone. This despite the adrenalin rush she had so clearly experienced collating with me, for a short time, the potential evidence and facts prior to the interview with the DCI. How that interview, to take place without her having slept for three nights, would impact on her, and what her state of mind would be in I simply could not imagine as I waited alone in that corridor. I didn't feel the need to pray very often, but that evening I prayed to God she would be OK and not fall apart emotionally.

Surprisingly the interview finished after only half an hour and I was allowed back into the room, the detective and solicitor having left. I was even permitted a small embrace with my wife despite her being still shaken from that last experience. For several minutes Libby was able to brief me about some of the questions she had been asked by DCI O'Mara. Equally important she was able to recall some, though not all, of her answers. For instance she told him about how she came to be arrested and in that situation in the first place, from her point of view. She mentioned the sightings we had experienced of what we thought were strange and dodgy-looking people; the looks she had received from the wild and maniacal-looking bloke; the bumps she had taken when she thought the same guy deliberately walked into her, not once but twice; how she had reacted the second time it occurred and anything else she could recall about the pair that she failed to recall when talking to me earlier.

Amazingly, looking back at the pressure she had been under those last thirty-seven hours, she went on to give the DCI an unbelievable suggestion. First she told him the name and address of the chemist's shop she visited back in Birmingham to buy my travel pills. Secondly, she made a cheeky suggestion to him: she had dared suggest to him that he would locate the name of the female that we suspected of being involved with Johnson's disappearance, if he spoke to the manager at the chemist shop. The manager if he was well-organised she went on to say, would be able to check out who had either been absent from his shop or on holiday from any staff rota he had for any given time. Further, the cheeky minx said, the rota would verify which staff had been away on the days that happened to coincide with the dates of the break we had taken too. Later in the evening she would tell me she received a polite reprimand from the officer for suggesting to him how he should go about his investigation. Had he known her previously he would have known it was the way she was as Libby was always totally honest and up front with all and sundry. If he knew how many crosswords she completed each week he would know she was a regular sleuth. I needn't have worried for her health because she was by no means intimidated by the DCI's questioning when she realised he really was listening to her explanations. The information regarding places and occasions that we had seen our two suspects she confidently divulged to him in her inimitable way. She told O'Mara that she herself had become vaguely aware of Johnson decades ago as a new teacher in London having lived in the same block of flats as him. And that information only came back to light when she met Johnson as he was the tour rep for our trip to Cologne!

It became later obvious to us that officer O'Mara, or one of his staff, would at some stage have to contact the police in Birmingham following the information given them by Libby, if only on the off chance that the two suspects were heading home and back to Birmingham. They had after all, if my eyes had not deceived me, got off the Eurostar at St Pancras and most likely made for home. At least it was worth considering. Checking the name of the assistant in the chemists in Birmingham would be a mere formality once they had contacted the shop's manager even if it was late at night. Libby was adamant that the assistant must have been involved. If that was so then confirmation of her travel arrangements and her possible involvement and that of her accomplice, might be gained from any train tickets and hotel reservations that they had made. Then if it was them, to us it would have been a mere formality to find out how they conveniently managed to arrange to travel and parallel our itinerary with the information given to her by Libby. Before leaving the room DCI O'Mara told Libby that she must stay put for the time being though we could be reunited.

That was how I found myself in a long embrace, with Libby, in the interview room while being watched by her WPC chaperone. Neither the ideal place nor our idea of fun but we were past caring at that stage. We spent most of the rest of the time talking about the family with me bringing her up to date about our daughter, the grandchildren and telling her of the best wishes sent to her by our recent acquaintances

After an absolute age, but what was in fact only an hour and a half, the DCI returned to inform us that both our cases had been opened and thoroughly searched and had also been subjected to a thorough set of forensic tests before being returned to the safe area in the police station where I had been asked to leave them when I first arrived. It seems that little operation was undertaken whilst we had been waiting in the interview room and obviously without our knowledge. I took his comment to mean that we were clean through and through having proved several issues the main one being that we had nothing to hide. O'Mara told us that the two cases that had been left on the train, different in colour from ours but with similarly named labels, by the people we had placed in the frame as suspects, had also been opened and tests conducted to ascertain who owned them and what the contents were. That was all he would tell us at that moment and it was noticeable he made no mention of the missing tour rep Dennis Johnson. Having given us a partial update of progress made so far as he was able he beckoned us to accompany him to a much more acceptable looking suite somewhere deep inside the police station. After refreshments he moved us again to attend a custody sergeant who astounded both of us as he bailed Libby to stay in London and attend the same police station the following day and before noon. I had to pinch myself to check I was not dreaming while Libby produced a smile as wide as Westminster Bridge she looked so happy. However, conditions of her bail also included the surrender of her passport until released from bail, or in the event that she was charged further it was to remain in police possession. Her remaining possessions were returned as was her phone.

'Does that mean I'm free to go?' she asked the officer jubilantly.

'Not yet' was O'Mara's reply, 'I said we still get to keep your passport until you are discharged absolutely or charged again. Until one of those actions take place you can be called back for further questioning at any time. However, for the moment would you may collect your cases and leave the station. We have phoned for a taxi to take you to a hotel of your choice for the night, but you pay.'

Holding hands we both turned round to see our cases had been placed ready for us to collect at last. We had been there for nearly five hours and were both so shattered after all the shenanigans that had preceded her questioning in the afternoon let alone the evening's questioning which only served to make her tiredness worse. Neither of us had eaten all day but we were maybe understandably not at all hungry. All we needed was a room for the night if only to lie down and crash out if that were possible. A kindly police officer had recommended a hotel nearby to us and when the taxi arrived curtly reminded Libby that she had to return the following day, Wednesday, or else face arrest!

Lo and behold the taxi driver was the same one who had dropped me off earlier in the evening and he remembered me too. After he dropped us off we checked into the Corus Hotel as quickly as we could and then took the lift to our room on the fourth floor. Once inside the views from the room would, under different circumstances, have looked really attractive but the king-size bed at that moment looked far more inviting. We crashed out not even bothering to remove our PJ's from our cases. Libby eventually fell asleep in my arms after she told me she had not closed her eyes or slept since her arrest on Monday morning.

Chapter Nineteen.

The night seemed long and the chances of any quality sleep impossible. We were both wakened regularly not by any noise around us but by an inability to relax, our arms and legs moving endlessly as we struggled to find a comfortable position on the bed. Whispering to each other to see if either was still awake in the early hours or just chatting to each other about who we thought could have been involved in the disappearance of Johnson seemed to take up most of our time. But, when I heard snoring next to me I knew at long last that Libby, utterly exhausted, was asleep. I rolled over and attempted to sleep myself.

With absolute certainty that there would be further interviews for Libby to undertake that day we both found ourselves wide awake at five-thirty. We chatted, reminiscing not only about the problems we had recently experienced but also about the direction we were going in from then on as a couple. The discussion ran out of steam as we realised everything depended on Libby's release and so we sorted out some fresh clothes, a luxury for Libby and then we showered. Sitting talking again drinking coffee, we both kept an eye and one ear on the early television news. The six o'clock news that morning certainly held our attention when its second item mentioned that police had discovered that a horrific murder in London, so gruesome that experienced detectives described it as being one of the worst they had come across. As we stared at the screen open–mouthed the newsreader quoted a police statement saying the murder involved a body that had been found at St Pancras railway station in two cases. The body had been placed in two suit cases abandoned on a train returning to St. Pancras station the day before. The newsreader said the investigating police wished to interview two people who had travelled on the same train as the suitcases. And that was it. There was no mention of any names, neither the victim nor any other people involved. We looked at each other and then back at the TV in utter astonishment. However the newsreader went on to say that the next of kin of the murdered person had been informed. We looked at each other again in stunned amazement, in fact total shock as the newsreader moved on to another item of news.

At any other time I would have flashed a smile her way safe in the knowledge that she would be freed at last. Not that day. I made another coffee feeding our caffeine debt as we came to terms with what we'd heard seconds earlier when the phone rang taking us both by surprise. I answered it with trepidation and with Libby looking at me totally speechless thinking that it might be bad news for her I spoke into the phone. It wasn't bad news as such, though it was DCI O'Mara who had interviewed Libby at length the day before who told me there had been further developments overnight in Libby's case. He said investigations were still proceeding and he asked us to return by taxi to the police station immediately. I looked at my watch it was six fifteen. Libby looked at me her eyes dancing in her head when she asked nervously what the call was about. I quickly told her what O'Mara had said and that we had to return and asked her if she wanted any breakfast, make-up, more coffee or anything else. Only the toilet she said mockingly meaning, I supposed, that she was again nervous and anxious but above all, beginning to feel insecure again about what we might be told. It was all and ifs or buts. If only the policeman had given us the slightest inkling of what the overnight developments had been she might have relaxed.

As it was before we could both get to the toilet the phone rang again only that time the voice at the other end of the phone informed me gruffly that our taxi had arrived and the driver was waiting downstairs impatiently. Scratching my head I knew it wasn't us that had phoned for the taxi yet immediately after that second phone call there was a knock at the door. Libby froze and looked at me. Now who was it? Looking through the spy-hole I could see it was a hotel porter, who, when I opened the door asked us to hurry and not to keep the taxi driver waiting. I told him we would be on our way pronto. He said we were to leave our luggage in the room because the hotel's manager had been told to cancel the maid for the room that morning, not that we'd made much use of the room at all: only the bed, shower, coffee maker and TV and not the toilet.

In the taxi we flew quickly through dark and wet London streets towards the police station. Even at that Godforsaken time traffic was heavy. During the journey, unusually, the taxi driver never spoke a word even when Libby asked if he'd heard any news on the radio that morning. At the police station I paid off the driver and we went up the steps holding onto each other tightly. Even we'd hardly spoken a word on the journey from the hotel because the anticipation was too great at what we thought might have been about to happen. I had a good idea what had passed through my wife's mind all the same but felt totally inadequate and unable to allay her fears. Would it be her day of judgement?

At the top of the steps by the main entrance we were met by DCI O'Mara who opened the door for us with what passed for a smile on his chubby and cheeky mature face before inviting us both inside the warm dry building. The portents looked good for Libby if that was his attitude. After that positive greeting he whisked us down a corridor and into an interview room where the Custody Sergeant, present when Libby's bail conditions were set the day before, was again present that morning. I must say the manner displayed by the DCI had changed from that of interrogator to congratulator and he amplified that by much handshaking as he began to tell us of some of the overnight developments even before we had sat down.

Developments had begun to take place whilst Libby was being questioned the previous day about the terrifying encounters and collisions with people, as yet unknown, she had experienced in Cologne and Aachen to DCI O'Mara. It appears the Met Police had immediately set in motion a series of strategies to check out and confirm or deny Libby's evidence following the appearance at the railway station of the two mysterious cases. The officer explained that the West Midlands police had located the manager of the chemist's shop in Birmingham fairly swiftly where Libby had stated the suspect woman worked. Having established her name, age and address from the shop records and more importantly where we were concerned the manager had been able to confirm she had been 'on holiday' at the same time as we had. The manager further substantiated she had asked for and taken two weeks annual leave, but that he was unaware of any of her further plans.

I asked DCI O'Mara if he knew why the woman, if she was the one, had been so enthusiastic in following us and why she seemed so intent to implicate me and my wife in Johnson's disappearance. He declined to answer my question and after a brief pause in proceedings to answer the phone he left the room for several minutes. Despite being offered coffee, which we refused, we spoke about DCI O'Mara's change of attitude towards us both when he greeted us that morning and in the interview. We were reflecting on some of the evidence that Libby had spoken to him about when he re-entered the room.

On that occasion he was more forthcoming about our two suspects. He told us that the woman assistant in the shop was wanted for questioning as there were issues involving her that did not add up. The woman and her companion had indeed used false names in German hotels clearly believing they could cover up any possible future trail leading back to them. O'Mara said that however much the pair thought it was a clever the ploy it was bound to come unstuck eventually because they had foolishly bought their rail tickets on the internet. The woman had to pay for them by card in her own name and the tickets were sent to her home address in Birmingham. Once her bank details were traced the police had all the evidence it wanted to prove the couple had been in Germany. Further the DCI said that customs officers in England were able to confirm the couple had travelled by Eurostar because all seats are reserved and are always allocated in advance of the person travelling. In addition DCI O'Mara stated that they were unbelievably naïve because they had to show their passports at the various controls including to the overly-officious French Customs officers at St. Pancras adding another nail in their coffin.

Libby sat open-mouthed throughout all of the policemen's brief conversation and at a suitable let up was moved to ask if the police could trace everyone going on holiday. The officer replied that in the majority of cases they were traceable, the passport controls being the catalyst in such an operation. He continued saying

'It transpires by an incredible coincidence that Maria Allsebruckovski was formerly Maria Johnson the ex-wife of Dennis Johnson.'

Libby gasped at that revelation.

'Her companion Volodymir Bondachuck' he continued, 'was previously from Kiev in Ukraine and had lived with her for several years. Those are the names of the two suspects the police are looking to question in Birmingham.'

He went on to say the police had all the proof needed that they travelled together to and from Germany as partners and were as of that moment on Wednesday wanted for questioning with regard to the disappearance of Dennis Johnson.

'So have you arrested them or not?' Libby enquired expectantly.

'I'm coming to that slowly now,' a tired-looking DCI said before continuing 'On returning from London to Birmingham by train on Tuesday night they broke their journey and left the train at Coventry a stop or two before Birmingham.'

'Why would they do that?' asked Libby.

'I'm coming to that now if you please. They took and drove a car from the railway station car park where they were captured on the station CCTV. They were acting very furtively at the time they were getting into the car checking to see if they were being watched we presume. We got a really good full-on facial of the woman from the camera. Anyhow the car they used did in fact turn out to be Allsebruckovski's and was driven by Bondachuk back towards Birmingham.'

'So am I free to go or what?' interjected a frustrated Libby.

'Let me finish and I'll come to that' the increasingly fraught DCI replied. 'They travelled down the A45 trunk road towards Birmingham at well above the speed limit believing they were home and dry having completed their two objectives of removing Johnson and implicating yourselves with the crime. However, they failed to take notice of the speed cameras they passed at regular intervals well above the sixty mile an hour speed limit for the road.'

The DCI then paused and drank a well-earned glass of water all the time Libby watching and waiting with her left leg over her right leg twitching away. The tired Officer went on to complete his de-briefing with us telling us that the suspect's car was stopped for speeding by traffic police near Meriden. Bondarchuk, when breathalysed was found to be way over the legal limit. It was as he was cautioned and arrested for the drink drive offence that they were both asked for identification. The car number plate was genuine and did belong to the car and the car was with the rightful owner. But it was when they asked Bondarchuk for his identification that he panicked and gave the game away after being told he would probably go to jail for a succession of motoring offences. Those offences would include speeding, being several times over the legal alcohol limit to drive, having no driving licence and therefore no insurance and the suspicion he was wanted for a hit and run accident in Birmingham.

Libby flashed me a look at that point and almost half a smile. More importantly it then meant that the game was really up for Allsebruckovski and Bondarchuk. The senior officer went on to finish his summing up telling us that

'The arresting officers were ordered to send for back-up which arrived almost immediately enabling the suspects to be separated in two cars and driven to Steelhouse Lane police station in Birmingham where they were charged on several accounts. Bondarchuk, realising he was going away for a long time in gaol, sang like a bird implicating his partner. So much so apparently that she admitted her part in the conspiracy almost straight away after being cautioned. They were coincidentally also wanted for questioning about none payment of hundreds of pounds of parking fines.'

I looked at my watch. It was well into the afternoon though you'd never have known it from the look on Libby's face that had assumed a much happier state with the information put to us by DCI O'Mara.

'How did they know we were on holiday with Pineapple Rail Tours and with that particular tour rep?' Libby enquired.

DCI O'Mara told us that Allsebruckovski had a sister who just coincidentally lived on the same housing estate as Johnson.

'During a weekend visit to her sisters' he continued, 'she had seen Johnson waiting at a bus stop one Saturday morning and so had followed him. He, going about his business had visited the Pineapple Tours main office perhaps having gone to get particulars of some future tour he was to undertake we'll never know now. Anyway, under caution in Steelhouse Lane she confessed to having later phoned his company asking when and where he was going away because she had travelled on some successful tour with him previously and wanted to do so again. Sadly as it transpired, somebody at the company gave her the information she wanted and the rest is history.'

'But why me?' asked Libby 'why me for pity's sake? What could she gain from implicating me in any of her grisly work?

'Well you remember you had said that when you began teaching you could vaguely recall at some stage meeting Johnson on the communal stairs in the block of flats you both lived in? Well she was his then girlfriend and an extremely jealous lady who it also transpires was such a control freak that she thought you and he had an affair at some stage. In her eyes you would eventually become the reason for the break-up of their marriage. Such was her jealousy and control freakery that simply by saying hello to him you became a target of hate and vitriol' the Chief Inspector concluded.

'But how on earth did she recognise me after all those years?' Libby persisted.

'Simple' the Chief Inspector carried on 'from your prescription drugs for the travel sickness your husband needed and you collected one morning before your holiday.'

'But they were in my married name weren't they?'

'Yes but the name was on computer and your records threw out your maiden name. That is what clicked in her mind after all those years. Oh and by the way before you ask if you hadn't realised already Johnson was the unfortunate victim in the cases.'

'That makes me feel sick. How did all that come about?' Libby asked.

' Well he'd been lured to the hotel room of the two suspects with a promise of forgiveness for his dumping of Allsebruckovski all those years ago and the promise of some free booze as well. He couldn't resist the booze which became his downfall. How did he know it was Allsebruckovski? They met in your hotel lobby in Cologne quite by chance one day when Johnson called back for a beer and recognised her from all those years ago poor bloke. We think she must have been checking out the guest list to see if you were on it! Apparently in the Birmingham nick she flipped and kept screaming that Johnson had it coming to him calling him a filthy philandering bastard. What of the partner Bondarchuk, Allsebruckovski's lover? He had previously been a butcher in a shop in Kiev in his native Ukraine. But I'll leave you both to guess the rest rather than recall the gory details. Finally to let you know they also stole the luggage labels off your cases whilst they were parked on a platform in some trolley on Cologne's station which was why your labels with your names came to be on their cases.'

I looked at Libby when that last piece of information was given to us and smiled at her when I saw the significance of the Chief Inspector's last comment dawn on her.

'So that's where our labels went, they weren't lost at all they were stolen' she muttered.

'Right in one' I said to her.

DCI O'Mara had by then stood up and walked over to us both to shake our hands and tell Libby 'Libby Russell you are free to go and are no longer under suspicion, the case against you is dropped.'

He then shook our hands and wished us a happy anniversary before departing once more into the bowels of Paddington Green Police station. That left the attendant female PC to tell Libby again that she was free to go visit the bail officer and get her release from the bail order as all charges against her were dropped.

The sheer relief on Libby's face as the moment sank in I don't think I'd seen in all our time together. If I am honest, after all the difficulties and pressure of those previous few days, I began thinking if I'd ever see her smile again. Only the trial of the ex-wife of Johnson and her lover to go through and perhaps life would return to normal.

When all the paperwork and formalities were completed we both looked at each other before giving each other a big hug. Tears of absolute relief and joy ran down both of our cheeks as we realised the impact the last few days had on our lives. And before we returned to our hotel for a sleep and some relaxation we intended to celebrate not only Libby's release but also our forty years of marriage which had been placed on hold.

Yes we would have a drink to our forty years of marriage to each other. God did we need to get away from that police station though not before I'd asked another taxi driver to divert from taking us to our hotel and drop us off at a bar on the way.

Neither of us bothered to look back at the police station out of the taxi's rear window. We were just so relieved to be on our way but I did ask the driver to drop us near the Low Life Bar that was within staggering distance of our hotel. Although the name of the bar summed up our last two days the celebration champagne we had was ice cold and very dry. If we'd been able to stay awake back at our hotel when we eventually arrived there not quite so sober our 'personal' Ruby Wedding Anniversary celebrations could have begun there and then. But those things just had to wait a little longer.